Athena Butler, the twenty-year-old descendant of an ancient bloodline of psychics, yearns to live a normal life. She wants a career in art, a boyfriend, independence. Her clairvoyance has taught her, however, that people can be false and dangerous. Although warned to keep her psychic gifts a secret, she's recruited by law enforcement to help search for a serial killer and to uncover a terrorist cell that threatens her own diplomat father.

She bonds with an intriguing, handsome man, Kas Skoros, who knows her secret and accepts it. Of the same bloodline, his own mother is precognitive and predicts they are meant to be together . . . someday. Kas realizes that life is too uncertain, but he can't resist his growing passion for the strange young woman.

Still, they face obstacles beyond their control. Can Athena and Kas overcome these obstacles? More importantly, can Athena stay alive long enough to fulfill her dream of a normal life?

This novel was previously published.

Athena's Secrets

ISBN: 978-1-4874-2194-6
Cover art by Martine Jardin

Published by eXtasy Books Inc or
Devine Destinies, an imprint of eXtasy Books Inc

Look for us online at:
www.eXtasybooks.com or www.devinedestinies.com

Athena's Secrets
The Delphi Bloodline Book 1

By

Donna Del Oro

Dedication

I dedicate Athena's Secrets, Book One in the Delphi Bloodline Series, to all those readers who know what I mean by clairvoyant tendencies. May you develop those tendencies and listen to your inner voice.

CHAPTER ONE

The Coltswolds Academy for Girls, Surrey, England 1998

One moment nine-year-old Athena Butler was sitting on the floor, holding hands with her friends in their *Mates for Life* circle. One of them, Cynthia, was relaying a bawdy joke her older sister had told her during her weekend home. All four were giggling, their eyes wide with gleeful shock. The next moment Athena felt the barrage, like a pelting hailstorm into her brain.

I knew they'd be shocked, tee-hee, I haven't even told them the naughty ones, such prudes, don't get your knickers in a knot, no, mustn't think that, Athena has a brother, why look so shocked? She should know what a dingle-bob looks like, tee hee, it's so disgusting, like a banger without the mash, funny but disgusting! Will I have to confess this to Father Dillon? Oh bother, I won't, it's nothing, just silly words, dingle-bobs, Susan's brother calls it his Johnson, I've heard it called Bobby-boy—Oh lordy! Susan saw her brother and his girlie friend doing it, really doing it! Shall I tell them? She saw him stick it in between the girlie's legs, it was as stiff as a stick–

The sharp images and intense emotions hit Athena's mind and sent her reeling in panic. Not at first, but the words and images kept pelting her brain.

Stop! Was she losing her mind? Going mad?

Fear clutched her heart and she collapsed in a heap, screeching as if a massive headache had struck. She clutched her head on both sides, tried to cover her ears.

The other three girls flung apart as if struck. They stared at her with looks of horror.

Another jumbled mess of emotions swamped her. She shrieked at each new barrage.

Athena was only dimly aware when the three other girls backed up in their confusion and surprise. One ran off. But every time the other two touched Athena, the frightful barrage of thoughts and emotions overtook her. She screamed, squeezed her eyes shut and heaved hysterical sobs.

Curling herself into a ball, Athena heard the headmistress run into the girls' dormitory room.

Her three friends clamored for Miss Barkley's attention. Athena had suddenly flipped out, one of them cried, had gone mad and they had no idea why. A few minutes before, Athena was laughing along with them. Then suddenly she was shrieking as though in great pain.

Miss Barkley didn't believe them, said they were exaggerating or pulling a prank. Athena felt the woman shake her shoulder, and suddenly the barrage struck again. She screamed and curled further into herself. Aware of the commotion she'd stirred up, she knew Miss Barkley could see no physical injuries of any kind. The woman's thoughts intruded into Athena's mind as she held her hand to Athena's forehead.

The child's having a seizure. Good god, I must call an ambulance.

Miss Barkley turned quiet for a moment, then abruptly took her mobile phone out of her pocket. The plea she issued to the EMTs was to get there as fast as humanly possible.

Was that it? Was she in the throes of a seizure? A seizure of the brain? Any human touch scorched her mind, making her flinch violently from any contact, causing her to shrink from the next round of pain. A seizure? She knew a girl her age who had epileptic seizures, but those seizures rendered her unconscious.

Meanwhile, Athena had stilled into a fetal position and was no longer whimpering, but breathing shallowly. Although cocooned into her ball of blackness, Athena could hear everything.

"Take her to St. Bart's," ordered the shaken headmistress to the two EMTs who arrived minutes later. "I'll ring her parents in France. The father's with the Foreign Service."

Athena knew the woman found refuge in officiousness. She'd seen the headmistress flustered before. Her response to confusion was action and orders.

"Pack her suitcase, children. I do believe Athena Butler may leave us for a while." They began to weep. "I am so very sorry, but what else can we do? I shall keep you girls informed as to her progress at St. Bart's."

"I think she's catatonic," one of the two male EMTs said. The other hushed him up before saying, "I'll start a drip line, sedate her."

Athena knew what that meant and didn't mind. That meant she would fall asleep and the pain would go away. She felt the EMTs strap her into a gurney before she felt a prick on her arm. She didn't squirm or cry out, for suddenly she felt no pain. Craving sleep all of a sudden, she let the sedative work its magic, drip by drip through an IV line.

She could hear Miss Barkley helping the girls pack her suitcase, still interrogating them. What were they doing when Athena collapsed? Had they drunk or smoked anything? No, no, nothing, just telling jokes and holding hands. Miss Barkley told the EMTs that she needed to call the Chief of Staff of the psychiatric ward of St. Bartholemew's. It was the county hospital less than ten miles away. The woman promised the three girls that she would check in on Athena later the next day.

That promise quieted their tears, and for that Athena was grateful. She hadn't meant to frighten anybody.

Athena felt herself lifted and carried downstairs. Strange, how clear and still her mind had become. The mysterious images, thoughts, and emotions had disappeared. She wondered how soon her parents would come to the hospital. The psychiatric ward of St. Bartholemew's sounded frightful. Wasn't that for people who went mad?

Was that what she was, mad? Mad as the hatter in the Alice in Wonderland book she loved? Good golly! Would they strap her in a straitjacket, like she heard they did with psychos at St. Bart's?

If so, how dreadful! She'd been so looking forward to playing rounders, hockey, and tennis that spring. She was certain they wouldn't let a mad little girl stay at school with the others.

She began to weep. Silent tears.

Her thoughts in turmoil, Anna Butler stared ahead as Doctor Nasritti, the on-duty night shift physician on St. Bart's psych ward, led her and Trevor Butler down one corridor of St. Bart's psych ward. A tall, burly orderly stood by a locked door but moved aside as they approached. The physician paused and looked through the door's steel-grid window.

"Mrs. Butler, we had to restrain the child. She was alternately violent and catatonically stiff. I feared she would hurt herself. These restraints were necessary, I confess." He stopped when the mother loudly sucked in her breath. She was looking past him at her child, the girl's arms, legs, upper torso and head constrained by wide, leather straps as she lay imprisoned on a hospital bed. The bed had no railings or sheets, nothing nearby that a violent patient in the throes of a psychotic break could harm himself with.

A wave of dizziness hit Anna. The physician and the big orderly caught her shoulders as she sagged. She immediately shook them off and glared at them both, her face turning livid.

"Take those horrible things off her! I can't believe how you could treat my child in this way—" Anna choked up and sputtered into silence. Tears erupted and ran down her heated face, and as soon as the physician unlocked the door, she pushed past him and approached her daughter's bed. Anna and Trevor exchanged a long look as she composed herself, wiped her face with her gloved hands and then, her hands working and tugging, began unbuckling the straps. Trevor stood frozen, shaking his head, overcome, Anna knew, with emotion.

With a nod, Doctor Nasritti gave tacit approval to the orderly to help her unfetter the child.

"Please," Anna ordered the man, "do not touch her. Just the straps. Then leave us." She glanced over at her husband. "Trevor, please wait for us outside. I know what to do."

"There's an observation room, Mrs. Butler," the physician said, "Hospital protocol dictates that I watch and interject my help if necessary. Mr. Butler, you're welcome to join me there."

Anna nodded distractedly, her focus never leaving her daughter. "Yes, thank you." She turned to give her husband an encouraging smile.

Nasritti rested a troubled gaze upon the pair as if waiting for the girl to rise and attack Anna in a frenzy. He was obviously prepared—he'd brought a hypodermic syringe loaded with a powerful sedative just in case.

She drew a deep breath to calm herself. It was all she could do to keep from attacking the man herself. Reason returned, fortunately. He couldn't know. None of them could know.

And if she had anything to do about it, they never would.

* * * *

Athena lay still, her eyes closed, her breathing shallow and labored. Though not yet conscious, she floated in a dream-like state. Slowly she began receiving images and emotions like a television antenna. At first her body's muscles contracted and she flinched, beginning to curl again into a fetal position. But the flow continued uninterrupted, like a river that refused to clog up or detour, and this flow changed everything. This flow slowly relaxed Athena's rictus of fear.

A warmth born of love and familiarity flowed with those images and emotions and worked like a tranquilizer upon her mind and body. Athena recognized what flowed into her mind, memories from their shared past, images of her favorite dolls, her books and bicycle, her room at their London townhouse, her mother's warm embrace, her handsome father's broad smile, the big, brown eyes of her brother, Chris—whom her mother called Christoforo, in the Italian way. Images flowed of Nonna in Como, her Zio Giancarlo, the mountains and lake she so dearly loved and visited every summer, ever since she was born. These thoughts penetrated her cocoon of defense and reassured Athena that she was indeed very sane.

She hadn't lost her mind. Indeed, her mind had expanded ten-thousand-fold. Instead of the gradual coming on of Anna's powers from age two to ten, as her mother had often told her would happen, Athena's powers had gushed forth like a burst dam. She remembered that her mother had tried to warn her this might happen. But she was only nine—holy heck, how could her brain prepare for such a thing?

Our minds work differently than others, figlia mia. But we can adapt, like all humans are built to adapt. What you feel now, the fear, the pain, will lessen as your mind adapts to the new situation. After a while, this influx of information from the minds and feelings of others will be normal and your brain will learn to ignore it all, or work around it. Your mind will adjust, and you will learn to shut it off. I learned. You will, too.

Athena's protective cocoon lifted and the white noise stopped. Her conscious mind rose up, and her normal senses took over. She heard electric buzzing and felt the cool vinyl under her fingertips. Then she heard her mother sigh, followed by a quiet sob. Although not yet fully remembering where she was or why she wasn't lying in her dormitory room, Athena realized for the first time in her life what the powers her mother had told her about were really like. She had a lot to learn, she knew that, but she was no longer rigid with fear. And so she opened her eyes and looked at her mother. Her hand lifted to touch her mother's face.

"Don't cry, Mummy. I'm awake now. I think I understand."

"Oh, my baby girl. *Figlia bella,* I'm so sorry it came like this."

Athena nodded. Who could she blame? Certainly not her mother. Her mother had warned her, but how could she have understood such a miracle? Such magic? Such a curse?

One thing was clear to her. "Take me with you to France. Please, Mummy. I want to go with you and Daddy and Chris."

Her mother bent over and kissed Athena's hand, which then glistened with her mother's tears.

"Yes, we won't leave you again." Her mother turned to look in the direction of the mirrored window, and her expression became fierce. An explosion of angry Italian followed before her mother settled down. "We need each other to get through this. Your father did not understand . . . but now he does. No more English boarding schools. They're not for you, *amore mia.*"

Athena realized now how different her mother was from her father. The miracle had never come to her father, just her mother, and Nonna and Nonna's mother before her. A long line, Mummy had told her, all the way back to the ancient world of Greece. To the priestesses of Delphi. Athena wondered about that, but before she could do or say anything more, her eyes drooped. The trauma of the past night had wrung her out.

Miracles . . . and curses . . . were indeed exhausting.

Chapter Two

Ten years later, Washington, D.C.

Athena trudged up the concrete steps of the Art Institute, lugging her weekender bag on wheels. The bag strained to support her painting supplies. A large gessoed canvas was strapped to its extended handle with bungee cords. Most of the students there had similar devices to transport their work. Not everything fit into a nice, neat portfolio. But the more paint Athena bought, the heavier her bag. Still, hauling the bag was cheaper than renting a locker at the school. As long as her parents were covering tuition at this private school, she would do her utmost to contain costs.

She looked around her. The sycamores nearby, naked on this bone-freezing November day, stood like stalwart sentinels over the entrance. Despite her being ten minutes late, due to the late arrival of her replacement at the coffee shop, Athena paused to admire the patchwork bark of the closest tree, its palette of colors in the grays, browns, and mauves. Could she capture that unique mix of shades with her palette knife? The sycamore's bark beckoned for capture in oil.

Such beauty.

No time.

She shook herself and continued on her way, through one of the double glass entrance doors and on up the stairs to the third floor painting studio. A secondyear student at the Art Institute, a prestigious private art college a subway's ride from her parents' Alexandria condo, Athena had graduated two years before from an American private high school, the same college prep school where her brother, Chris, was currently enrolled. There had never been a doubt in her mind what field of study her college degree would entail. An avid artist since she could wield a crayon, she'd gained admission based on a thick portfolio and hearty recommendations from a variety of art teachers and gallery owners. Already, she'd had a small exhibit of her landscapes and still lifes in an Alexandria gallery and a small but prestigious gallery in Kensington, their English home.

As she entered the vast painting studio, she noted their instructor wending her way around the easels, pausing to make comments about the students' work-in-progress. Their assignment that week: Paint a portrait from a photo, using oil or acrylics, and choose a palette and style that reflected the mood of the piece and the essence of that individual.

Her friend, Mikela, looked over and, with rolling eyes, made a head gesture, as in "Watch out, the Wicked Queen has a bug up her ass." Her straightened, flowing black hair in a Cher hairdo, Mikela came over to Athena's easel as she began to set up her tools.

"She's busting all our humps today," said Mikela, leaning over and touching Athena's shoulder. Her African-American friend was tall, statuesque and worked as a part-time photographer's model while she attended the Institute. A fact that Athena found exciting if a bit scandalous, for her high school mates had been as conservative as their parents. Though her major was Interior Design, Mikela loved to paint almost as much as Athena. Her friend returned to her easel but threw back over her shoulder a warning gesture.

When Mikela touched her, an image intruded into Athena's mind, along with an emotional message. Her friend's thoughts were on other matters today. Lusty ones. In Mikela's words, she was as horny as a horndog. Whatever that was. Without thinking, Athena replied, "Don't worry, your bearded man is coming along nicely."

Mikela did a double-take. "Dude, how did you know I'm painting a bearded man? You can't see my canvas. I didn't tell you 'cause I wanted to surprise you."

"Didn't you?" Athena assembled her paints, brushes, and bottle of mineral spirits on the table next to her easel. She mentally kicked herself as she prepared the one-inch wide brush she'd need for the pale background, which she'd start first. The outline and some of the details of the man's face had previously been drawn onto the canvas, but she was waiting for . . .

For what, she couldn't say exactly. Inspiration, a power from The Flow, that mysterious Otherworld that her mother had guided her into and out of over the past so many years of her youth. Athena pulled out her photo.

"I thought you mentioned it last week," she added innocently, "Anyway, I knew you'd paint him. He's your, what shall we call him, the new squeeze in your life? Oh, look here, Mikela, what do you think of this chap?" Although Americanized, thanks to her father's posting in the states for the past eight years. Athena still lapsed into British terms and slang although lately, mostly on a whim or for humor. Any time she wanted, she could turn on the Brit talk and make her American friends smile. Sometimes she milked it, other times she even forgot she'd slipped back into her former accent and idioms.

"Ah, you're going English on me, are you?" Mikela gave her a peculiar look, even as she did her best upper-class British imitation. "Trying to distract me, luv? I know I didn't tell you I was painting Jerry. I swear, Athena, someday I'm going to find out how you do that. It's some parlor trick, or you're some friggin' psychic. Now let me take a look at *your* model." A slow smile stretched her pretty, red-lipsticked mouth as she took hold of Athena's five-by-seven colored photo. "Ooo, he's a hottie. How do you know him? And what's that uniform he's wearing? That's not a British army uniform, is it? Thought you had no boyfriends in England."

Athena elbowed her friend while she tacked the photo to the upper left corner of her canvas' wooden stretcher. Professor White, their hypercritical painting instructor, was fast approaching, a perennial frown fixed to her face. The woman walked like she was stalking her prey.

"He's just a friend of the family. He is the son of my mother's distant cousin. I think he's a sheriff's deputy, lives in California."

"Good looking," Mikela added, her black eyebrows arched with curiosity, "Are you sure you don't have a thing for him? Like a crush from afar?"

"Of course not. Besides, he's too old for me. My mother wanted me to paint him, that's all. She wants to give it to her cousin as a Christmas gift. I don't know why."

In fact, Athena did know why. Her mother had confided a secret about the Skoros family, the California-based, Greek-American family that her cousin, Lorena, had married into. Lorena Skoros was of the Delphi bloodline, according to her mother. They had met each other in Como, at Nonna's after Papa Trementino died four years ago. There, at lake's edge, the three older women—Nonna, her mother, and Lorena—had kissed cheeks after giving her a solid gold medallion. On one side was an embossed Athena, the ancient goddess of knowledge.

"Well, that's bizarre," Mikela said, "Why would your mother want you to paint his portrait? He's not your boyfriend."

Athena shrugged. Lorena was the mother of four handsome, strapping sons and possessed precognitive powers that surpassed even her mother's. The woman had seen a foreshadowing of tragedy within her own family, the sudden death of one of her sons. But Lorena wouldn't tell Anna which son's death she had foreseen. Therefore, she wanted Athena to paint all four sons, beginning with the youngest.

She put off Mikela's curiosity with a shrug. "She wants portraits of all her sons. I'm just starting with this one."

Was it this young man's fate their cousin Lorena had foreseen? After all, he did work in a dangerous field, law enforcement. Athena stared at the photo, ignoring Mikela's stare. The man's dark eyes appeared to sense his pending demise. His thoughtful, even gloomy stare into the camera made her shudder.

I hope he's not the one.

Engrossed in his photo, Athena looked up to find her instructor glowering at her. Edith White was a middle-aged woman of average height and weight who seemed to have the Napoleonic complex of a short man, as if she were always trying to compensate for her insecurities by criticizing others'. Their theory for her denigrating behavior towards others was that she was so insecure in her artistic merit that she often ridiculed others' work with simply a frown and a peremptory shake of her head. White was not Athena's or Mikela's favorite instructor at the Institute, but despite all, the woman knew her painting techniques. She was a capable painter and had celebrated many one-woman exhibitions in the most renown galleries in the D.C. metropolitan area. They knew this because she displayed the promotional posters of her exhibitions all over the studio's walls.

"You haven't begun, Miss Butler?" White said, scowling at the white-gessoed canvas. On the white surface, an outline of the subject in pencil was visible. "And you were late, I noticed."

"Yes, I'm sorry. I work every morning at the Starbucks down the street. We were swamped, and the other barista came in late. Drop by, Professor White, and I'll treat you to a free coffee drink." Athena tried a weak smile, but not even her offer would dislodge Doctor White's scowl today.

"I told everyone to prepare for today's class by painting in the background, to spend class time on the subject, itself. You haven't even begun the background."

Gee, she's like a pitbull with a bone. "I made a sketch, but that's all. I haven't decided on the palette yet. Perhaps you can suggest something."

Though Athena had already decided the mood direction and color scheme of her portrait, she knew enough to soothe the always ruffled feathers and insecure ego of their instructor by soliciting her advice.

"Hmm," White murmured, gazing at the photo of the handsome dark-haired sheriff's deputy, the closeup photo an obvious professional one meant for the Sheriff's online roster. His proud mother, Lorena Skoros, had sent it to her cousin, Anna, the month before. His thick, dark hair was parted on the side, his mouth masculine but sensual, his jawline and chin strong and angular. Her mother wanted Athena to capture his other qualities, his intelligence, and courage. Her mother knew him well enough, but Athena had never met him. How could she capture a stranger on canvas?

With her imagination, that was how.

And the aid of last night's dream, a romantic fantasy in which she'd flung herself into his strapping arms and he'd kissed her passionately. They'd begun shedding their clothes when, unfortunately, she awakened. Long before their romance could reach a satisfying climax.

God, I am so horny. I do have to get out more. A heartbeat later. *I need a boyfriend.*

Mikela had returned to her easel a couple of feet away, but Athena knew her friend was eavesdropping.

"He's a friend of the family, but I don't know him," explained Athena, feeling more than a little foolish. Her focus turned back to the painting and the sketch she'd made. Tempted to touch Doctor White to find out what the woman really and truly thought, Athena nevertheless resisted the impulse. Going into the dark troubled corners of that woman's mind was a temptation she found wise to resist.

"I see," was White's noncommittal response.

"I mean, because I don't know him, I'm not sure how to portray him. He's handsome, to be sure, but other than his intelligence and courage, which according to his mother and mine, he has in abundance, how can I show these traits?"

Athena waited for the woman's pearls of wisdom, or at the very least, a modicum of guidance.

Doctor White gave a loud harrumph and gave a dismissive shake of her head.

"That is the very challenge of this assignment," she said archly and moved on to scrutinize Mikela's canvas.

Right. Well, thanks a lot.

Her gaze returned to the young man's face, and then his trim build in a pale gray snug-fitting shirt. She got nothing. Maybe if she emailed him or called him and heard his voice, she'd get a clairvoyant feel for him. Then it hit her. She would portray the young man full of hope and optimism, just as his proud mother was wishing beyond the vagaries of Fate that her son would be spared an untimely death. That she was mistaken. After all, their powers weren't foolproof. At times Athena received images and thoughts that were difficult, even impossible to interpret. They were first and foremost human beings, and humans were always fallible. That was one of the lessons her very wise mother had taught her these past ten years.

"Really, Miss Vega? Another boyfriend?" Doctor White's assessment of Mikela's choice of subject had already met with mockery. "A world of topics surrounds you, and all you can paint are your boyfriends." The woman made a tsking sound. "Your background is too busy. Your focal point will be lost in all the jumble. The focal point being his face, or perhaps that is exactly your objective."

Poor Mikela. Nothing could please their instructor.

Doctor White moved on out of earshot. Athena peeked around Mikela's canvas and observed her friend's angry flushed cheeks.

"Hey, never mind what she says," Athena said.

"I know, don't get my knickers in a knot. Ain't worth it," was Mikela's flippant stance. "I'll paint Jerry so hot, even Doctor Cold Fish will pant over him."

Athena gave her friend a thumbs-up and returned to her subject. His dark eyes challenged her to see into his very soul. *Okay, Mr. Keriakos Skoros, let's see what you've got. You sexy-but-too-old California chap.*

She dipped her wide brush into the spirits, squeezed it dry and then swabbed up a bit of pale gold acrylic paint. No, too dark. She wiped it on her palette, then added some Arctic White to the dollop of pale gold and made a rough, stucco-looking mixture, then added some medium to dilute the mixture a little. Whenever she thought of California, she imagined hills of pale gold grass. Or colorful stucco houses with palm trees swaying next to them. With her palette knife, she'd give the background a somewhat rough texture. With that in mind, she slowly covered the background. His dark, good looks—well, they'd stand out against such a background. His handsome face—she'd imbue his face and eyes with hope and optimism.

Background first. Mr. Skoros' soul next.

Hope and optimism. Everyone needed it.

Anna drove from the Georgetown restaurant, where she'd just had lunch with Trevor and his secretary, Winston Blake. They were knee-deep in preparations for an evening reception to honor and culminate the British Prime Minister's visit to the United Nations General Assembly. Her help was necessary, and both Trevor and Winston depended on her to engage the PM's wife during the UN's two-day assemblage. Since this was to be the PM's wife's first visit to Washington, Anna was expected to take the woman under her wing and entertain her with visits to the Kennedy Center, various monuments and, of course, a special observation of the Senate floor in the chamber. A formal dinner at the White House was on the schedule, naturally, and therefore a shopping visit might be included. The PM and his stylish wife, Anna reminded her husband and Winston, had very little free time for fluff, but by the end of their lunch meeting, Anna had agreed to make a list of possible forays among the D.C. *glitterati* and places of interest.

She took a right-hand exit off Dupont Circle, then drove another four blocks and down into the parking garage of a station of the Metropolitan Police. She punched in the security code given to her and watched the steel bollards recede into the asphalt. A policeman at the booth checked her ID, made a phone call and within a half-minute waved her in. She took the prescribed visitor's parking stall number and turned off the engine of her BMW sedan. Puffing into her leather gloves, Anna closed her eyes to center herself. These visits always disturbed her, shook her to the core. Still, she could not stop herself. No more than she could stop the sun from rising in the East. Her husband would disapprove if he knew—no, he'd be furious if he knew what she was doing twice a week.

Trevor, a lovely man in his own right, bore more understanding and patience than the average man. Didn't he occasionally say, with tongue firmly in cheek, that his forbearance was one of his finest qualities? To marry a gifted clairvoyant and father a daughter who'd inherited her mother's *whatever-it-was* required the forbearance and wisdom of a King Solomon.

Anna quite agreed, and she made a point to remind him of her gratitude and admiration. After all, men needed that kind of affirmation in the face of interminable mystery.

The elevator rose with seeming slowness while Anna's quick mind turned to thoughts of Athena. Her daughter had thrived in the U.S., had loved her private school in the Virginia countryside, as did her sixteen-year-old son, Chris. Having Athena under the family's roof had enabled Anna to gently guide her beautiful blond daughter along the treacherous journey of their shared mental powers.

With Anna's guidance came the wisdom of secrecy, also. She'd admonished her daughter to keep her clairvoyance a secret from everyone at her school, from their social circle of ex-patriot Brits and those who worked with the British Foreign Office to their American friends and acquaintances, from their Butler family in London to their neighbors in Alexandria. Only Nonna's family in Como, Italy knew the truth and extent of their powers.

Trevor insisted that his career not be jeopardized by any claim of *psychic powers* for fear such a claim would make him a laughingstock. Laughingstocks did not keep positions in the Foreign Office for long unless they were willing to languish in some god-forsaken part of the world. *How would you like a post in Timbuktu, my dear? Well, then . . .*

Poor Athena, to be burdened with such powers and such a secret. However, her daughter had wisely agreed for the benefit of her father and their family as a whole.

The elevator doors hissed open. Standing there to greet her, a tall, husky man of whom she'd grown quite fond. Detective Gino Palomino—she even adored his name—shook hands with her. His touch sent a frisson up and down her spine. The man was in a dark mood. Her stomach, full from lunch, plummeted down to her knees. Bile rose in her esophagus and tears sprang to her eyes.

"I'm so sorry," Anna said.

"You know, then?" the detective asked, staring at his hand, then at her gloved hand. His angry gaze traveled up to her face. "You know we found her? Right where you said she'd be, where you saw her. Under that pile of discarded cardboard and rags, by that old, broken streetlamp. That sonuvabitch, he strangled her and left her in that alley. And he left no trace evidence behind. He's either extremely clever or extremely lucky."

Detective Palomino, of Major Crimes and Missing Children, looked bereft. A predator and killer of children was loose in the city, and all he could do was look to Anna for help. Their investigation had met a series of dead ends and no leads.

Poor man. Poor child.

There would be others unless she could help him stop the monster. She would do her best. In the final analysis, this was *her* burden. *Her* destiny.

Her secret.

Chapter Three

The onslaught of images and emotions struck Athena's mind. In an instant, she knew she was going mad. Stark, raving mad. In response, her brain's gelatinous mass exploded into a thousand pieces. Like a ball of jello blown apart, slimy pieces of brain splattered all over. Somehow, her head still intact, she shut down emotionally and curled up tightly within herself.

Athena woke up fully. Blimey! That old, recurring nightmare still plagued her. Her memory of that terrible time, when she'd had a psychotic break—or as close to one as she'd ever experienced in her life—always returned when her delta brain waves rapidly morphed into theta waves. It was like those movies of a submarine crashing up and out of the water. Sudden and explosive. Always jarring.

Or, put another way, as her subconscious receded, seemingly yanked downward, and her conscious mind shot upward. This was one of many facts about her mental powers she'd learned over the past ten years from her mother. At least, this was the way Anna had explained this phenomenon to Athena. Athena considered the explanation more theory than fact. One of many theories about their powers of clairvoyance.

Ten years ago the reverse had happened, a rapid descent from alpha to theta waves, more rapidly than her nine-year-old mind could handle. Mental overload and fear had sent her into a sharp, spiraling descent into her subconscious mind. Somehow, in that theta state of dreamlike images, her conscious and subconscious mind overlapped and merged. And in that state, somehow, she was able to access other minds. This was how her mother explained it, anyway. All it took was a physical touch to trigger this jarring descent.

Now, the descent into merging brain waves wasn't jarring.

The phenomenon was rapid, in the blink of an eye, a fluid transition that didn't affect her physically, except that her mind flooded with another person's images and emotions. And now, she could turn it off like she could the faucet at the kitchen sink. It took concentration and willpower to block the flow, but she'd worked at it over the years and, with her mother's encouragement and training, had mastered the ability. Otherwise, her mother had explained, the flood would be constant and exhausting. And she'd grow to hate another person's touch.

In Athena's view, she'd mastered the curse.

Workshops at the Claremont Institute of Psychic Research in Virginia these past eight years of their American posting had revealed modern theories about this rapid transformation in brain waves. She and her mother had attended a couple of these workshops as she continued to develop coping mechanisms for her extraordinary clairvoyant powers and as her mother sought to explain these powers. The mental discipline required to turn her clairvoyance off when people touched her had been difficult for Athena at first, for she had to overcome her natural curiosity to know what others were thinking. The Claremont Institute helped her gain control of that strange state where theta and alpha merged.

There were numerous other theories, Athena had learned, that sought to explain the psychic powers of women like her mother, her grandmother, Lorena Skoros and all the other women in the Trementino bloodline.

All very strange and perplexing, Athena knew. But then,

wasn't life itself rather strange and perplexing? Her mental powers were just one aspect of her entire life. Right now, improving her artistic abilities and somehow finding a boyfriend was more important to her. Those two goals ranked higher on her priority list than probing the mysteries of her clairvoyance.

Smiling, Athena hopped out of bed. She had the guest bathroom all to herself, since her brother Chris, preferring to be boarded, remained at school in Virginia until Thanksgiving and Christmas breaks. Her father had already left for work, and her mother, she could hear, was downstairs in the kitchen. Already she could smell the aroma of freshly brewed coffee, her and her mother's preference over her father's morning tea. She showered, then blow-dried her long blond hair and swept it back into a simple ponytail with a fluff of bangs. Afterward she dressed in her ubiquitous faded jeans, sweater and scuffed brown ankle boots. She added a soft coral lipstick, her only makeup. Today, her sweater of choice was a cream-colored cable-knit her talented mother had made for her one Christmas, over which Athena added a wide brown belt. The look was plain compared to stylish Mikela, but it was *her* look.

Her mother was bending over the tiled counter, reading the newspaper. Athena tiptoed up behind her and wrapped her arms around her mother's waist.

Anna squealed in mock shock. "You bad girl, sneaking up on me like that!" Anna turned and hugged her, her dark eyes downcast.

The images Athena had caught from her surprised mother were unmistakable. Mum was at it again, helping the cops catch bad guys.

Athena withdrew and poured herself a cup of black coffee. There were scrambled eggs on the stove, along with blood sausage—which her father loved—and pork'n'beans.

Although she and her mother tended to stick to toasted bagels or thick, grainy bread, toasted and heaped with jam, she filled a small plate with eggs and beans. Just then, however, the dark, gruesome images that flowed from her mother's mind overrode Athena's hunger.

"Mum, what disgusting crime are you trying to solve now? Man, if Dad finds out, he's going to be pissed off." She scampered over to the toaster and snatched a warm bagel half and smeared it with cream cheese and strawberry jam, then made a face and left it on the plate. She'd be lucky not to barf up her coffee and cream.

"Such an ugly phrase, 'Thena, this *pissed off*." Her mother frowned but returned to the newspaper, lying flat and opened on the counter. A polyglot, her mother was fluent in three languages, English being her third, Italian and French her first two. In addition, her German was passable. She had done translation work for publishers since she was in her twenties.

"Mum, it means angry."

"I know what it means, 'Thena. You startled me just then while I'm trying to take my mind off this horrible case that Detective Palomino is stuck on. I'm not succeeding. I keep thinking, thinking, wishing I could see more. I feel so helpless . . ."

"Mum, you know what Father thinks about that. He's afraid you'll get hurt trying to help the cops."

"Police, you mean, Athena. Don't be afraid what your father will think if he knew. I think he already knows. He has his way of finding out. On the Embassy staff, there are Her Majesty's spies, you know. Your father told me at lunch yesterday that MI-6 has detected a possible threat during the UN's General Assembly. The entire Embassy staff's on alert." She brought her mug of steaming coffee over to the table and sat down next to Athena. "My work with the Metropolitan Police is child's play compared to MI-6 spies and what they do to save lives. My life's work is small, but I must do it."

Athena understood what her mother meant, but because she too, like her father, disapproved out of concern for her mother's safety, she remained silent.

Anna smiled. "If any of your friends ask what I do, simply say I'm a translator of books. No one needs to know I'm also a forensics consultant. That's the way I'm announced to the police station. Detective Palomino tells them I have a forensics background in anthropology." Her mother glanced up at Athena and smiled ironically. "I'm not even sure what anthropology is." She gave an exaggerated Italian shrug, so like Nonna's expressive gestures.

"Oh, Mum, of surely you know what that means. I only hope you know what you're doing," said Athena, her tone of voice ominous. The dangers of which, Athena knew, her mother ignored. What else could she say? Her mother had a desire to help eradicate wherever she felt evil ruled. What better place to help the police than the murder capital of the United States, Washington, D.C.?

Turning contemplative, Athena dug into her plate of scrambled eggs and beans. Hunger pangs had returned, so she took a bite of bagel and savored the taste of the strawberry-flavored cream cheese. When she looked up, her mother's dark-eyed gaze fixed her. Mum wanted to talk.

Uh, oh. More cop talk.

"You know I feel compelled to do this. So far, only the Medical Examiner and Gino—Detective Palomino—know the truth. The other day, he took me to the Police Morgue to view the girl's body. A young girl of twelve, so sad. Her poor body, small for her age"—her mother glanced up to see Athena in mid-bite—"well, this sick man likes them young and for the present, African-American. This monster sees himself as a hunter preying upon the most defenseless."

Athena suppressed a flare of nausea but put down the bagel. Even her heavily creamed coffee felt slick inside her throat, making her feel sick.

"Mum, please . . ."

She looked up to find her mother gazing at the kitchen window with a faraway, haunted look in her eyes. "Anyway, my job is to gather clues to help the police investigate. When I touched the girl, I saw his hands on her throat. They were white—he's a young, white man—and his knuckles are bruised. All red and bruised. I told Detective Palomino all this. I sensed this predator's thoughts. He roams the poor black neighborhoods and looks for little girls who are alone. What Americans call latch-key kids. Somehow he gets the children to trust him, and when they get close enough, he grabs them, overpowers them and shoves them into his black van."

"Black van? Like a delivery van?" Despite warning herself not to get involved—didn't she have enough problems in her life—Athena was intrigued. "Did you see him wearing a uniform? Did you see his face? If you did, describe him and I'll sketch him for you."

Anna scowled. "No, I wish I had. No, *Dio mio,* his face eludes me. I just saw his hands and the black van." Anna's dark eyes were in a deep glaze, so Athena waited. Then her mother sighed deeply and refocused her gaze again on Athena. "Thank you for offering, but no, I could get nothing more. If I do, I shall ask for your help. Your rendering skills are so acute, so keen, a sketch of this madman would be very helpful. Nevertheless, Detective Palomino is following what few leads I could give him. It's so frustrating."

Athena said nothing as she pushed away her plate of eggs and beans. "What kinds of leads, Mum? You mean that he's young, white and drives a black van? That must cover thousands of men in the D.C. area."

Her mother shrugged again. "I was not completely useless. I sensed the man's knuckles were inflamed and causing him pain. He didn't wear gloves, even in this cold weather, so the monster either wants to get caught by leaving fingerprints, or . . ."

"Or what, Mum?"

"Or he has an urge to feel their skin, their fear when he grabs them. The M.E. didn't find any fingerprints on the victim and the police have found no prints at the dump sites. Gino thinks he's not going to stop, so he has ordered his team of detectives to pursue all the possibilities."

"Like what?" Athena sipped her coffee until it cooled, then put the cup into the microwave to nuke it up to the heat level she liked. While that was happening, she wrapped up the bagel in a square of foil. She'd eat it later during her break at work. Once her stomach had settled.

"One is the possibility the man is a street fighter—I have no idea what that is. Gino claims it's what some desperate men do to make money. That would explain the bruised knuckles. Or he works with his hands and scrapes his fingers. The other lead I gave him, he drives a black van with signs on the sides. Those magnetic signs he takes off, but these signs cause the girls to trust him. The detectives on his team were very pleased that they had these leads, anyway. They are going to canvass the neighborhood where the child's abduction took place, ask if anyone saw a black van with a tradesman's signs. That's what Gino told me before I left."

A red flag of warning raised to Athena. "Mum, how many detectives know about you and what you're doing to help Detective Palomino?"

"I don't know," she mumbled into her raised cup, "maybe four. Palomino's team of investigators. Why?"

Athena studied her mother's still pretty face. For the past ten or more years, since her father's posting in Lyon, France, Athena had kept her mother's unpaid occupation a secret because she knew how fulfilled and gratified her mother felt after each case was solved. The price her mother paid, however, for doing such selfless work was noticeable on her countenance. Every additional line around her mother's full mouth, the deeper crow's feet around her expressive brown eyes, the additional gray hair were all results, Athena felt, of her mother's chosen work. This kind of community service and its potential risks were beyond the call of duty. The dedication took its toll.

Not to mention the fact that if her work became public, especially in the criminal world, the whole family would be in danger.

Athena returned to the table where her mother sat, apparently lost in her world of predators and murdered children.

"The more people who know about our gifts, the more danger we're in. You keep telling me that, Mum. You've always told me to keep our powers a secret. That there's a danger if our secret gets out, and that includes Dad and Chris, too. Doesn't Father have enough to worry about with his job at the Embassy? You told me ten years ago we must keep our clairvoyance a secret. Have you changed your mind?"

Cradling the cup of coffee in her hands, Anna locked gazes with her Athena. One hand reached out and clasped Athena's. Immediately, sharp images and strong emotions flowed from mind to mind.

Athena reeled in surprise. "Nonna's mother risked her life? During the war? Do you mean World War II? She risked her life? How?"

Her mother smiled slyly. "Yes, of course, World War II. *Dio,* we're not that old. My mother, Nonna Trementino, was very brave. She gave readings to the Nazi officers that occupied that part of Italy and because she wove the truth with the lies and did this so skillfully—yes, they believed her. So when the opportunity arose to help the Italian Resistance, she told the Gestapo chief the lies that saved an entire village from certain death."

For the first time, Athena began to understand her mother's motivations for helping the police. "Every generation of our bloodline has done something like this, Mum? Nonna, too?"

"Yes, with our gift from God comes an obligation to do good. To do something that makes a difference. But . . ." Anna paused and looked pointedly at the cup on the table that her father had used during his breakfast. " . . . we must be cautious and careful at the same time. Do you recall the ceremony at the lake? With Nonna and Lorena Skoros? When we gave you the Athena medallion?"

"Yes. Each one of you told me in turn, *For the greater good and to honor God*." Athena looked down and fingered the gold medallion that hung on a gold chain. Then she frowned. "But Mum, you're walking a kind of tightrope. And sorry,"—she stood up, uneasy with the turn of their conversation—"but I don't feel the same obligation to work for the greater good. It's all I can do to keep up with my studies and my part-time job." She glanced at her watch. Her shift started at nine, and it was already eight-forty. "Shit-on-a-brick, I'm due at work in twenty minutes."

Anna looked up, disappointment creasing her face. "What an expression. Where did you learn—no, don't tell me. I don't want to know." Instantly, she brightened. "Before you rush off, show me the painting you did of Lorena's son."

Athena glanced at her watch again. *Shit*. She was always late. Late to work, late to class, late for dinner. Her entire life was like a treadmill, and she was always running to catch up.

Still, a few minutes more of mother-daughter bonding wouldn't hurt. Her morning shift at Starbucks, from nine to one, was ideal for her. Close to the Art Institute, the store was a hub for students and local artists, a place to work and socialize. On the down side, there was a lot of stress on the job, even though her manager was an easygoing boss whose true-life work was metal sculpturing. A fellow artist, he seemed to understand her tardiness. Still, everyone had a breaking point.

"Okay, I finished it two nights ago," she said, then went to her portfolio in the large living room, where she had a corner all to herself. Her easel stood, a silent reminder that another work in progress would draw her back to the corner later that night.

Carefully withdrawing the twenty-two by twenty-four inch canvas on a wooden stretcher, she held it up for her mother to see. It wasn't her best portrait, but it was fine, considering she knew almost nothing about the subject. Aside from her nighttime fantasies about the guy. Which, of course, had nothing to do with reality.

"I might need to do more work on it. You see the rising mists in the pale gold background. I saw him there, like somewhere in the early morning sunshine with the pale ochre hills in the background. He likes to walk there, I think. Wish I could've seen more of *him*."

"Oh, 'Thena," her mother purred, "that's very good. It looks just like Kyriakos. I like what you did . . ." Her voice trailed off as she studied Athena's treatment.

"Since your cousin Lorena has foreseen Keri—"

"Kyriakos. They call him Kas, short for Kyriakos Alexander Skoros," her mother clarified.

"Kas's possible death, I wanted to give him a different look, like he's determined to cheat death. A confidence and hope. The poor guy probably needs it." She shook her head from side to side. "How sucky is that! His mother says he's going to die in a car crash."

Shrugging thoughtlessly, as if her black humor would fall on deaf ears, Athena almost laughed. Then she saw her mother's shocked look.

"First of all, she hasn't told me which of her two youngest sons she saw die in that horrible dream. Secondly, you don't believe that Lorena can see the future, do you? You think this is all nonsense?"

Stung by her mother's look of outrage, Athena narrowed her eyes defensively and refused to budge. "No, Mum, I don't believe that your cousin can see the future. Precogs only exist in sci-fi movies."

"Well, let's hope in this case Lorena is mistaken. Even what you call *precogs* make mistakes . . . I would think. Speaking of whom, Lorena Skoros and her family have invited us to visit them for Thanksgiving weekend."

It was now Athena's turn to be shocked. "But-but," she sputtered, "I can't go. I have to work that weekend."

Her mother stood up, all five-foot-five of her erect and stubborn. "Oh no, you don't. While your father's in England that week on government business, you and Chris are coming with me to California. And there, *bella figlia mia,* you will see for yourself what my cousin is capable of." She took another long look at the painting and softened a bit. "Lorena will be happy to see this portrait of her son. Kyriakos, he's the youngest of the four sons. Very handsome, intelligent, well educated. And unmarried."

Stunned, Athena watched Anna turn away and walk to the sink. *So that's it – they're playing matchmakers, the two cousins. They're trying to hook us up – me and a guy who's almost thirty. Un-friggin'-believable!*

The women didn't merely have clairvoyance and an obligation to do good in their bloodline's DNA. They were smart and determined. Not to mention sneaky and conniving.

Well, Thanksgiving was two weeks away. She'd think of something to get out of it. Mum's hidden agenda. Like she wasn't busy or content enough doing police work on the sly.

The cute guy—Tony something-or-other, a Polish name, she thought—was working that long Thanksgiving weekend. And she wanted to work it, too. Her miserably uneventful social life depended on it.

She'd shown Tony her portrait of the sheriff's deputy in the break room, her huge portfolio propped obtrusively against the cabinet, making him almost trip over it. She'd caught him in mid-fall, had received a swarm of feelings—all positive, all lusty. Tony liked her, was attracted to her, even desired her. That very day, she'd begun to send out to him her flirty vibes. He looked encouraged but hadn't yet asked her out, though she knew he was building up towards it.

She just had to stay in town by herself. With everyone gone, maybe she'd do a little entertaining of her own.

Chapter Four

Athena took her first break at eleven that morning, and since she'd eaten little for breakfast, her hunger pangs were acute. The bagel she'd wrapped earlier at home had to suffice, she knew, for there wasn't time to nuke up a breakfast wrap or English muffin. She was slurping down her orange juice when Tony poked his head around the door of the break room.

"Sorry, gorgeous, but we need you up front. Another crowd's arrived. Barb's getting her drinks mixed up and Fergy's looking frantic."

He shot her a brilliant smile before disappearing. Barb was the new girl that Athena was trying to train at the brew bar and Fergy was the store manager, a talented metal sculptor who subsidized his income with a steady paycheck. As he often said, the paycheck paid his rent and groceries, but his sculptures fed his soul. Another poor artist with high-minded ideals. They surrounded her. Heck, she was one of them.

Gorgeous, she mused, jumping up and tossing the rest of the bagel away. She took one more swig of juice and wiped her mouth with a napkin. A quick look in the mirror by their lockers reminded her that she was anything but gorgeous. Neat and clean, yeah, but not gorgeous. Her bangs plastered across her forehead from perspiration, her face flushed from hurrying for two hours over a warm machine that spit out hot brewed coffee and steamy milk. Her coral lipstick had long since worn off and there were dark, bluish shadows under her eyes. In her opinion, the green tint of her eyes was her only saving grace, and it pleased her that Tony—tall, cute, curly-haired junior at American University—found her not loathsome to look at. At least the other good feature—her long blond hair, shot through with strands of brown, caramel, blond, platinum—was something she could be a little vain about. Long, thick and wavy, her hair came compliments of her father's genes. Her body type, too, was her father's. Her figure was average, neither slim nor plump, but her taller than average height compensated and made her legs look longer than they really were.

Oh well, I am what I am. Gorgeous or not.

The store was suddenly packed. Five minutes earlier, no more than ten customers were sitting around the store. Now, the line in front of the counter sported twice that number. Half a dozen empty cups, labeled and ranging in size from tall to venti, greeted her alongside the left machine, and Barb was frazzled, close to a tearful meltdown. Athena patted her back and whispered to her.

"Go take a break, I'll take over. Go on. Come back in five, okay?"

A shaky Barb smiled gratefully and left. Athena threw a look over at Fergy, who was shooting up his thick black eyebrows. To his credit, he didn't leave his post at the register and had decided, she assumed, to trust her judgment. After whipping out two drinks and calling them out, Tony joined her and took over the other brew machine. He touched her shoulder briefly, but the touch sent a shockwave down her arm. And an image just as shocking.

An image of her and Tony, naked as jaybirds, his body behind her, pumping against her—she almost dropped the cup in her hand.

"Good idea, Athena," said Tony, "Nice of you, too. She was on the verge of breaking down. When she comes back, I'll send her to the register to calm down."

For a moment, she stopped what she was doing and looked at him. His facial expression gave away nothing remotely close to his salacious thoughts. Well, maybe something. A reddish spot dotted one pale cheek, and his deep blue eyes burned with laser intensity when he turned them her way. Her heartbeat raced as she realized that he did indeed want her . . . badly.

Wow. Tall, cute, curly-haired Tony was going to become her first lover. He just didn't know it yet.

A week later, Athena came downstairs from her room to find her father having a whiskey-on-the-rocks in the living room. He was staring at the corner where her easel stood, a cloth covering the current work-in-progress. Another cloth-covered canvas, the one of Kas Skoros, rested at the foot of the easel. She'd add a touchup or two, and then spray it with fixative one more time. Her mother would take it with her on the flight to California and present it to the Skoros family as a gift.

Her father was home an hour early, so Athena had to do a double-take. Pleased beyond words, happy to see him, she bounded over to greet him. He smiled at her.

"Yes, luv, I promised not to look. Some sort of surprise for the Skoros family, am I right?" her father said, tossing her a lopsided smile.

Trevor Butler was the scion of an English family that could trace its roots back to King William the first and the Norman Conquest. He was tall, at least six-foot-three, slim in build although easing gently towards a stocky middle, with a full shock of graying dark blond hair. It pleased Athena that she'd inherited his physical looks and his wry sense of humor. She considered him a success. He'd risen from small-town Yorkshire barrister to a couple of stints in the House of

Commons, then on to Foreign Service work in Turkey, Croatia and France, ultimately landing his current plum assignment, Cultural Attaché to the British Embassy in Washington, D.C. Her pride in him knew no limits, and they were close in ways that were different from the bond she felt with her mother.

As soon as she gave him a fierce hug, her mind was hit by a jumble of images which transmitted so lightning fast that she couldn't read them all. One image lasted longer than the others: Sunshine, ocean waves, palm trees.

"Are we going to Florida for the holidays?" she asked him after they released each other.

"Blimey, Thena, will you shut that off? I keep forgetting how you read minds. It's quite disconcerting. Respect my privacy, will you, luv? Not to mention, I must remind you, that some of my thoughts are officially classified government information."

Immediately chastised, she said, "Sorry, Father, I forget sometimes." She wrapped an arm around his waist. She watched him glance again at her easel in the corner. "Don't even think you're going to get away with a peek. This is *my* classified work, at least until I finish it. The one on the easel, it's a Christmas surprise for you and Mum."

Actually, since she was taking Portrait Painting this semester, she'd decided to do an interesting portrait of her parents in the chiaroscuro style, a style which the French painter, Georges de la Tour, made famous during the seventeenth century and Caravaggio expanded upon. People's faces and upper torsos were lit by a single candle, so two-thirds of the subjects were in darkness. The result was very striking, very dramatic. She wanted to see if she could get it right, just like de la Tour and Caravaggio.

Her father sat in a nearby wing chair, his feet propped up on a matching ottoman, and invited her to join him. Athena could hear her mother speaking to their housekeeper-cook, Tilly, who came in three afternoons a week to help with domestic chores. Athena's bedroom and bathroom were off-limits, for she preferred to clean those, herself. Chris' room was always a disaster, especially after a weekend home from boarding school. Athena had taken before-and-after photos of the miracle that took place when Tilly whirled through.

"Mind if I join you with a Coke and Jack, Father?" She went over to the credenza bar and looked back at him expectantly.

Her father frowned his disapproval. "Thena, I don't want to condone hard liquor. Wine would be better," he added.

She sighed, "Okay," and instead poured herself a glass of *prosecco* from a bottle in the bar's small fridge. They held up their glasses towards each other.

"Cheers," they chorused. Athena approached and clinked glasses with her father.

"You're becoming a bloody American, luv. They're the only ones who do that. Maybe it's time to return home for good. Or at least the continent. What do you think?"

She knew her father was teasing her, taunting her more likely, for he loved his assignment in D.C. and knew she loved the Art Institute. They were a five-hour flight from London, so if government or family matters called him home, the visit was always short-lived.

In response to his teasing threat, she screwed up her face. "Very funny, Father. Just for that, I think I'll become a naturalized American. Now tell me about the palm trees and sunny beaches."

Having already shed his jacket, Trevor leaned back in his shirt sleeves and loosened his tie, then took another sip of Scotch whiskey and wiped his mouth with the back of one knuckle.

Athena looked on patiently, admiring his vibrant blue

eyes and handsome features, wondering if she'd ever fall in love with a man half as good-looking, intelligent and as accomplished as her father. Would she ever get married?

"Indeed, I shall. And you'll be very pleased, I trust. Your mother and I are flying tomorrow to California, San Francisco to be precise. Sir Arthur's number one and number two men were unavailable, and so it has fallen upon me to christen, so to speak, the new consulate-general in San Francisco. As you know, your mother's cousin lives nearby and your mother plans to stay on for the Thanksgiving holiday next week. I'll fly back on Sunday. I won't have much time with you and Chris, just overnight to sleep and grab my thick overcoat, and then it's on to London for some briefings having to do with the PM's visit in January. You'll be in charge of hearth and home this weekend, luv. Now, I know you told your mother you didn't want to go, but when Christopher comes home for the holiday on Sunday, you and he will fly out to California on Monday to join your mother." He sighed audibly. "Lots of comings and goings this weekend. Do you think you can handle all the responsibility, the solitude, the freedom for two whole days?"

As his news sank in, Athena's thoughts ran to the possibilities that had just opened up to her. It was Thursday evening, and that meant she'd have the condo to herself for at least two days and two nights. Most of the weekend, in fact. Chris was due home Sunday by noon, and they'd be flying to California on Monday. Suddenly, her objections to the Skoros visit dissolved. As long as she had a couple of days of freedom to do as she pleased, a week in California didn't seem so frightful.

A glance at the leaden sky outside the living room window, and having heard the news report of more snow flurries in the next few days, made Athena's spirit soar. Instantly, the promise of a little sunshine and sandy beaches sounded divine. Then she frowned.

"I've heard San Francisco is cold in the winter. The Skoroses live near Sacramento. Isn't Sacramento inland? There're no beaches or palm trees there. Is it even sunny in the winter there?"

Her father shot her a droll smile. "You were always so geographically savvy. Yes, it's inland, closer to the mountains but the Skoroses have promised you and Chris either a skiing holiday or a visit to the ocean. They expect it to hit the high seventies out there next week. It's not Florida but . . ."

Athena laid on a thick English accent, "It sounds divine, Father."

Her father's eyebrows cocked and he studied her for a moment, then sat back and closed his eyes. Fatigue lined his mouth and crinkled the corners of his eyes. "Think you can handle the freedom, luv?"

"Of course, Father. I'm not fourteen." Her voice sounded convincing, to her ears, anyway. "Have you forgotten, I'm turning twenty December first?"

"Ah, indeed, so true. I've been so busy of late, I need to catch up on your news. So, luv, any boyfriends? Or at the very least, male admirers in your spotlight?"

If Athena didn't know better, she could swear her father was the psychic of the family. How could he know . . .

"I have a date tomorrow night," she said, but added quickly, "it's a double date with Mikela and her new boyfriend. A guy at work. His name's Tony Grabowski. We've worked together for almost two months now. He came to our store from the Starbucks in Georgetown. He's a junior at AU, majoring in computer science."

She'd rushed through his *bona fides,* so it didn't surprise her when her father blinked his eyes and gazed upon her with open curiosity.

"Your first date with . . . this Tony?"

"Uh, not really. It's our second one. Tuesday night he took me out for pizza."

Afterwards, their French kissing had evolved to heavy petting in his car, thank heavens, and she'd managed to keep her clairvoyance shut off the entire time. Why spoil a fun time by doing a Peeping Tom? Maybe she'd finally lose her virginity tomorrow night. In two weeks, she'd turn twenty, and she was bound and determined not to be a twenty-year-old virgin with no love prospects in sight.

"Why is this the first I'm hearing of this young chap? He is young, isn't he? You're not dating that forty-year-old manager, are you, luv?"

Athena giggled. "No, Father, Tony's twenty-one, very cute, very smart."

"Good lord, is this serious, Athena?"

The question took her aback. She had no answer for her father. What could she say? Tony would make a good first lover—or at least she hoped so—but marriage, kids and a mortgage were unthinkable at this point in her life. In a way, she'd lived a very sheltered life in spite of her cosmopolitan upbringing. And her yearning to explore, to live, to experiment was making her want to burst out of her skin. But she was willing to take baby steps instead of sprinting ahead.

When he refused to look away, she searched for a reply. A sanitized, redacted reply meant for parents' ears only.

"Well, I don't know, Father. I don't know him that well. We're attracted to each other, that's all I can say. You know my track record regarding the opposite sex. Not very good."

"That's certainly not because of your looks or manners, luv. You're a pretty young woman with outstanding artistic talents. You're intelligent and kind. Any young man with half a brain would be lucky to attract your attentions. If you're referring to that obstacle, that clairvoyance of yours, well . . ."

Her father never called it a gift, like her mother always did. *Their gift from God* was how her mother expressed it. Nor did he call it a curse or miracle. She thought he regarded it as another sort of talent or ability, like a musical ability. If she could've played a beautiful rendition of Beethoven, however, her father would've considered that a more practical, more admirable ability. Although he never said so, Athena thought her father regarded her artistic talents as more useful, more marketable than her clairvoyance.

Unbidden, a few memories of her high school crushes and the resulting humiliations flooded her mind. As soon as she had allowed in the thoughts and feelings of her high school boyfriends—all two of them—she'd learned the truth. They wanted her body—oh, how they wanted to do things to her body. But they really considered her a freak, once they realized she knew things about them that no one else did. Their innermost secret thoughts and desires were accessible to her. And she was shocked by them. When she naively let it slip that she knew their secrets, they recoiled. What did she expect? That they'd be impressed by her gift, her powers? They were shocked down to their teenaged sneakers that she knew somehow, that she had invaded their minds. The word had spread like a virus—Athena Butler was a freak. No one had ever asked her out after that.

She had no date for the junior prom or senior ball. She had no dates at all her last two years of high school. A social pariah.

What a fool she'd been. Now, at least, she could control her invasions into other people's minds. It was difficult, but she knew the price she'd have to pay if she didn't.

Athena swallowed back a swelling of pain and downed the rest of her sparkling wine in one long swallow. If she didn't control this . . . this curse of hers, she'd end up a dried-up old maid. She just knew it.

"Father, I think I finally got it under control. My clairvoyance, I mean."

"Good to hear that, my darling girl. Men don't like to share their private thoughts. Not even your dear old dad." He took another sip, leaned his head back. "Let me know when dinner's ready. I might take a cat nap."

She stood and placed her wine glass on the credenza's marble top. "Okay. I'll see if Mum and Tilly need help."

On an impulse, she leaned over him, stroked his lanky forelock—how gray it was getting—and planted a light kiss on his forehead. Again, images and thoughts flooded her mind. *Too bad, Father. I want to know why you're so tired all the time.*

What she saw gave her a jolt.

CHAPTER FIVE

In the kitchen, Tilly, a stocky middle-aged black woman, was blending together the ingredients for a fruit torte while her mother tossed a green salad. The look on Athena's face must've raised an alarm, for her mother's hands stopped mid-air.

"*Dio mio,* 'Thena, what happened?"

"Father," she murmured miserably, "he's getting death threats? The ambassador, too, and the PM."

Her mother shot her a quelling look but continued tossing after sprinkling some dressing into the wooden bowl.

"You shouldn't have looked, 'Thena. You know how your father feels about that." Tilly was the only one besides Detective Palomino and his team who knew about their clairvoyance, and she, too, was sworn to secrecy. In return, her mother gave the woman readings, so it was not surprising when her mother spoke so offhandedly about their abilities in front of her.

Athena stared at her mother, scowling until Anna put down the salad utensils and threw up her hands in a surrender gesture. "This is part of the work. British diplomats, and I daresay diplomats all over the world, receive letters, phone calls and emails all the time from angry subjects. Or others. People who have been denied travel or work visas, people who face deportations, people who oppose the political party in power. Islamic terrorists, too. You've seen the Embassy on Embassy Row, 'Thena. It's like a fortress, and it's well guarded. You've been there."

Indeed, Athena had visited the Embassy several times. Located at the northern end of Embassy Row, the British Embassy looked like a country estate surrounded by acreage, security patrols, surveillance cameras, watchdogs. The airspace was monitored by the American military. The car her father traveled in to and from the Embassy was bulletproof, and his driver was former British Special Forces. Security details were assigned to all of the diplomats.

"I know all this, Mum. This time it's different. It has to do with the Prime Minister's visit here in January, doesn't it?"

Her mother glanced over at Tilly. "Add some mandarins and water chestnuts to this salad, Tilly. I must speak with my daughter in private."

At her mother's gesture, Athena followed her into her father's downstairs study after passing the entrance to the living room and looking in on Trevor. She closed the door behind them and took a seat on one of the club chairs.

Athena, alerted by her mother's need for a confidential talk, did the same, her focus never leaving her mother's face. "You're scaring me, Mum."

"Don't be silly, 'Thena. I just don't want Tilly to hear this. She doesn't need the worry. Yes, this is different than the death threats your father and the others at the Embassy usually receive. MI-six has picked up some chatter that concerns them. Some kind of plot by an Islamic group associated with the Chechen rebels in Dagestan. The warnings have come from, of all places, Russian intelligence agents who have informants within that group. InterPol agents have also confirmed this threat. Something about East European mercenaries working for this Islamist group and possibly carrying out the deed. You know that when we were stationed in Lyon, France, your father developed relationships with agents at InterPol Headquarters there. One of his assignments is to liaise with InterPol wherever we are stationed.

He has absolute confidence in these people, and they have confirmed that a plot to disrupt the PM's visit is definitely in the making. They've followed a money trail, and now they believe these mercenaries have accepted a contract to carry out something horrible. The Embassy doesn't know exactly what or when or where. Everyone is on alert."

"But the PM's visit isn't until January. What can they do before then?"

"Carry out their preparations. Gather intelligence on all Embassy personnel and their families. Thus, we must all be vigilant. This is one reason why your father is relieved that we'll be in California while he's away in London. InterPol suspects this team of mercenaries is already in the U.S. and making preparations. Even here in D.C."

Athena felt her insides grow cold with dread. "Already in the U.S.? How can the U. S. State Department allow these people in?"

Her mother gave her an exaggerated Italian shrug. "Who knows why? The Americans let anybody in, it seems. They give out visas like balloons at a carnival. Besides, we don't know exactly who these people are. They're traveling under aliases. False identities. False passports. InterPol suspects that these mercenaries were denied British visas, so they are coming here to target the PM. So whoever the prime minister sees when he comes here is also at risk. That includes your father and the rest of the Embassy staff."

Realization hit, making Athena's mouth gape open. "The diplomats *and* their families? And the American president?"

"I'm afraid so. There are no details as yet, so we can only be extra cautious. Tell us, for example, if you sense someone means you harm. Use your clairvoyance if you sense something's not quite right with somebody. Be careful when you take the subway. Let your father know if you think anything is amiss. In fact, when we return from California, your father wants me to drive you to work in the morning and pick you up after your classes. Chris' boarding school is fenced, and there will be security details assigned to us and to the other families of Embassy diplomats. We won't know who they are, however, or what they look like. They'll look like everybody else and they will blend into the background. For this weekend, while you're alone, I would like you to stay home. Don't go out by yourself. Just stay in, 'Thena."

Athena groaned. "Mum, I have a date tomorrow night. I can't break it, I won't break it. You know I rarely have dates—"

Anna patted Athena's knees, her dark brown eyebrows furrowed in thought. "No, of course, we can't stop living, can we? I'll have your father assign you a security detail, just until you and Chris get on that plane for California Monday morning. By the way, the plane tickets are on your dresser. It's a seven-AM flight, so it's up to you to get Chris there on time. One of the Skoroses will meet you both at the airport. Maybe I'll be there, too. It'll be an adventure."

Athena wasn't listening. Her thoughts swirled around the change in plans for her weekend of pleasure. Suddenly, she didn't feel so lust driven. The least she could do was have the foursome come back to the condo after dinner and clubbing. Maybe have a late-night snack and let Mikela and her boyfriend slip out at some point. Tony had made it clear that he wanted to spend the night with her. She was determined to make it happen. She might not get another chance for months.

Was it so awful to want to be like other young women and have a sex life?

Her mother looked down at her hands and nervously twisted her wedding ring around. *Oh god, there's more?*

"'Thena, there's something else. I'm expecting a call from Detective Palomino. He's been following up on some leads I gave him this afternoon. I saw one of the signs on the black van, some kind of plumbing service, which he claims does not exist. I couldn't see the van's license number, more's the pity." Her hands fisted in her lap as her mother shook her head with exasperation. "I wish I could have seen more, because I'm so afraid that man will strike again. Anyway, if the detective calls, tell him I'll be back on November twenty-ninth. Perhaps by then he'll have caught the *bastardo*." Her mother's eyes widened, and she made a hurried sign of the cross.

Her mother was so old-fashioned in some ways that she still felt guilty swearing in front of her children. Athena smiled wryly.

"S'okay, Mum. I swear all the time. So you see, that's one sterling example of yours that I can't possibly follow. I guess I'm bound for hell—" She broke off when her mother scowled. "I'll tell Detective Palomino if he calls. Do you think he's getting closer to finding that sick asshole?"

Her mother rolled her eyes, then nodded. "Yes, he's getting closer. The sooner, the better. The man's evil, he has a choice but he has no conscience, no empathy for those poor little girls. He must be caught and put away for good." Her voice catching, Anna put a hand to her heated face, as if to remind herself that a semblance of their normal life beckoned her. "Now, let's put dinner on the table. Your father and I have an early night tonight. Our flight's at eight tomorrow morning. Thank god it's a private charter, otherwise we'd have to be in the security line at six. Horrors!"

They stood up together and as they did, her mother touched her arm. "Whatever you have planned, cancel it. You must stay in this weekend. Alone."

Athena pulled her arm away and changed the subject. "You're taking the painting I did of Lorena's son?"

Her mother brightened. "Oh yes, she's going to love it.

You will love them, 'Thena. The Skoros family is . . . well, unique. Smart people with a strong love of family. You would like Kyriakos and his three brothers. They're all tall, dark and handsome."

Dutifully, Athena nodded. *Don't push it, Mum.*

She gathered her things together and made a beeline for the front door.

Not as tall, dark and handsome as Tony, I bet.

CHAPTER SIX

No sooner had Athena begun her morning shift at Starbucks than her cell phone vibrated. She noted the caller and when she got her break, she went into the back room and returned the call. Detective Palomino answered on the first ring and Athena identified herself.

"My mother wanted you to know that she'll be out of town until November twenty-ninth," she dutifully explained. "She left this morning and won't be able to help you out for the next week or so."

There was a pause before he spoke. "That's unfortunate. I've set up a lineup of possible persons of interest in this case. A result of your mother's excellent leads. I was hoping she'd come down and maybe give us a hint or some direction. We have such little physical evidence to go on."

"A lineup? You mean, where suspects line up against the wall, and a witness identifies the criminal through a one-way window?"

"Yeah, something like that, Miss Butler. We have a neighbor of the latest murdered child, who recalls seeing the driver of the black van."

"Then why do you need my mother's help if you have an eyewitness?" Athena asked.

She heard the detective clear his throat and lower his voice. "Our witness is not the most reliable. He's the drug addict neighbor who was supposed to be watching the child after school while the mother was at work."

That gave her pause. "I'm sorry. My mother told me the

little girl was taken from a poor black neighborhood."

"Yes, that's right. Your mother told you about this case?"

Athena's first reaction was to blurt out the truth, but she demurred. Would her mother get in trouble if she said yes? Still, what was the harm? Compared to a child being abducted and murdered simply because she had the bad luck of being raised by a poor woman who couldn't afford proper child care? What unspeakable suffering did that child endure—and all the others the sick bastard had tortured and killed?

"Yes, she did," Athena admitted, "Everything, in fact. Uh, Detective Palomino, my mother told you about me, didn't she? That I'm clairvoyant, too?"

"Yes, she did." There seemed to be tense silence on his end.

An idea struck Athena. Once, during a workshop at the Claremont Institute of Psychic Research in nearby McLean, she, her mother and other clairvoyants had participated in an experiment. The results had amazed even her as she and the others handled objects each one had brought in.

Hmm, well, why not?

"Detective, do you know what psychometry is?" When the man replied with a hesitant *no,* she went on, "It's when a clairvoyant can touch or handle an object that belongs to someone and receive information about that person. Y'know, insights, facts, images. What I'm thinking is that I can maybe help you today. If you allow me to touch something that belongs to these men in the lineup. Do you think it's worth a try?"

"Hmm."

Did the man think she was a veritable fruit loop? When Fergy entered the room to rummage through a box of frozen breakfast wraps, she stood, ready to return to the brew bar. Tony was fielding the orders at the espresso machine while she was on break.

Finally, Palomino came back on the line. "Sure, let's give it a try. The lineup's set for noon. I'll have one of my detectives pick you up at eleven-thirty. Where are you right now?"

She gave him the store location and hung up while flagging down Fergy on his way back to the front of the store.

"I'm so sorry, Fergy, but I've got to leave today at eleven-thirty."

"What? And miss the lunchtime crowd?" Fergy looked fit to be tied.

"I know," she said, practically wringing her hands, "but it's police business. I have to go."

"What've you done now, Athena? Parked in a handicapped zone?" He disappeared around the corner, obviously not wanting to deal with her request at the moment. His avoidance of "No" was, she knew, his tacit approval despite his annoyance. Poor Fergy. He was too kind and understanding, but she knew also that there was a list of oncall part-timers who could come in at a moment's notice.

As she walked back to her post behind the left hand espresso machine, Tony threw her a quizzical look.

"What's this? You're leaving early? Fergy wants me to call a replacement."

Instantly, she made the decision to, well, not exactly lie but embroider the truth a bit. Tony couldn't know, not yet anyway, about her clairvoyance.

"It's a police matter involving my brother, Chris. I've got to go."

"We still on for tonight?" Tony asked, darting her an anxious look as he steamed a pot of milk.

Her thoughts lingered on the phone call and what she was hoping to accomplish, but she managed a halfheartedly enthusiastic *Oh yes.*

For the next hour or so, she wondered uneasily why she

had volunteered to help Palomino and his team of homicide detectives. Getting involved in this case was maybe not one of her better ideas.

Well, stupid, hope you don't live to regret it.

Detective Juan-Pablo Ochoa turned out to be much younger than she expected. She guessed he was in his late twenties, but when they shook hands after he showed her his badge and ID, she realized he was older. Maybe early forties.

"You have a young face for someone with three children," she said as they walked to his unmarked Crown Victoria parked at the curb.

He flashed her a smile before he stowed away her art supplies in his back seat. Settled in the driver's seat, Ochoa looked over at her buckling up in the passenger seat. Dressed in a turtleneck, slacks and sports jacket, he was good-looking with dark, wavy hair and a deep olive complexion.

"Your mother told you?"

Surprised that he would doubt her since her mother had been working with Palomino's team for over a year, Athena gently placed her hand on his forearm. He stared down at her hand, then raised his dark eyes to her face.

Athena smiled. "No, and she didn't tell me that your eldest daughter plays piano very well. Or that your middle child, a boy, has a complete set of Star Wars figures on his shelf. Your youngest son is hyperactive but then,"—she shrugged—"he's only two. He loves those Ninja turtles."

He shot her a grudging nod of respect and pulled out into traffic. "Y'know, I told Palomino this was going to be an exercise in futility, but maybe I was wrong."

Athena darted him a look. "Your very religious mother named you after Pope John-Paul, didn't she?"

"You picked that up, too?" He took a right turn towards

the freeway ramp.

"No," she said, "I guessed. Hispanic, Juan-Pablo." When he barked a short laugh, she began to relax a little.

"You speak Spanish?" he asked her.

"A little. We lived in Madrid for two years after France. My father's posted all over."

"Sounds like a great job. Your mother says you and your brother are worldly for your ages." He laughed. "I should consider diplomatic work. My wife would never go for it, though. She likes the good ol' USA. Her family left Cuba years ago and here is where she wants to stay."

Athena nodded in understanding. "It's a nomadic life. You make friends and then have to leave them. Y'know, Detective, I've never done this before. Worked with cops, I mean. If I get it wrong, will you arrest me? Like, for obstruction of justice or something like that?"

He chuckled. "No, but the squad will never let us forget it. We've kept a low profile on your mother, passed her off as a forensic consultant. That gives her entry into the morgue, our station, even crime scenes. But, believe me, some of them have guessed what we're up to and they've given us gobs of grief. When we get results, however, that shuts 'em up quick. And we've gotten lots of results, thanks to your mom."

Genuinely shocked, Athena asked, "My mother goes to crime scenes?"

"Oh yeah. She's got a strong stomach. She's given us solid tips on a lot of homicide cases. She's the real deal. I was a skeptic at first, but she's come through and proven herself time and time again. My question is, are you the real deal? So far, it looks like it."

This revelation about her mother made Athena realize how committed her mother was to use her gifts to help the police solve crimes. Ochoa's last question caught her off-guard. She honestly wasn't sure how to explain how their clairvoyance worked.

"Am I the real deal? I don't know. I guess so. I've never tested it before . . . well, except at the Claremont Institute of Psychic Research. They—the scientists there—seem to think I'm the real deal. I guess you and the other detectives have to decide for yourselves. I mean, today I might get nothing. I don't know. My mother believes this gift of ours comes from God. What do you think, Detective Ochoa?"

He glanced over at her, then turned his attention to merging onto the freeway. "Hmm, could be. Maybe it's like any other gift. Any other special ability. Does it come from God, nature, mankind? Is it built into our DNA? Our brains? Who knows? We don't care, all of us. Palomino's team. We just want results so we can get the bad guys off the streets."

She nodded. "I can't play Bach on the piano or Strauss. Not even Chopsticks. I suck at just about everything except art. And clairvoyance. Ah, here's a factoid. Did you know that fifteen percent of women—just human females of all ages—carry a fourth photoreceptor in their brains? All other humans have only three photoreceptors. Isn't that amazing? A neuroscientist discovered this. So is this clairvoyance ability just a gene mutation? Like an extra photoreceptor? A gift from God? Why would God want fifteen percent of human females to have the ability to see subtle shades of color that no one else can see? Are these abilities just random acts of nature?"

"Beats me," Ochoa said, taking an exit ramp and following a street that took them directly to an underground garage. He flashed his badge and ID to the patrolman at the gate, after which the wide steel gate swung open. "So do you think this ability you and your mother have is the result of a gene mutation?"

"I don't know. I often wonder about it," Athena said,

"The Institute we've taken workshops at doesn't know the answer to that, either."

They chatted while he directed her onto an elevator, Ochoa talking more about his family in an attempt, she knew, to get her to relax. Inside, she felt like a bundle of Mexican jumping beans. A police station. Was she going to get the wrong man arrested? Athena grew quiet as the elevator rose.

She'd never been in a police station before. Suddenly she realized what she carried in her purse, a satchel she slung over her shoulder.

"Detective Ochoa, I forgot to tell you. I have a canister of pepper spray in my purse. Is that okay?"

"Better give it to me," he said, grinning, "I'll give it back to you when we leave. Sometimes someone from the SWAT team comes in with one of their bomb and chemical sniffing dogs. Let's play it safe and not make anyone nervous or go ape-shit."

She smiled broadly at that and gave him the canister, which he pocketed in his sports jacket. Minutes later, Ochoa led her through a bullpen of desks, ringing phones, lit computers and people scurrying about, then down a long hallway and into a small conference room. Sitting at the oblong metal table were three men, older than Juan-Pablo and looking stern. Instantly, Detective Gino Palomino stood, shook her hand and introduced himself, then the other two men on his team did the same.

Athena had recognized Palomino immediately from her mother's thoughts. He had a very prominent widow's peak framed by a shock of thick, salt-and-pepper hair, penetrating, light brown eyes, and a large, hooked nose. He was happily married, and one of his sons was already in college. A young football player on a scholarship, his name was Gianni and Palomino was very proud of him. The other two men, Abe Rosen and Joe Bosco, were also in their fifties, both divorced, hardbitten and cynical. Their handshakes told her a lot more, but she said nothing. This was not the time to show off.

Palomino sat down next to her, asked her if he could get her anything to drink and when she said no, he clasped his hands on top of the table.

"Do you know anything about this case, Miss Butler?"

"Athena, please." She looked down as he spread several closed files out in front of her. He didn't open them yet. "Yes, a little. Children, girls, are being kidnapped, raped and then strangled to death." When she grew silent again, Palomino prompted her with, "Anything else?"

"Just that, my mother saw a black van with signs—fake signs for a fake business. A white guy in his twenties. He's very disturbed."

Ochoa, glancing down at the closed files, spoke up at this point. "Athena's never done this before so let's take it slow and easy."

"How old are you, Athena?" Detective Palomino asked gently. He kept his large, clasped hands on the file folders as if reluctant to let her see what was inside.

"Nineteen, almost twenty."

"I called you down here because we have a time factor problem. Your mother won't be back until the twenty-ninth, and we can't hold these guys more than twenty-four hours. We had five in a lineup. A neighbor, admittedly an unreliable witness, said he could identify who took the latest victim. None of the five passed muster. This witness couldn't identify any of the five in the lineup. So we're back to square one, basically. Unless, of course, you can help."

Athena placed a hand over Palomino's clasped ones. At first, he stiffened but after a few seconds, he relaxed. His hands were cold but after a moment, images came through, making her nod in understanding.

"I see, all those guys own black vans and live not too far from the neighborhood where the girls lived. And they all have police records. Right?"

Detective Palomino gave a small nod. "We're holding them a few more hours, hoping we'll get something from you. Then we'll have to cut them loose. We're at our wits end here." He glanced up at the other men as he cleared his throat. Obviously, he felt uncomfortable about opening the files. When he did, Athena sucked in a deep breath. She knew what was in them.

There were forms and typed reports in the files, but the photographs drew her attention. Postmortem photos of four little girls, no older than ten or twelve, Palomino assembled in front of her like a horrible scrapbook. All of the girls bore red marks on their small throats, where the killer had strangled them to death.

"I don't know how much your mother has told you about this case but we know we have a serial killer at large, a predator of the evilest, most despicable kind. He preys on the most innocent, most gullible and helpless in our poor neighborhoods. Little girls who aren't supervised very well after school. We need to stop him . . . now. So if you're here on a whim or fancy, please don't waste our time. Believe me, we take this seriously and we don't appreciate anyone who doesn't. Know what I mean? Everyone at this station and in those neighborhoods want us to catch this guy. We've put in thousands of man hours into this case, and the only solid leads we've gotten have come from your mother."

Athena nodded soberly. Gingerly, she touched the photos but got nothing. All she felt and heard was the quiet sobbing of the medical examiner who had done the autopsies of these children. The spirits and minds of these little girls had already gone. There was nothing left but hollow shells. Mass converting back into energy, and then waiting for the next conversion into mass again.

The cycle of life and death.

Athena looked up at Detective Palomino and waited.

"We have the jackets of these men, who're right now in holding cells," he said, "I heard what you told Ochoa about psychometry."

"Yes," she said, looking around the room. "I do very well with objects that belong to people. If you give me something that each of these men owns or wears, I might be able to help you. Better than if I just look at them. I can't touch the men, can I?"

"Without them seeing you, no," said Palomino. He looked up at Ochoa and hooked a thumb at the door. "Bring in their jackets in any order. Just pile them on the table here. Let's see what she can do."

Five minutes later, while Detectives Rosen and Bosco were off attending to their supposed eyewitness, Ochoa was sorting out on the metal table the five different jackets. The first was a dirty suede sportcoat. Another a black nylon parka style, a third a fleece lined, plaid lumberjacket-style coat. The fourth another parka with a hood, this time dark green, and the last one a brown corduroy like the boxy barn jackets the farmers in England wore. Before Athena stepped up to the end of the table where they were spread out, Ochoa gave her transparent vinyl gloves to put on. "Hope these don't interfere with your psychometry, but it's protocol."

She nodded, pulled on the gloves and began to touch each one, taking her time. She felt the lining, the collars, the sleeves. Then she put her hands into the pockets, all cleaned out and emptied when the men first came in.

Palomino handed her a box of tissues, which she took absently and set aside, continuing her silent probe into the stark, sad lives of these five men.

All of the men had lived hard lives, bereft of love and security. She wondered how people endured without both, but these men had, somehow. Their life stories were varied, one coming from a middle-class family with educated parents, who had beaten him so severely and had broken his arms so many times that Athena could feel his pain every time he put his arms through the sleeves.

She grabbed a tissue and frowned. Wiping her eyes, suddenly realizing her vision was blurred with tears, she went back to the first jacket. The dirty suede sports coat. Instantly, she stifled a sob.

She saw it. The killer had once worn this jacket. She saw him gazing at himself in the mirror while wearing it. Trying out his disguise. The dyed, shorter hair. The baseball cap. The weight gain. Each time he killed, he changed a part of himself. As if showing everybody he was either too smart to get caught, maybe . . . or as a way of showing himself and the world that he was in control. Maybe he was admitting to himself that with each heinous act, he was changing into a beast beyond help. Beyond redemption.

Like the movie, The Portrait of Dorian Gray. With each heinous act, the handsome young man, Dorian Gray, grew more and more vile and vicious but his looks remained the same, handsome, young, virile. His painted portrait, however, morphed into a hideous and grotesque monster, reflecting the man's true nature. Athena sensed that the killer was looking to see if fate would punish him in some way by altering his appearance. When fate didn't punish him, he altered something about himself. He seemed to be obsessed with this notion.

She wiped her eyes and nose, swallowed down the lump in her throat, took a fresh clump of tissues and dried her face. Then she pointed at the jacket. The dirty suede sports coat.

"The man who owns this jacket is either the killer or knows the killer. They sometimes swap clothes. I think they're good friends or related."

Palomino and Ochoa exchanged pointed looks.

Her knees turned to rubber, so she sat down.

What she had learned was an epiphany. Human monsters looked like normal people. No wonder they were so dangerous.

Chapter Seven

"Are you sure?" asked Ochoa. He exchanged glances with Palomino.

Athena shrugged. "Yes, as much as I usually am when I use psychometry to do my thing."

Palomino told Ochoa to go and run the man's sheet. Whatever that meant. Silently, she dropped the suede sports coat and backed up against the wall. Invisible waves of evil seemed to ripple from that jacket, as if the killer's nature had imbued the object with his twisted mind.

Suddenly her thoughts churned into a tumultuous mess of doubts. What if she were wrong? What if she'd misinterpreted what she saw? What if she caused the wrong man to be arrested?

After Ochoa left, the leader of the homicide team gave her a studied look and held out a chair for her. She acknowledged his gesture with a faint smile, sat and sank her head onto her folded arms on the table. Drained physically and exhausted mentally, she bent over. Sitting quietly usually restored her sense of well-being but this time, her mood remained dark and gloomy. Her stomach felt nauseated, as though she'd just had a small bout of food poisoning. Her head ached.

"Are you okay, Athena?" Detective Palomino inquired gently.

"No," she said honestly, "but I will be. I just need to shake it off. It doesn't always affect me this way, but what I saw made me sick." A moment later, she pulled out of her large hobo bag her small sketchbook and a plastic box of pencils. "I need to make a drawing of the man I saw in the mirror."

"Mirror?"

"I saw a man wearing that jacket and looking at himself in the mirror. He was wearing a baseball cap, sunglasses. Trying out a disguise, I think, like trying on a different look. I couldn't see much of his face but his chin . . . it was rounded and had a deep dimple. A cleft, y'know."

Her right hand flew over the page, then slowed down to shade in the area around his covered forehead and eyes, his jawline and neck. That was when she recalled what she'd seen in the mirror. A scar on his neck. The left side. Or was it the right side? Her hand paused and went to her own neck. Her thinking was a little muddled.

"The scar was on this side, my left side—his right side in the mirror—but that's a mirror image. So it's really on his left side. A long, curved line, as if a knife had tried to slice it."

Two minutes later, she handed the sketch to Detective Palomino. "I think he's your killer."

Palomino narrowed his eyes and scowled until Ochoa returned, holding a computer printout with a photograph of a man. Ochoa's voice bubbled over with excitement.

"The guy with the suede jacket's got a younger brother with a mile-long sheet and a bunch of aliases. Look at this," he said, holding up his printouts. Palomino gazed at the printouts, then at Athena's sketch before blinking a few times.

"Look at this," the lead detective echoed, matching up the two pictures. "Definitely the same chin, a cleft chin. This person of interest's doing his best to cover his appearance. Says here his last known address is Minneapolis. Get rid of the witness, have Bosco and Rosen trace credit card activity, banking, ATM and cell phone use. Bet he's been in town the past six months, about the time the first murder began. Take Miss Butler back, then lean on . . ." He glanced over at Athena. " . . . the owner of that suede jacket."

"Right, boss. Be right back." Ochoa smiled over at Athena before exiting the conference room again. The man's excitement was palpable. The vibes in the room ricocheted off the walls, it seemed. She looked over at the suede jacket, its evil emanations diminishing by the second.

"Good work, Miss Butler, but I can understand how difficult this must've been for you. You have afternoon classes?"

She lifted her head and nodded. Today a male model would be posing nude for their portrait painting class. Her spirits rose. She and Mikela had anticipated this new development. The sickness in her stomach receded.

Ochoa returned with a note, which Palomino read over solemnly. His eyes flared for a moment as he nodded silently to himself. They exchanged another meaningful glance before the team leader wrapped up their meeting.

"Thanks for coming, Miss Butler. We'll call you again," said Palomino, "when you return from your week in California. We'd like to use both you and your mother in the upcoming months. Your skill with that sketchbook will come in handy. If you agree, that is."

She said nothing but held out her hand in parting. After the detective shook it, she said, "You should see a doctor, Detective. Right away. You have an ulcer that hasn't been treated. It's about to start bleeding." She shrugged. "Just saying."

He frowned and looked thoughtful as he ushered her out.

"You did good, Athena," Ochoa told her as he escorted her to the elevators. "Didn't know about Gino's ulcer. He's been eating Tums like candy. Guess it's not doing him any good. He hates doctors. Says they always bring bad news. Anyway, we might collar the perp, thanks to you."

"You mean, I gave you a solid lead in the case?" she asked, picking up on their cop lingo.

"Oh yeah," chuckled the detective, "more than solid. I'm not saying you've cracked the case, but you might've just given us the key to unlocking it. We've had a problem because the jacket owner has a bonafide alibi for each kidnapping and each murder. Now we need to track down his younger brother. I can't say any more than that. We've got a lot more work to do. The guy's in the wind."

He wouldn't elaborate or explain what he meant, so Athena just smiled. Her stomach and head felt better as her thoughts turned to her afternoon painting class. She'd be a half-hour late, but that was becoming a habit. Which wasn't impressing ol' Professor White. Then she brightened, recalling what Mikela had said on Wednesday.

A male model, Professor White had announced. A *nude* male model, Mikela had whispered a moment later, her eyes lighting up. Soon, Athena decided, she'd shake off this sick miasma. She shivered as the elevator doors closed on the homicide squad's floor.

And if she could help it, she'd never do this again.

Chapter Eight

The strobe lights flared in Athena's vision, then banked off and swirled around the dance floor in their crazy syncopation-to-the-drumbeat rotation. She smiled at Tony as he gyrated on the backlit checkerboard dance floor, but the truth was that her carefree mood was all for show. The day's events lingered with her, especially her experience at the police station, and she was not in a mindset to party tonight. Too bad. Tony was expecting hot sex at the end of their date. He figured this was a booty call, and to be honest with herself, she'd looked forward to that night, also, for over two weeks.

How perverse she was to change her mind like this.

Not wanting him to see her pasted-on smile, she whipped around on her stiletto heels, her long ponytail swinging like a pendulum. He put his hands on her hips, steadying her in place, as he came closer and ground his pelvis against her bottom. They were ass-grinding and she felt nothing. Just irritation with herself for encouraging Tony's attentions and bringing about this situation.

Well, holy bloody hell.

Too emotionally exhausted to turn on her clairvoyance antenna-receiver, she was moving *blind,* so to speak. Nothing came through, which was fine with her. She'd seen too much ugliness that day, enough to last her all year. Maybe an entire lifetime.

Glad to have the night off, she gave her mood room to expand. Whatever part of her mind controlled the on-off switch of her clairvoyance radar was relieved, no doubt. And so was Athena, in her very core of being. *Give it time off, for Pete's sake.*

"You're so hot," Tony cooed into her ear, "I can't stand it anymore. Let's get the hell out of here and go to your place."

She leaned her head back onto his shoulder. It was so nice to have such a tall guy to lean on. "I don't know . . . I'm so wiped out. The week's been torture."

"Didn't you say you had the place to yourself? No parents? No brother?"

His gentle but steady persistence was breaking down her reservations, so that by the time they returned to their shared table with Mikela and her current hottie, Jerry, their glances back and forth were signals. After Jerry, a senior at Georgetown, kept probing Tony with questions about his classes and his professors, Tony signaled it was time to go.

"Hate to run, dudes," Tony said laughingly, "it's been a blast, but this gorgeous girl and I have some private catching up to do. Understand me?"

Mikela and Jerry laughed obligingly, a moment before Mikela leaned over and whispered to Athena, "I want details when you get back from California. Second thought, can't wait that long. Text me tomorrow."

In Tony's car, an older model BMW sedan, he shot her a glance on their way to her parent's condo in Alexandria. He looked a little angry.

"What's with this Jerry? He kept drilling me like he thought I was lying, like I couldn't be a junior at AU. Plus, who wants to talk shop when we're out with a couple of hot babes like you and Mikela?"

The darkness hid her frown, she hoped. It was strange for Tony to take offense at Jerry's casual get-to-know-you questions, since the two men had never met before even though they went to the same campus.

"He was just trying to be friendly. It's just Jerry."

"Yeah, trying to pump me for information," Tony interrupted, squeezing the steering wheel with both fists. Another glance her way, as if inquiring about her sudden silence, and he morphed quickly into a more jovial mood.

"What you need tonight, sweetheart, I've got. I know you've led kind of a sheltered life . . . from what you've said. It'll be great. I guarantee it!" The last was a mimickry of a men's clothing TV commercial and Athena had to chuckle. But it was a forced chuckle. She decided that she didn't want Tony to be her first lover.

Something was missing.

Yeah, good ol' fashioned love.

So what does love have to do with it? This is just animal lust, pure and simple.

Her mind conjured up the photos of those dead girls. Maybe that was what the killer thought . . . Just lust and power over another human being.

She shook off the police station's dark mood. What about her? Tonight? Did repressed lust for years and years justify doing whatever she pleased now? With whoever she pleased? Even with a man she didn't love?

Bloody hell, yes!

"You're over eighteen, babe, that's all that counts. We're gonna make each other feel really good tonight. I've got some moves, baby . . ."

Athena darted him a weak smile. Tony was trying hard to put them both into a warmer mood, but she found his seductive skills lacking. Nothing he said or did that night could erase from her mind what she'd seen that day at the police station. The photos of the little girls, the tragedy in those men's lives, the man's face in the mirror. The sketch she'd made. Creepy, sick, evil . . .

In exasperation at her own black turn of mind, she shut off those thoughts, and her mind kept drifting back to her afternoon painting class' nude model. Not completely nude, for he'd worn a teeny-tiny Speedo. Martin Larsen. A Scandinavian hunk, all sinewy muscles, washboard abs and long legs and arms. The looks he kept tossing her way all during their sketching session were smoldering. From their sketches that afternoon, they would begin their painting next week, focusing on flesh tones and counter-palette tints for the shadowing, another technique Prof White was fond of using.

She would miss the class while in California, but she'd catch up after Thanksgiving break. Athena kept thinking about those looks of Martin's, speculative ones that settled on her every time Professor White said to take a break and stretch his legs—a five-minute one every thirty minutes. Martin would walk around their easels, not making any comments, but just slapping his arms and thighs in a thin wool robe he wore during his breaks. More often than not, he'd pass her way, looking at her and her easel but saying nothing. Just smiling, like he approved of her skills.

He was divine. Martin Larsen, a blond-haired god who reminded her a little of her father in his RAF uniform when he was younger. If that was more than a little pervy, then so be it. Athena felt smitten for the first time since her last heartbreak back in high school.

Too bad for Tony, she thought. Just bad timing. Between her subdued emotions all day and her salacious thoughts about her painting class's new model, Martin, Athena was in no mood to lose her virginity that night to Tony or anyone. No matter how cute and tall he was. Not when a long-legged, hunky blond like Martin Larsen lived and breathed and shot her flirty, approving glances.

She tried to tell him that when he parked his car at the curb outside her parents' condo complex, but he wouldn't listen. He nuzzled her neck and lowered his voice to a whisper. He was nearly pleading, and Athena felt guilty for leading him on. The least she could do was be hospitable.

"C'mon, baby, just let me in for a few minutes. Gotta use the john and y'know, I'm hungry, too. Can you make me a sandwich?"

"Sure," she said, letting him kiss her deeply, a French kiss that had the opposite effect from what was intended. When they broke apart, she added the lie, "My father's coming home early, so you can't stay. And my brother, Chris, too. We'll have to do it another time, Tony. I'm so sorry."

No longer feeling apologetic, she felt annoyance crawling up the back of her skull. She had to make this quick. Let Tony down easy and shoo him out the door. She unlocked the front door, shed her nylon-quilted jacket and hung it up on the foyer's coat rack. He did the same with his parka. Then all of a sudden he took her into his arms and, like an octopus, was all over her, touching her breasts, her bottom, the inside of her thighs. Hiding her revulsion, she extricated herself after a couple of kisses. He looked so downhearted and preoccupied, she had to cut the tension.

"I'll make you a ham and cheese sandwich. Is that okay? While you go to the bathroom?"

"Great," he effused, rubbing his hands up and down his jeans. "Your bathroom?"

She smiled. Maybe he wasn't going to give her a bad time, after all. They worked together, so she was counting on him to be a gentleman, after all. If worse came to worse, she was ready. In the car's darkness, she'd taken out the small pepper spray canister from her hobo bag and now carried it in her jeans pocket. Her sweater tunic concealed it, but she was praying she wouldn't have to use it. It would make working with Tony so much more difficult if she had to make him gag and vomit. Wouldn't it?

"Down the hall, third door on your left."

While he was gone, she set about putting a sandwich together from the salad scraps and ham and Swiss cheese slices she'd munched on since her parents left. She poured a glass of water for herself and a glass of milk for Tony. Then she waited on the bar stool at the kitchen counter. It seemed like he was taking longer than necessary, but she didn't want to go roaming down the hall to inquire. That would be rude.

When he finally appeared, he was beaming. "Had to take a look around. These are such great digs. What do your parents do again?" He took a big bite of his sandwich, standing up next to her, before taking a seat on the adjacent stool.

She'd told him once that her father was a British diplomat at the Embassy and her mother was a translator of books, but she reminded him again.

He nodded, wolfing down half the sandwich in less than five minutes. The milk went next, all in a couple of long swallows. Funny, his mood had completely changed and he was now a total gentleman, contented with everything. In fact, he seemed in a hurry to leave. Athena didn't know whether to feel reassured or disappointed.

Would her relationships with men ever improve? Even the young men who were attracted to her seemed to lose interest fairly rapidly. What was it about her that put them off? Her intensity? Her painting passion? Maybe they sensed she was . . . different?

"Father moves around so much with the Foreign Office," she explained, looking for a neutral topic of conversation, "we never know where we'll be posted next. Rather, where he and my mother will go next. We've been here for almost six years, and I like it. So does my brother. I'll be staying here and finishing up my degree at the Art Institute whether or not Father gets an extension here. Chris, too. He has his heart set on Stanford. Father is mortified that he won't go to Cambridge, but Chris likes sunshine and beaches." She was rambling on, anxious to avoid his octopus arms and a possibly difficult situation.

They chatted a bit about the coffee store, their manager, and the newbies they had to train, Athena nervously steering his attention away from sex and what was supposed to have been a night of lovemaking. She needn't have bothered. When Tony finished his sandwich, he stood up, leaned over to peck her on the cheek, and then shrugged into his parka. Yes, he was in a definite hurry to leave. And she was flooded with relief.

To borrow American slang, how dope was that!

"See you tomorrow?" she said, holding him back for one last kiss. Like, no hard feelings?

Instantly, he grew attentive and focused on her. "Sure, I'm on duty. Nice and early. What about you?"

"Not 'til nine, thank goodness." A tense silence ensued. Come to think of it, she reminded herself, there had been a lot of tense silences all evening. She didn't know what to think of it, except that Tony had probably found another girl. Suddenly curious, she thought about switching on her clairvoyance and taking a peek into his mind, then decided against it. Whatever Tony was thinking, it probably wouldn't be very flattering.

Like, what a royal bitch of a tease.

Maybe he was entertaining thoughts of another girl. Anyone but her. No, she didn't want to take a peek. Better leave him alone.

"See ya, Athena," he said as he turned to go. He turned back and shot her a strange look, a mixture of satisfaction and something else.

He's saying goodbye.

He hurried down the exterior staircase and disappeared.

"Good night," she murmured into the cold darkness.

The next morning, she showed up at Starbucks all ready to make it up to Tony for the lackluster evening—with a cheery greeting if nothing else. But he wasn't there. Fergy looked fit to be tied. Everything about the man's demeanor, from his fists to his bulging eyeballs, was apoplectic. He'd called half a dozen part-timers, and only one was available on such short notice to take Tony's place. It'd take him thirty minutes to get there.

"He quit!"

"Tony Grabowski?" She couldn't believe it.

"Just called it in, just minutes ago. No reason, just quit." Fergy raved inside the stockroom. "Judy's at the counter, barely holding her wits together. Thank goodness you came in or we'd be up shit creek."

She consulted her iPhone. No text or email or phone message from Tony.

"I wonder if he's all right," she said, stowing her bag and jacket and throwing on her apron. The newbie at the espresso machine looked frantic, and the line by the cashier was ten-deep. "It's so bizarre, Fergy. He's never missed a day," she added. She sent Tony a text but got no reply. She called his cell phone, but the number had been discontinued. Unfriggin-believable, she decided, her mind on full alert now.

Why not use her psychometry skills? She felt stronger and rested, emotionally and psychically. Tony seemed to like the job, although lately, he'd been tense and a little curt at times. Athena surveyed the immediate area of the espresso machine, ignoring for a moment the lineup of cups with orders marked on them with black ink. No, nothing that she could see that he'd handled lately. The evening shift last night would have obliterated any trace of Tony Grabowski from his shift the morning before.

It was a mystery. Why all of a sudden, right after their date? Why now? It couldn't have been anything she did or said, could it? She seldom prayed, much to her Catholic mother's consternation, she knew, but now she prayed. She didn't love the guy, of course, but she did like him. So she hoped and prayed that Tony wasn't floating in the Potomac River somewhere. Why he would be, she had no clue. She was overreacting, being morbid, but she just had a feeling something was wrong.

She glanced around the back room and spied two green aprons. One had a stain from the defective lid of a caramel syrup container, one that had spilled on Tony yesterday morning. Athena grabbed it and held it in her hands. A jumble of words, a trace of anger and fear—

Sick of this place . . . gotta move on . . . get the dough and split . . . gotta do the job at her place first . . .

A frantic Fergy popped his head in. "Athena, what're you doing? I need you out front!"

Startled, she dropped the apron on one of the boxes. "Okay, okay, I'm coming."

What's that all about? Tony's in trouble? What's he afraid of?

Maybe, after her visit with the cops yesterday, the world just seemed a darker place.

Darker and more dangerous.

CHAPTER NINE

The mystery of Tony's disappearance from work still remained unsolved by Sunday morning when her father flew in. He was dropped off by his driver in the black Range Rover, followed by her brother Christopher, who appeared at their condo, fresh off a soccer match practice.

Father and son both howled their delight at each other, shadow-wrestled for a bit before catching up over the next several hours. Athena observed the two in Chris's bedroom as her brother threw his clothes into a soft-sided suitcase for their Thanksgiving visit to California. Her father paced from the master bedroom suite, slowly and methodically folding heavier winter clothes for London, simultaneously sharing with Chris his opinion of the next Manchester match with Madrid. From his room, Chris, stopping to sniff lighterweight shirts and his casual jeans for teenage-boy odors, called out his opinions of both teams and all the others in the EU and British Isles leagues.

She leaned against Chris' door jamb, her head swiveling as though she were at Center Court in Wimbledon, and registered barely half of their bantering. Soccer bored her to distraction now that she'd seen American football first hand. The brute force of the blocking and the sheer courage of the running and passing games were as hypnotic as the Roman gladiator spectacles at the Coliseum. At least, the sheer physicality was what fired up her imagination, especially after seeing the movie, Gladiator.

Their mock fury over the weekend's soccer matches made

her roll her eyes, but she enjoyed watching the two favorite men in her life. Her father, the tall and slim Nordic desk-warrior, had passed on his physique to both her and Chris. Their long faces, square jaws and high foreheads were cookie-cutter copies, but that was where the physical resemblance ended. Chris had inherited his mother's thick, curly, auburn-tinted brown hair, chestnut brown eyes and light olive complexion. Athena had inherited his pale skin, blond hair and bluish-green eyes.

In personality, too, father and son were both gregarious and loved people. Chris was highly intelligent like her father but, of course, the psychic powers of her mother's bloodline—what Nonna called the Delphi bloodline because of her stories about the ancient Greek priestesses—had kept to their true course and had shunned the male offspring. It's in the mitochondria, Chris had said once. Lucky Chris. Through an accident of conception, he'd avoided the burden, the curse.

The family secret.

Whatever.

Finally, as they wound down on the latest goalie's errors on the field, Athena jumped in. "Father, you just came from California. Did any of the Skoros family attend the new consul's welcome party in Sacramento?"

Blinking as if he were seeing her for the first time, he came over and wrapped an arm around her shoulder. "Sorry, my dear, we've been ignoring you. Just had to catch up on the football. Mobiles and what-not, not the same as talking in person." He glanced over at Chris and exchanged a typical male time-to-share-the-wealth kind of look.

"I'm just curious," she said mildly, "about the Skoroses."

"They all came—well, all except the youngest son. The sheriff's deputy. He was on an emergency rescue operation somewhere in the mountains. You and Chris'll like them.

The elder Skoroses, well, they're rich as Croesus. He's into real estate development, owns shopping centers all over northern California. He's very Greek and she—Lorena, your mother's cousin—is very Italian. The four sons, well, Chris will love the two younger ones, Alex and Kas. We didn't meet the two older boys. They're married, involved in running the Skoros empire. I imagine Alex and Kas will be showing you two about. They're both good-looking ladies men, my darling daughter, so watch out."

"Father, they're too old!"

Her father suppressed a smile with a smirk aimed in Chris's direction. "Thirty and twenty-eight. Hardly. They said they'll take you out on some adventures, skiing in the Sierras or jet skiing on the lake. From the Skoros estate in the Sierra foothills, you can go from jet skiing on Folsom Lake to snow-skiing in the mountains. You'll both have a jolly good time."

"I don't know," she admitted, "hope it's worth missing three days of work and class."

"Hey, I go for that, Dad," effused Chris, "Better pack swim trunks. You, too, 'Thena, unless you don't want them to see your thunder thighs."

She fell for her brother's bait. "I don't have thunder thighs, cross-eyed Chris"—a rather lame retort, she felt—"I've lost five pounds in the past month, I'll have you know."

"Yeah, how? You eat a ton on the weekends."

"I do not," she shot back, "I work hard. Which is more than I can say for you."

Chris sneered, which sparked an old rivalry for their father's attention. "Still no boyfriends, eh?"

A quick glance at her father told her he'd heard that a million times before.

"Come now, Chris, you know your sister has discriminating tastes. Which, by the way, I heartily approve of. We wouldn't want just any bloke hanging around, would we?"

"Any ol' bloke, Dad, would be a welcome sight compared to zero, zilch, *nada, rien*. I'll have to hook her up with some of my high school pals before long."

Athena grabbed the nearest pillow and threw it at Chris's head, which prompted him to throw it back. And thus ensued their thousandth pillow fight while her father vanished into the relative peace and quiet of the master bedroom suite.

Twenty-four hours later, as she and Chris left the jetway at the Sacramento International Airport, Athena spied her mother first, waving and smiling broadly. Apparently, her mother, looking relaxed, was having a good time with the Skoroses.

Through the floor-to-ceiling windows of the terminal, the sun shone brightly, not a thunderstorm or snow-bloated cloud in sight. Excited, Athena felt in her hobo bag and found her sunglasses. Ah, California. They were right, it was sunny, and everyone, including her mother, was wearing cropped pants or Bermuda shorts and colorful tops. She could get used to this.

Chris nudged her as they approached their mother. "Remember, I got dibs on the jet ski."

The three hugged and kissed as though they hadn't seen each other in years. Her mother's custom, very Italian, which they relished following.

"Are you alone, Mum?" Athena asked. Not a Greek-American nearby, from the looks of it.

"How was your flight? Oh, I'm so happy to see you both! You'll have such a good time. No, I'm not alone. The boys are downstairs in the baggage claim area, waiting to meet you."

The boys? Did she mean the two younger Skoros brothers?

She nudged closer to her mother as they followed the disembarking passengers down the escalator to the floor where revolving conveyor belts disgorged all shapes and sizes of bags and boxes.

"What are they like?" she asked. Before her mother could reply, she gestured down below at the base of the escalator.

Two dark-haired men stood slightly apart from the others and immediately fixed on them as they approached. Both were tall, broad-shouldered and handsome, and obviously brothers, so alike in appearance there could've been no doubt. The shorter, cuter one, in khakis and a navy polo shirt, wore a wide, rakish grin. The other, slightly taller and huskier, more rugged with a dark stubble, wore jeans and a plain black, short-sleeved tee shirt. Athena recognized him immediately—the sheriff's deputy whose portrait she'd painted for his mother.

He locked his dark eyed gaze onto hers and frowned.

Most men she encountered didn't react that way to her. Just the opposite, in fact. Usually they stared with eyebrows raised, as if speculating about her. It wasn't until later that they frowned.

Her mother made introductions.

"Alex, Kas, my son, Chris. My daughter, Athena." The cute one, the ready charmer, Athena thought, bumped Chris's fist and took her hand in both of his.

"Very nice to meet you, Athena," he said, "Athena, the Greek goddess of war, knowledge and wisdom."

She opened her clairvoyance channel and held his hand a second longer. What surprised her was the image of a brick wall. Red brick, solid and high and thick. In surprise, she looked into his light brown eyes. They glittered with merriment. This was some kind of a joke.

"And this is Kas," her mother continued, indicating the taller, more rugged looking brother. Shyly, although she didn't know why, she held out her hand but couldn't look him in the eye. Again, all her mental channel gave her was a vision of a high wall, this time a gray fieldstone one covered with pale green lichen.

"War, knowledge or wisdom? Which one are you, Athena?" Kas asked. He held her hand firmly, as if he had no intention of ever letting go.

She could not penetrate that gray fieldstone wall. His dark brown brows deeply furrowed, he stared her down. Athena broke the stare and glanced at her mother.

"They know about you, Athena. The Skoros brothers have had years of practice with their mother, who's like you and me, dear. If they don't want you to see into them, they've learned how to block us out. With literally mental walls."

Finally, Kas let go of her hand and stepped back. Both men then smiled, Alex tucking his hand around her arm and sidling up to her. He lowered his baritone voice to almost a whisper.

"Hope you don't mind, but we've learned over the years how to keep our private thoughts to ourselves," he said, winking at her. "We can do a wall for minutes at a time. At least until our mother gives up and lets go."

Athena liked Alex's breezy smile and easy way of disarming her. The other one, Kas—the one whose portrait she'd painted—kept his distance and walked ahead to the baggage carousel.

"So, pretty girl, you never answered Kas. Which are you, Athena? The goddess of war, knowledge or wisdom?"

"At this point in my life, I'm afraid, none of the above. Certainly not the first, working on the second and wondering if I'll ever attain the third."

He laughed, and Chris scoffed. "Wisdom, Athena? Huh, never in a million years."

Kas turned around at the baggage carousel and shot her a

lop-sided grin. When this taller brother smiled, he became better looking, less intimidating though from the back, his shoulders appeared even broader and more solid. She found herself studying him while he had his back turned, watching the carousel. There was something about him, a quality of integrity and reliability that held her interest for a few moments. And something else she couldn't define.

Her mother tucked her hand into Alex's other arm and smiled at them all. Then she gave Athena *the look.*

Ooh, no, Mum. Don't even try. He's gorgeous – Alex, the cute charmer – but still way too old.

What was Alex, thirty? He looked twenty-five. The other one, Kas, looked like a weary Atlas, carrying the burden of the world on his very broad, capable shoulders. He was the youngest, but he looked older than Alex. World weary. Dark, mysterious but too mountain-man, too serious.

Funny, how just being around the Skoros brothers evoked a lot of the Greek myths she'd learned in high school. If Kas was Atlas, who was Alex?

Her heart skipped a little.

Ah, yes. Adonis.

CHAPTER TEN

Later, Athena would recall their sojourn in California as a blurred series of scenes and conversations. With the Skoroses providing the opportunities, the next four nights and three days passed eventfully. The first evening Athena and Chris met the family patriarch and matriarch and tried not to show how overwhelmed they felt by the family's trappings of wealth. Her father had provided them an upper-middle-class upbringing and lifestyle, but the Skoros family showed her what real wealth was. More than a rented townhouse condo in Alexandria or an old family townhouse in a venerable neighborhood of Kensington, London. The Skoroses had acreage and a mansion that would rival Earl Spencer's country estate.

Lorena Skoros was petite, her short, curly hair kept dark brown and stylish, as were her clothes, befitting a woman a little younger than seventy years of age. Her dark eyes, like her younger sons', were lively and penetrating. Athena got the impression that she never missed a thing. She was especially warm and cordial with Athena, a possible reason made clear by Alex the next day as they were sightseeing in Napa Valley among the wineries. He was playing guide around the Castillo Amoroso, the newly built castle and headquarters of a popular winery. Meanwhile, he expanded on his family's dynamics.

"Mom's prescient, a prognosticator, or as she calls it, an old-fashioned seeress. She said she had a dream that Kas would someday marry a tall blonde and have children, at least one daughter that would carry on the psychic gift. Well, I never argue with Mom, but Kas challenges her predictions all the time. He said in so many words that he'd never marry a blonde, no matter what she looked like. Blondes weren't his type, blah, blah, blah. No one's going to influence him. Free will and all that. Mom just smiled and said, You'll see."

While her mother didn't look surprised, Athena was stunned. All she could murmur was, "No wonder he avoids me like the plague." Alex laughed and said he wondered if she'd picked up on that.

"He's avoiding all tall blondes, so don't take it personally."

"He's not my type, either," she retorted smoothly. "You can tell him that for me."

Alex laughed, a boyish kind of laugh that reminded her of playgrounds and ice cream cones.

"Papu, he's the brains of the family business, but now that George has taken over as CEO and Leon's COO, he's not involved in the day-to-day operations. With my fiancée, Papu plans where the next big project is going to go. We do the rest. He appointed me CFO, thanks to my major in accounting and economics, so I work the numbers and set up the financing."

They discovered that the two older sons, George and Leon, would join them all Thanksgiving Day and bring their families with them. The younger generation of Skoroses were all involved with Skoros Enterprises, and all of them shared both the work, the responsibilities, and the financial gains.

"What does Kas do? Besides being a deputy sheriff?" Athena looked at the tapestries hanging in the medieval-looking dining hall, trying not to appear too interested in the Skoros's family business. She'd never met a family of multimillionaires.

"He's on call with the Sheriff's Search and Rescue Team, so it's part-time. His job with the family business? He's a hands-on kind of guy and former military police, so his day job is liaison with the contractors and construction crews. He doesn't take bull from anybody, and he knows how to juggle details. After a shopping center is built, he supervises the site managers for Leon."

The entire family impressed Athena. Philip Skoros, the eighty-year-old patriarch of the family, was taller than his wife and chubby, although when he hugged Athena, she could feel his firmness as if there was more muscle than fat behind his rotund belly and barrel chest. He was American born but loved to hold to Greek traditions and food. Their first evening at the Skoros estate—the evening before their Napa wineries tour—the dinner meal wafted garlicky dishes like hummus and pita bread, tzatziki sauce and lamb skewers or kabobs, and tabouli and rice pilaf. There were two cooks and two servers who kept the dishes coming over a three-hour period. By the time a tray of baklava was brought out and sent around the large dining table, Athena's throat had clamped shut. Chris looked like he was going to barf up half his meal.

While Alex kept a continuous and entertaining stream of conversation going all day Tuesday, as they wine-tasted among the vines and then had lunch at Castillo Amoroso, he wrapped up his summary of the Skoros family. He then shocked Athena by bringing up the topic she had studiously avoided mentioning.

"You don't have to feel squeamish about my mother's dreams," he said good-naturedly, "even though she's been accurate about ninety percent of the time. We take her precognitive dreams in a philosophical way. If it's meant to be, it's meant to be."

The three of them were having lunch in the vintner's castle, built in 1985 as a replica of a parador the owner had stayed in while traveling in Spain. Chris had run off with Kas into the mountains to ski. Although the weather had turned warm and sunny that week, the month before had seen at least six inches of snowfall in the Sierras, and avid skiers were taking advantage of the cold nights and snow-making machines to get an early start on the season.

Athena glanced at her mother, who was gazing at something across the large banquet hall. Well, there was no way to broach the topic but to plunge into it.

"Alex, what do you and Kas think about your mother's dream? The one about you and your brother?"

"Oh, the one she told Anna about," he said, getting her mother's attention. "Don't feel upset about it. Kas doesn't take any of Mom's predictions seriously, but this one, he is. He's making sure we don't fulfill Mom's prophetic dream. She hasn't told Pop for fear it'd give him a heart attack, which it probably would. The old man has gotten frail these past couple of years, and he's a lot like Kas, worries about everything, every detail. She told us, though, so we could avoid fate, as she calls it. How's that even possible? Avoiding fate? Me, I don't worry about it. I live in the moment, or at least try to."

Alex took a sip of his syrah and shrugged. "Here it goes. She saw one of us dying in a car crash, but I was driving and Kas was the only other person in the car with me. Well, naturally, that creeped us out at first, and we questioned her. Are you sure I'm the one driving? Do I hit another car, or does the other car hit us? Do I lose control, that kind of thing. She was kinda vague on the details. Her dreams come in a flash from god-knows-where. Some other dimension, she says. None of us have the Sight, y'know. She says it's just handed down in the female line and she's had no daughters. So here we are, with a mother—" He paused and looked first at Anna, then Athena—"as you well know, Athena, with a mother who has these powers of Sight and Prophecy and none of us guys can see beyond what we're doing this very minute. It's strange, but we're used to it."

Athena saw her mother nod in understanding. "Yes, I can imagine how my husband and son feel about me, and about Athena."

Athena's stomach roiled. She hated her freakiness—it was like hating the color or texture of your hair. What could you do about it? Ignore the freakiness? Or embrace it?

"So this prophetic dream of your mother's? Do you believe you can keep it from happening? The car crash and . . . everything?" she asked bluntly. Alex stared back at her as if weighing for a moment how he was going to reply. She hoped he would choose total honesty, for she hadn't much use for people who sugar-coated reality.

"Kas believes we can. So that's good enough for me." He gave a short laugh. "Just like he can avoid falling for blondes."

Anna smiled at Alex and toasted him with her glass of wine. "Here's to tolerant, open-minded husbands and sons. God bless them. And here's to cheating fate. Our powers aren't etched in stone, and god knows we're anything but infallible."

Joining in, Athena raised her glass of wine and tapped the other two. "Yes, that's so true, Mum, we aren't. But I doubt we'll find open-minded men outside the Skoros family. They're in a unique position, don't you think? They've grown up with a mother with our powers. Same with Chris and Father. They're the only other men I know who don't let it bother them. At least, not all the time. Which is probably why I'll never get married. Finding men who don't mind us reading their minds is impossible."

Alex studied her for a moment. "Mustn't give up on the male gender. Others might find your powers—and your mother's and my mother's—absolutely awesome. Intriguing and wonderful."

"Only if you're a cop and need help solving a crime," said Athena, looking pointedly at her mother. She hadn't had the chance to share with her mother her experience working with Detectives Palomino and Ochoa, and how she'd felt afterwards.

Her mother placed a hand over hers. "I know all about what happened. The detective called and brought me up to date. He hoped I wasn't upset about your getting involved, but he was desperate to try anything. He was very impressed with you, 'Thena. They had no record of their Person of Interest even having a brother, or what the man's family background had been like. The younger brother had changed his name. Anyway, you helped them enormously, *figlia mia*. They haven't located his brother but they're working on it, he says."

When Alex looked over at them, puzzled, her mother elaborated on the case she'd been helping the Metropolitan D.C. homicide detectives with. He turned to Athena, respect and awe mirrored in his dark eyes.

"You're helping the cops, too?"

She squirmed a little in her chair. The images that flooded back after having touched those jackets made her lose her appetite. She winced and pushed her plate away.

"Well, I'm not sure I want to keep doing it. I saw a part of life that freaks me out. I never want to see that again."

She suddenly realized how hypocritical her stance was. Wasn't the horror she saw that day part of life, too? Wasn't it too late to sugar-coat her own awareness of the dark, violent side of human nature?

Her mother's intense stare caught her attention. She

hoped she understood her squeamishness. When her mother smiled, she thought maybe she did.

"I'm happy you haven't had to experience first-hand the ugliness of humanity," Anna said softly, gently, "but if you are willing to continue helping, know that your art and all the beauty you can create will sustain you through the darkness. Your art will give you a wonderful escape."

She hadn't considered that before, that her love of art and painting would be a refuge from the troubles and horrors of life. And she realized something else just then, too. Her mother was warning her about something. Warning her that because of her unique clairvoyant powers, Athena would not be able to avoid those very horrors of life. Maybe she had a role to play that she could no longer avoid.

No, that's a role I never want to play again.

Alex's eyes lit up as the server approached with their dishes. "Ah, that reminds me. I thought your portrait of Kas was, well, awesome. Mom loved it, too."

"Yes, she told me last night. Kas said nothing about the painting. What did he really think of it? Please, I can take the truth."

Alex screwed up his face, then grinned.

He must not like it. Athena scowled and snapped her napkin over her lap in an impatient gesture. "Oh, don't tell me. Kas thought I made him look too handsome, too clean-shaven and soft. Not macho enough."

"You'll have to ask him yourself. I wouldn't want to spoil the fun." Alex could barely disguise the impish delight behind his grin. The man was irrepressible and charming but occasionally exasperating. Still, Athena liked him.

However, with such an oblique response from Alex, Athena had nothing more to say. She dug into her shrimp salad and shrugged. *Oh well, can't please everyone.*

Of course, he didn't like it. I'm a blonde.

Wednesday was another unseasonably warm day, so Alex took Chris and Athena on the lake in the family's ski boat. Kas would've come, according to Alex, but he had an early morning call. The Sheriff's Search and Rescue Team was needed in the mountains to track down three skiers who had wandered off one of the trails just before closing time the day before. The team suspected the three had gotten lost and couldn't find their way back. They'd probably spent the night on a forested slope and were scared to death. Or one or more of them was hurt, and they'd decided to stick together. It was good the temperature hadn't fallen below fifty Fahrenheit, although in the mountains it had sunk to close to freezing.

In any event, at six that morning, according to Chris, Kas had thrown on his one-piece Vortex suit, snow hiking boots, grabbed his equipment and headed up to the team's rendezvous site at Boreal Ridge. He had no idea when he'd be back. Instead, Alex allowed Kas' dog, Spartacus, a black-and-tan German shepherd, into the ski boat for the thrill ride.

The wind whipped in their faces as Alex skippered them around the lake, slowing down to mosey into coves and small inlets created by the American River's south and east forks. For several minutes, Athena had her arm slung around the dog, relishing his furry coat and savoring his enjoyment of the ride. When they hit a few wake bumps from other boats, she cinched her arm more tightly around the dog so he wouldn't get tossed off the stern. Spartacus turned his pointy head in her direction, and Athena could swear he actually laughed. The sound that escaped the dog's throat was like a girl's high-pitched yawn. Athena smiled and hugged the dog's neck.

Images flashed through her mind of the dog and Kas' various experiences with Spartacus, their long walks together on the property, the human's tenderness as he fed and cared for his pet, the dog's deep, emotional bond to his two-legged friend. By the time they returned to the Skoros dock, Athena felt like she knew a side of Kas she'd not yet seen. The dog kept to her side on the trail all the way back to the house a half-mile away, as if he'd sensed something special about her.

Thursday morning, while the kitchen staff scurried about, she helped her mother and Lorena set the dining room table. With Alex's help, they'd extended the table to accommodate sixteen and placed china and crystal glasses and goblets according to Lorena's direction. After which, a bedraggled Kas joined them briefly to look in on the arrangements. He'd slept late apparently, having put in a full day the day before with the Search and Rescue Team. As he leaned against the French doors and drank coffee, he capsulized the rescue situation.

"We were in the Sheriff's helo and found the skiers on the backside of one of the lower mountains at Squaw Valley. When they heard us, two of them ran out from the tree cover and flagged us. We lowered to about forty feet and realized one of the skiers was hurt. So another deputy and I harnessed up and zipped down our line with a gurney. Strapped up the injured skier and ran the line back up so the two on the helo could grab him. Then they winched up the remaining two skiers, who were suffering from hypothermia, and got them wrapped up in special blankets. Pete and I had to wait on the mountain while the helo offloaded at the Squaw Valley first-aid station. An ambulance took the three to the Truckee hospital. We set our flares to guide the helo back to us. The helo pilot is new, and in all the excitement we weren't sure he'd set his coordinates. Anyway, we had to put in a stint at the hospital to fill out paperwork at our Boreal field site. Then it was back on Interstate Eighty for the drive back home."

Chris stared. "Wow. Awesome!"

Kas cheeks colored. "These guys were lucky. Not all our rescues end up like that. Wait'll they get the county's bill."

His mother asked why he hadn't joined them for dinner the night before.

Kas said he'd met some friends at a watering hole in Auburn. At that point in his story, he glanced over at Athena, then looked down at his coffee.

He was with a girl.

Why that should've mattered, she didn't know. But when Kas suggested to Chris and Alex a turn about the lake on the jet ski, she thought quickly. She wanted to go with him.

"Sorry, bro," interjected Alex, "I promised Chris I'd take him down to the American for a coupla hours of fishing." He turned to his mother, palms up and out. "Don't worry, Mom, we'll be back by two or three at the latest. I'll do bar, make cocktails for everyone."

Lorena pointed her finger and waggled it. "Cocktails at four, Alex. Everyone's dressing up a bit, so don't make the poor boy late."

Athena turned to Kas and blurted out, "I'd love to go jet skiing!"

Despite Kas' dark, fulminating look, Athena added excitedly, not waiting for his refusal. "I'll go up and get my bathing suit on."

Although she'd been jet skiing before, she couldn't hide her excitement. Not even from herself. She ran up the staircase.

She was finally going to get some alone time with Mr. Macho Man.

Chapter Eleven

Kas didn't speak much as they left the house—actually, the house was a three-story mansion in Italian Revival stucco with limestone railings and pediments.

He mentioned how Spartacus seemed glued to Athena's side, his tongue flopping out happily, his tail wagging excitedly.

Keeping her channel closed, she wondered if Kas was jealous of the dog's attention. "We're pals," she said.

Kas led her down the back terrace steps to the gravel path behind the pool-patio area. They'd have to cross twenty acres—about a half-mile, Kas said—to the family's boat dock, the same path she'd taken the day before with Alex and Chris. Before they began, Athena bent over and rubbed behind the German shepherd's pointed black ears until he almost purred with pleasure.

Kas looked surprised. "He usually takes a long time to warm up to people."

Athena scratched under his long jaw. "Like his master, I suppose. We became friends yesterday during the ski boat ride. Spartacus told me a lot about you and how he feels about you. You're his sun and moon, his alpha and omega. He showed me all the things you do together."

Kas halted on the path. "You read my dog's mind?"

She didn't mean for her tone to be so defensive, but out it came, "Well, yeah. It's what I do. I was holding him in the boat, so yeah."

He shot her a crooked smile, then slapped a palm against

his thigh, a signal for Spartacus to heel at his side. The dog looked over at his master, looked back at Athena, gave a whine and then reluctantly moved away from her.

He mock-growled at his dog, which caused Spartacus to perk up his ears. "That's for being a traitor, boy. Telling this girl our secrets."

Athena grinned. "Don't worry, he didn't reveal secrets about any of your girlfriends. I don't think Spartacus knows or cares about that."

"C'mon, boy," Kas beckoned as Spartacus rubbed his fur against his master's leg. "You're something else, Athena," he added, "You're here three days and already stealing my dog. I suppose you want Alex, too?"

Astonished, she almost tripped. "What? I don't want Alex or your dog. And I certainly don't want to be friends with you."

He snorted. "No danger of that happening. You know that Alex is engaged?" Kas was gazing down at his dog, Spartacus, who was trotting alongside.

"Yes," she said, her chin up, "he told us. What's she like? He just said her name was Nicole and she's the daughter of your father's business partner. Another Greek-American."

"Nicole Papamichail. A GAP, Greek-American Princess. She's beautiful," he said, "spoiled, shallow and she'll make him happy in the short-term, miserable in the long run. But there you have it. No accounting for taste."

His frank reply caught her off-guard. She stared at his profile as they walked along. Maybe there was more to this guy than she realized. Kas wore faded blue jeans and a white t-shirt that stretched over his chest and back. He walked with a strong, relaxed gait and exuded a quiet self-confidence, as though he knew who he was and didn't pretend to be anyone different, a what-you-see-is-what-you-get kind of attitude. Take it or leave it. With a chip on his shoulder.

Athena had slung on sweatpants and a v-necked t-shirt over her solid black bikini. She wore no makeup and had hastily pulled up her hair into a ponytail. Her usual look, but not her best one. Oh well. Inside her chest, her heart pounded. *What's going on? Is this a panic attack? Why should I care how he feels?*

A flash of insight struck her.

"Kas, are you afraid of me?" she asked, expecting an outburst of mockery or ridicule.

He laughed shortly, but it was a self-deprecating laugh. "A tall, pretty blond-haired teenager who reads minds? Who's supposed to come along and save my sorry ass, somehow, some way. Now why should I be afraid of that?"

She chuckled, too. "No reason, I guess. Not if you don't believe in your mother's predictions."

That sobered him quickly, although he continued to wear an ironic expression.

"Y'know, we wouldn't have all this if it weren't for my mother's powers. When she and Pop first got started, she'd see a vacant field in the middle of nowhere and say, *Buy that field. In a couple of years, a big highway will come right through here.* So Pop did, and that started the whole ball rolling. We always take her to a location that we're thinking of developing. She tells us if it's go or no."

Surprised, Athena said, "I didn't know that. Wish Mum would have visions like that. She sees other things, creepy, ugly things. Killers and rapists."

"So I hear." They'd come to a fork in the path. Ahead of them, through a thicket of oaks and pines, Athena could see the lake glimmering in the sunlight. Kas took the path to the right. "Follow me," he said, heading for the boathouse that she could now see about fifty yards away, "we'll have to wear wetsuits. The air's warm, but the water's snowmelt."

"I live in D.C., so I can handle it. I can read minds but

can't do weather forecasting. Go figure."

Kas harrumphed. "I hear you work part-time at a coffee shop. Seems like you could make more money doing readings."

"My mother wants me to keep our clairvoyance a secret. Except for the police we work with. I guess it's safer that way."

"I know, my mother feels the same way. There's a history of the bloodline having problems when people find out the truth. There's always a group in society that doesn't understand, that take advantage or use them as scapegoats. I guess that means there's been some witch-hunting in the past, burning at the stake, that kind of thing."

She looked at him. He wasn't joking. The protective side of him was rearing up. "I've heard that, too. I thought it was just nonsense, Mum trying to scare me into keeping it secret."

"Can't be any harm nowadays," he said, glancing back and grinning. "Now you'd get celebrity status and your own reality TV show."

She couldn't help but laugh. "Not interested."

"Well, if you want to read me, go ahead. No skin off my nose. I'm sure what you see will either turn you off or bore you to death."

"Then I guess you're different from all the other men I've known," she tossed back. "Even my father doesn't like it. Men like their secrets."

"All the other men?"

"Figuratively speaking," she said wryly.

Athena noticed he frowned as he paused on the path and cut his gaze over to her. "Chris filled me in about you. You're nineteen. An art student. Single. Says you had a hard time when you were younger. With your clairvoyance, I mean."

"When it first came on, yes. Now it's okay. I manage." She shrugged and added, "I'll be twenty December first." Now she wondered what else Chris had told him. Probably how she couldn't get a boyfriend if her life depended on it. That she was a virgin desperate for love. God, no wonder Kas was put off.

"Don't believe everything my brother tells you about me," was all she could think of to say.

He said nothing as he entered the boathouse. Inside, he rummaged through a big plastic bin full of water ski paraphernalia, grabbed two wetsuits, two pairs of goggles and booties.

"You're Leon's size, I think. We only have men's wetsuits, so this might not fit exactly. It'll have to do." He handed her the smaller of the two and began to strip off his clothes until he was down to a small, black Speedo. Unable to stop herself, she stared at his wide, muscular back, his narrow waist and tight, rounded butt. When he looked back and saw that she hadn't moved, he frowned.

"What are you waiting for?"

She scurried to shed her sneakers, sweatpants and top. Standing in the cool air in just a skimpy bikini, she took hold of her wetsuit by its shoulders. The long zipper ran down the back, wouldn't you know. She struggled with the legs and arms, pulled and yanked, tugged and twisted, while Kas sat on a plastic chair and watched her, an amused grin replacing his initial show of impatience. There was no gruffness in his voice when he said, "Here, let me help."

He tugged the top part of the wetsuit until it covered her almost naked breasts, then tackled her back.

"You've got the body of a competitive swimmer."

"I used to compete in high school. Freestyle and backstroke were my specialties. Now I just paint."

He tucked the gold chain underneath the wetsuit before

zipping her up the back. She felt his hands rest on her rubber-clad shoulders and began to pick up an image, but immediately quashed it and turned off her clairvoyant flow. Out of respect for his privacy and a male's disdain for voyeurs, she told herself. In truth, she was afraid he'd find her severely lacking in feminine allure.

For his sake, she said, "Don't worry, I've turned it off. I'm not reading you."

"Good. Wouldn't want to shock your nineteen-year-old sensibilities."

She blurted out, "I'm older than my age. I'm not easily shocked." Oops, that sounded like an invitation. Embarrassed, she bent over and slipped on the rubber booties. Silently, he left her and went over to the far side of the boathouse, where a jet ski, a large, three-person SeaDoo, hung on wide nylon straps.

"We thought we were finished with it for the winter," he said, turning the crank manually and winching down the jet ski until it sat in the water. He unlatched the straps, checked the fuel gauge and then pulled a key on a floater chain out of a side compartment. "C'mon, get on behind me. Ever ride one of these? If you don't want to fall off, hold me tight around the waist but keep your weight centered. Move with me. Got it?"

She slowly mounted, excitement and fear surging through her. He counter-balanced her weight while she got settled behind him.

"Good," he added, "you've got good balance. Put on the goggles, we're going to get wet. Let me know if you get too cold."

The way Athena was feeling at that moment, blood pounding in her veins and arteries, her face flushed and her insides warm and liquidy, she didn't think she'd ever feel cold again. Immediately she changed her mind and decided to peek into his thoughts.

"By the way, how did you feel about my portrait of you?" She had to ask, and now was as good a time as any. If he said he hated it, so be it. She'd read him and learn the truth.

He backed up the SeaDoo and maneuvered a turnaround as he pointed the bow towards the open water. Before taking off across the lake, he worked the throttle a bit to juice up the engine. Then he turned his head to her side. His guard was down. No stone wall this time.

"I liked it. You captured a side of me that I forgot was even there. I looked young, idealistic. I'd forgotten I was like that once. You've got a lot of talent, Athena."

His thoughts and feelings revealed so much more than what he said. Now Athena knew he liked her. Very much. As much as she liked him.

She's a girl but looks like a woman. Wondering what it would be like to make love to her . . . she could even be the one Mom has foreseen in my future, or maybe not . . . don't even go there, just Mom's fantasy dream, wants me to settle down . . . Never mind, it's all nonsense even though it's superstitious of me to refuse to ride in a car with Alex, my own brother . . . just bullshit the way Mom manipulates us . . . Might as well not tempt fate, she tells us . . . she's right most of the time . . . Fate? Is this pretty girl my fate? Hell if I know . . . this girl, Athena, she's like a magnet, has a powerful pull on me . . . I've got such a hard-on for her . . . well, the cold water'll take care of that soon enough . . . I'm a big boy, I can resist her if I want to . . .

Do I want to?

Athena inwardly sighed as the wind whipped her face. The spray from the lake made them wet. She squealed with delight, and Kas laughed out loud.

"Hang on, I'm going full throttle." He turned the jet ski towards the concrete dam wall. Her thighs pressed against his hips as she clung to him. His broad back buffered some of the cold spray but wanting to look at the monolithic structure, she rested her chin against his shoulder. He turned his head and leaned it back so that the top of her head touched his temple. His first gesture of affection.

He was telegraphing something to her. An invitation to visit his man cave, the apartment he kept above the mansion's detached garage. Later that night.

Had she read him correctly? He smiled and turned his head away as the dam loomed ahead. Then he smoothly veered away, leaning into the turn. She leaned, also, not fighting the tilt of the jet ski. She trusted him and what his body could do. She trusted his mind, too, strange as that seemed. She barely knew him, and yet the man she'd captured on canvas was the real man all along. Maybe bruised and battered, but still there.

When they straightened and sped away from the dam, Athena suddenly realized what she was going to do.

Their mysterious attraction to each other wasn't going to do them any good, she realized. *No good at all.* They had different mindsets, different paths, too much baggage. She was too naïve, he was too cynical. Almost twenty and twenty-eight were a lifetime of experiences apart.

That didn't mean she wasn't going to take him up on his invitation.

She had to start learning sometime.

Chapter Twelve

Thanksgiving dinner was typically American with turkey, dressing, gravy and cranberry sauce. But it seemed that Papa Skoros, or Papu—his grandchildren's name for him—had insisted on a few Greek dishes, so Athena had her first taste of *spanakopita,* a flaky crust filled with a spinach and garlic mixture, and *dolmas,* grape leaves stuffed with ground lamb and rice. Very good, she thought. Papa Skoros presided at the head of the table, all sixteen places taken, his elder sons, their wives and children filling the seats that hadn't been occupied before. He held up a small glass of ouzo, a clear potent, anisette-tasting liquid—according to her table partner, Alex, ninety proof. The patriarch said a prayer in Greek, then toasted his family, their good health, his guests and the general state of Skoros Enterprises. His sons indulged him with hearty smiles and their own toasts, one by one, each one stamped with the speaker's own personality.

Kas' toast was the shortest, "To our guests from D.C. May they come again!"

At which point, Lorena Skoros, respendent in a high-necked, black-velvet cocktail dress and dazzling white pearls, spoke up.

"They will, I know it. I've dreamed it."

Alex turned to Athena and whispered, "If our Oracle of Delphi says so, it's gotta be true."

"I hope so," she said, sneaking a look over at Kas, who sat across from her and down one seat. He was speaking mostly to Chris and Anna but when he glanced up and caught her staring, he returned a grin. His blue eyes held hers for an instant before turning away.

Thanks to Alex's animated conversation and her second sampling of the ouzo, Athena enjoyed his wit and charm even more than usual. She noted, also, the warmth and affection which appeared to be a hallmark of their family gatherings. Even the five children, three boys and two girls, behaved well and listened to the adult chatter around them, taking part whenever they could. A pang of regret hit Athena as she recalled the somewhat reserved dinners with her father's family in London. There was no hugging or kissing with the Butlers. She and Chris had no family in D.C., and although they spent an occasional summer vacation with her mother's Italian family in Como, Athena missed the infrequent get-togethers.

When dinner came to a close, the caterers bustled about as everyone scattered to various rooms. Her mother and Lorena disappeared into Papa Skoros' study, Alex urged her and Chris to watch a movie recently released in DVD, while the children and their parents settled into the large family room with Papa Skoros holding court and taking each child in turn on his lap. Kas vanished, Alex said, to feed Spartacus.

After ten minutes of the high-octane action movie, Athena told Alex and Chris she was going outside for a short walk before running upstairs to grab her jacket.

She wasn't quite finished with Kas Skoros, whether he liked it or not.

In Philip Skoros' wood-paneled study, Anna sat on an overstuffed couch with her cousin Lorena. A lamp nearby cast a cone of light, but otherwise the room was dark. The two women clasped both hands in each other's and gazed into each other's dark eyes. They sat very still and quiet. Long minutes later, Lorena began to speak. Her voice was soft, calm and modulated.

"Anna, I've seen in my dreams this week much happiness and also much sorrow."

Anna Butler waited patiently, her gaze flickering now and then from Lorena's face—there was so much she wanted to ask her. But she knew she had to wait and let Lorena tell her in her own way.

"The danger and sorrow will come first, the happiness much later. Years later but it will come. You know that your husband, Trevor, is in great danger. The entire staff of the British Embassy are targets, but mostly the higher ranked officials. His enemy is powerful and wealthy, the great wealth coming from the bottomless coffers of their Saudi supporters. This time, however, the enemy has enlisted Eastern Europeans—mercenaries for hire—and has bribed a few Americans as well. They intend to carry out a series of explosions in the capital while these dignitaries are dining. I couldn't see the place, but an official banquet in honor of the Prime Minister might be one of them. Just know that the Prime Minister, his staff, the British Ambassador and other Embassy officials are the main targets. That includes Trevor, of course. Payback, I suppose, for Britain helping American troops in Iraq and Afghanistan."

She sighed deeply as her shoulders sagged. "I wish I could see more. I'm sorry."

Anna brought one of Lorena's warm hands up to her face and held it against her cheek. "You've confirmed what Trevor has already heard from their intelligence team."

Lorena nodded. "There's something else. Athena knows one of these Americans involved in this heinous plot. I think she has been friendly with him. I saw her with a dark-haired young man on the blurry fringes of this dream, so I believe it's related in some way."

Anna dropped the woman's hands and covered her mouth in shock. "How can that be?"

Lorena shrugged. "You'll have to ask her. But after this is over, the enemy will want revenge. Perhaps you and Trevor should transfer to another Embassy or Consulate. Leave the D.C. area. Go to another state or country."

It was Anna's turn to nod, but she frowned as she did so. "We can't leave now. Athena likes the Art Institute and Chris loves his school. This will have to wait until after they graduate in two years."

"I wouldn't wait, Anna," murmured her cousin. "The danger will be real, a kind of revenge against certain Embassy officials." She smiled tentatively. "There's an Art Institute in San Francisco if Athena should want to stay in this country and finish her education. There are many fine universities with good art departments. She is so talented. Chris said he could finish high school a year early with all the Advanced Placement classes he's been taking. Or he could finish up wherever your next post is."

Disheartened, Anna pondered her cousin's warning. Her family faced being torn apart because of this threat against the PM and the entire Embassy staff.

"Such a smart boy, that Chris. He wants to attend Stanford. My own four sons went to UC schools. They have good business minds, but they weren't smart enough for Stanford." She smiled indulgently at Anna, sympathy clearly etched on her expression. "If he comes to California, we'll look after him. Athena, too."

"Your sons are fine men, Lorena, and they seem so dedicated to Philip and the family business."

"Yes," Lorena said before her eyes glazed over, "they have their father's head for such matters. Kas, not so much, but he stays involved for his father's and brothers' sakes. Speaking of him, Kas and Athena . . . it won't happen for a long time. They have mistakes to make, problems to overcome. This is not the right time. You understand?"

"Yes, I think so." Anna looked down. A thought had crossed her mind.

"Yes," said Lorena, anticipating her cousin's question, "the police work is good for both of you. It gives you a sense of purpose. Athena needs it, certainly. She's a little lost and searching her way. Helping people, the law enforcement community in particular, is always a good thing."

"I agree it's a good thing for me. Athena, I'm not so sure. She sees life differently. Kas is devoted to serving his country, his community. Wasn't he in the military?"

"Yes, for four years. Then he went to UCLA, got a degree in business like his brothers. But he needs a sense of purpose, too. Making money in itself was never his main goal in life. Unlike George, Leon, and Alex."

"The two eldest, they seem to be such great family men. And Alex. What a character! We've enjoyed his company so much. He's been very generous with his time."

A shadow fell over Lorena's face, and she cast her eyes down into her lap.

"Alex, dear fun-loving Alex." But she said no more. She emitted a deep, ragged sigh and grabbed onto Anna, who helped her to her feet.

"Lorena, you must be tired. I can't tell you how much I appreciate your having us this week. And for sharing your dreams with me."

They walked slowly to the door. "I pray that some of the dreams will come true. Others, I pray that I'm wrong. So very wrong."

Anna understood completely.

Already familiar with the mansion and surrounding acreage,

Athena scurried down the terrace steps, skirted the pool and patio area, all lit up by motion-sensored outdoor lamps, and wended her way towards the large garage building. A two-story structure housed four cars and two small apartments upstairs. In the rear of the building, she found Kas and Spartacus, the dog wolfing down his meal in a giant bowl next to his doggie-igloo.

When he heard her approach, Kas stood up from the bench where he'd been sitting. He was wearing a Navy pea coat, and the air was so cold that his breath steamed with each exhalation.

"Just wanted to say goodbye to Spartacus," she said.

"You're leaving in the morning?" He gestured towards his dog. "Don't disturb him while he eats. He doesn't like it."

She smiled and squatted down, mindful of the dressy gray velvet pants and ice-blue sequined top she wore under her jacket but not really caring.

"Spartacus," she murmured softly. Immediately, the dog's black ears twitched and he raised his pointy face. He was at her side in a flash, rubbing against her leg, her side, her arm, making mewling noises deep in his throat as if he were whimpering.

"Well, sonuvabitch," muttered Kas. He growled in imitation of his dog, but Spartacus ignored him. Humor leaked through Kas's gruff voice.

Athena chuckled and stroked the dog's coat. "Ohh, don't be jealous," she scoffed, "he just likes me. Wish I had that same way with men."

"I think you're one of those dangerous women that all men fear. Y'know, the kind men fall hard for. And when she dumps you, you spend the rest of your life in a bottle, yearning for her."

She had to laugh. "You're telling me I'm a femme fatale?

You're the first who's said that. I'm more the freakish witch they run from."

He grabbed her ponytail and gave it a gentle yank. "You're a witch, all right."

"Are you saying, I should be flattered?"

"Oh, yeah."

Satisfied, Spartacus gave her one last snuffling, then returned to his food bowl.

"I'm getting a female companion for him," said Kas. "Every male needs one, I suppose. Spartacus gets lonely patrolling the property by himself and waiting for me to come out and play." He paused and stared at her as she stood up. "Athena, I'm going to be very busy this next year or so with the company. My brothers keep doing too good of a job. We're expanding by leaps and bounds. We've got three big projects going on."

Athena understood what he was trying to tell her.

This ends here. Before it begins. "I'm busy, too. At the part-time rate I'm going, it'll be two more years before I get my Bachelor's in Fine Arts. Well,"—she shrugged and ignored the ache in the pit of her stomach—"I'm glad to have met you," she said, then held out her hand.

She'd changed her mind. Unless she got another sign, she wasn't going to visit Kas that night. No way. She wasn't going to throw herself at him.

Kas's blue eyes drilled into her, then he closed the distance to envelop her in a bear hug, flooding her with wave after wave of emotions and images. He held her for a full minute—although she couldn't be certain, since time tended to elongate while she *read* someone's mind—before letting her go and stepping back. She stood there, dazed, unable to process it all, unable to speak. What could she do or say?

"It's up to you, Athena. Totally up to you." He lowered his head and kissed her. A dry, chaste kiss. He was holding back. But why?

He gazed into the darkness beyond their lighted area and shook his head. In disbelief? In self-reproach? As in, how stupid could he be for letting his guard down with her. She read the uncertainty and confusion in his mind, which was all the more surprising when he asked her, "You sure you don't have a boyfriend back in D.C.?"

For the first time all week, she thought of Martin Larsen, the gorgeous, blond male model in her painting class. Her lusting after him had vanished.

"No."

He said nothing for a moment before heaving a big, steamy breath. "The time's not right, y'know, but we'll stay in touch. I know I'll see you again. My mother says so, it's gotta be true, right?" He laughed, a bitterness edging his humor.

They stared at each other, turning shy with diffident grins. With a gesture, Kas suggested they walk back to the terrace.

"Mom says you paint portraits on commission. Like you did mine, only you didn't charge her for it. I want to give you a check for your time and effort for my portrait." He stuffed something in her jacket pocket despite her protests. "Stop it—this is also a down payment for something I want. I want to commission a portrait of Alex. You work from a photo, don't you?"

She made one last feeble protest, but he wouldn't take back the check, his hands palms up in a *stop* motion. They paused on the lit flagstone terrace under one of the carriage lamps while he pulled something else out of his pocket.

"I chose this photo of Alex. Now that you've met him and know his personality, I thought you could capture his . . . y'know, his . . ."

"His whimsical nature? His carefree, *bon vivant* attitude?"

Kas laughed shortly. "Yeah, something like that. Can you do that?"

She took the photograph. "I'll do my best. When do you need it?"

Kas shrugged. "Whenever . . . maybe in time for my mother's birthday in June." He raised his hand and touched her face. A vision came with the caress. A long, wet kiss, filled with more passion than she'd ever known in her life. He was strong and holding back for her sake. "Let's go in."

"Wait." She looked back at the huge structure that was the two-storied garage. "Is your place the one on the left or right? As you face the front?"

For a long moment, he stared back at her. His face was a confusion of conflicting emotions. Then his smile broke through. "The right. The left is Alex's. Lay off the oozo so you find the right one."

"When?" she asked him.

"About a half-hour after everyone goes to bed. Gotta clean up my place."

"Okay."

"You sure about this?"

She nodded. They smiled at each other.

As she followed him inside the family room, a sense of warmth and peace engulfed her. Finally, she understood. Her visit was like the time warps she read about in sci-fi books and saw in the movies. She'd gotten a glimpse of a future life, but the future wasn't ready for her.

Or she wasn't quite ready for *it*.

Still, she'd steal what she could from this magical evening. The adventure might have to last a very long time.

And keep her warm on many a cold night to come.

CHAPTER THIRTEEN

In her secondfloor guest room in the Skoros mansion, Athena looked closely at herself. Feeling flushed with excitement, she bracketed her face with her hands. Good lord, what was she doing? About to have sex with someone she barely knew, about to lose her virginity with a distant cousin's son? Was she mad?

She smiled into the mirror. No, she wasn't mad. She knew exactly what she was doing and why. Never in her nearly twenty years of life had she felt such a strong attraction to a man. But it was more than that. There was a connection between them that she couldn't explain, and it had nothing to do with Lorena's off-the-wall prediction about her and Kas ultimately getting together. Without doubt or question, she knew she could trust him. He would always be forthright and honest with her even though he might in the long run—or short-term—break her heart. Whatever came along, she felt ready for it. Even heartbreak was better than this . . . void in her life.

She smoothed down her gray velvet pantsuit and the ice-blue sequined tank underneath, took down her ponytail and fluffed up her hair. A freshening of coral lipstick and she was ready. There wasn't time to take a shower. Maybe they'd take one together . . . later, afterwards. A shiver ran up her spine. Oh yes, she'd love that. What would his long, muscular body look like under a spray of water? Exactly like she'd seen earlier that day when he stripped off his wetsuit. She'd noted the damp, dark chest hair that arrowed down his slim belly and disappeared into his skimpy Speedos.

Her pulse rate speeded up. Oh yes, Kas would look gorgeous. All primeval male beauty. All wet and glistening . . .

She snapped back to the present, exited her room quietly on tiptoes and found the back staircase that ran down to the rear of the kitchen by the laundry room and maid's quarters. The family had a live-in housekeeper who was a jack of all trades, but mostly cooked for the family and supervised the housecleaning service. Athena arrived at the side rear door, which opened on to the asphalt path leading to the garage. The two red lights on the alarm system wall panel stopped her.

She'd forgotten about the alarm, and she certainly didn't know the disarming code. Frustrated, she wondered what she could do. The house was dark except for a night-light in the kitchen by the sink. Wake up the maid? Call Kas on his cell phone? Except that she didn't know his number. Wrestling with her disappointment, she decided to go back upstairs and explain to Kas in the morning what happened. He'd think she was a silly twat—

The side door opened and a tall, dark figure turned and punched in the code, disarming the system. When he emerged into the dim light of the kitchen, Athena smiled with relief.

Kas.

"Sorry, I just remembered the alarm, and you wouldn't know how to turn it off. Last thing Betty does before going to bed, turns everything off and the alarm on."

He closed the distance between them and pulled her into a strong embrace.

"Wasn't sure you'd come, so when I saw you there—"

He lowered his head and kissed her, this time not the least bit chastely. Their lips meshed and mouths opened. With her mouth and tongue, she drank his moisture and did a lusty dance with his tongue. His mouth tasted of minty toothpaste and while half her mind regretted not brushing her teeth, the other half reveled in all the sensations his kiss evoked in her. His hands squeezed her hair and backside simultaneously. Her own threaded through his thick, dark curls, and then moved downward to cup his butt cheeks. Just as she thought, firm and muscular like the rest of him.

"Let's go," he growled.

"Yes," she breathed out. Her head spun, so she gratefully clung onto him as he wrapped his arm around her shoulder.

Moving out and up to his room above the garage happened in a drunken blur of time, but soon they were entangled in each other's arms and legs on his bed in a small bedroom towards the rear of the apartment. He undressed her, gently extricating her hair when it caught on her sequined top. She was down to her bra and panties—she'd worn black ones, thank goodness, not her virginal whites—when he paused to whip off his sweater and unzip his jeans. Their mouths had never strayed from a trail of kisses, which left her wanting more contact with his flesh.

"God, Thena, you take my breath away." A brief silence ensued while he shed his jeans. His arousal was evident in the animal-print cotton briefs he wore. He frowned and hesitated as if he'd read doubt in her face, but he said nothing.

She rushed to reassure him. "Kas, I turned it off—"

"I don't care—read me all you want. Doesn't take a psychic to know what I want. It's just—is this what *you* really want?"

She lay back on the bed, no longer feeling shy or wary. The act itself might hurt, but she didn't care. She could deal with physical pain . . . and emotional pain if it came to that.

"Yes, I want this with you."

"God help me, I shouldn't care," he rasped as he placed one knee beside her, the other leg still balanced on the floor.

"I want to know why. Why me?"

She smiled. "I honestly don't know. I've never slept with a man before . . . but I want to do this with you."

Kas exhaled a short, soft laugh. "Good enough for me."

They reached for each other, his smiling face lowering to nestle in the crook of her neck.

Oh yes, this—whatever it was between them—was going to be fine. Athena closed her eyes and her mind and surrendered to her senses.

His cell phone rang shrilly. Jolted back, Athena opened her eyes.

A girlfriend calling to check in? Or an emergency?

"What the f—?" His face raised up, contorted in disbelief.

"Are you on call with the sheriff's office?" she asked. Her breaths came in hard pants as she sat up on his bed. He nodded and reached into his jeans pocket.

"The unmarried guys volunteered. I can't believe the timing—" He answered the call and grew silent, his bare chest heaving up and down. One hand let go of her and raked through his hair. "You sure, Mom? I'm—I'm in bed—Okay, call nine-one-one. I'm coming."

His dark blue eyes swiveled to her, ran over her nearly naked body until his gaze met hers. Whatever it was, it sounded serious. He gulped for breath before swinging his legs around and thrusting them into his jeans.

"Who?"

"My father. Heart attack, or something like it. Alex is over his fiance's, I'm the only one here—"

"No, of course," she blurted and stood up. They both turned aside as they redressed in a hurry.

As he led her out his front door, he seized her around the waist.

"Next time we meet, Athena. Or maybe even later tonight if it's nothing. Maybe just heartburn from too much food and oozo."

"Yes, we'll see."

They held each other and kissed, then broke apart.

Wishful thinking on his part. There was no later rendezvous.

She and her mother joined Lorena and Kas for a tense, all-night vigil at the hospital in nearby Roseville while the elderly Philip Skoros fought for his life and while the surgeons operated on two of his main coronary arteries. By four o'clock, the entire Skoros clan had arrived. Four hours after that, when the family learned that the patriarch was recovering from the surgery, Kas took a break and drove Athena, her mother, and Chris to the airport.

He bade her goodbye with a quick peck on both cheeks and a soulful stare. Her mother said nothing to her as the three made their way through the security check lines. She didn't have to. Athena knew her mother surmised exactly what the elderly Skoros had unwittingly interrupted. It was no one's fault. The time just wasn't right.

Though she and Kas resisted the notion, a part of Athena was beginning to believe in fate.

Maybe there just was no fighting it.

CHAPTER FOURTEEN

Athena was back at work on Saturday, although her head floated in a fog. Her head was still in California, her mind and heart somewhere in Limbo Land, her thoughts consumed by her last night there. The resplendent Thanksgiving dinner, her short-lived sexual encounter with Kas, everything she'd seen through his touch, their mutual desire for each other. Processing it all was mind-boggling.

By noon, her boss, Fergy, had noted her lack of concentration and commented on it. At which time, she finally shook herself and tried to focus on what coffee drinks she was making instead of forgetting to put the caramel in the caramel macchiato or the hazelnut syrup in the hazelnut latte. By closing time, her eyes felt crossed, she had a jet-lag headache and, brrr, it was snowing outside.

Dammit to hell. Freaking snow. She longed for California's sunny warmth.

She longed for Kas' strong arms around her, crushing her to him. She longed for his passion, his kisses, his caresses. It was such a cliché of romance novels, but she found herself sighing a lot.

Kas' father had recovered but was still hospitalized. Two of the arteries going to his heart were ninety percent *occluded*, to use their medical term. Surgery that very night of the elderly man's admittance—stents put in those arteries to open up the passageways—had saved his life. Lorena expected a full recovery and was greatly relieved, as was the entire Skoros family. Kas had texted her the same news but had added nothing personal. Still, Athena now had his cell number and a way to communicate with him. She'd replied with hearty good wishes and an invitation, "Call me anytime." She wondered if he would. Even if he didn't, that outcome wouldn't keep her from thinking about him.

Bundled up in a wool fedora, scarf and heavy jacket, she grabbed her hobo bag and ran for the Metro. Pressure to bring her work up to date for her painting class weighed upon her. She intended to put in a long night of catching up. At once, a frisson of warning crept up her spine as she descended the steps to the subway platform, the Blue Line which took her closer to Old Town, Alexandria. Someone—that man with the red wool cap, black coat and hunched over posture—was following her, she was sure of it. Inside the subway car, she held onto the pole, cold even to her gloved hands, and glanced around. Steamy exhalations everywhere, but there he was, standing in the car two poles over, glancing at her but trying not to be obvious about it. She averted her eyes quickly but could sense his focus remaining on her. At the third stop, near Washington and King Streets in Alexandria, she got off and, pretending to pull up her thick sock, bent halfway around and noticed he'd gotten off, too.

With a renewed feeling of urgency, she pulled out her cell phone as she ascended to the sidewalk. When Chris answered—he was waiting until their father returned Sunday morning before going back to the academy—she told him to run down to the Hallmark store nearby and meet her there, that it was a matter of life or death.

By the time she reached street level, she was running all out, congratulating herself between gasps for wearing her ankle boots that day. The soles were thick and tready, gripped the snow like snow tires. The Hallmark store was filled to overflowing, a good place to seek refuge. When her breathing had settled down, she glanced outside the large plate window in front of the store. The red wool cap was nowhere to be seen. That didn't mean he wasn't close by, however. A few minutes later, Chris jogged to the front of the store, met her stare through the window, and shrugged his shoulders, like *what's the big deal*?

Athena joined him for the short walk over to Prince and Pitt. Their condo building welcomed them as she laughed off her creepy feelings and told him about the guy in the red wool cap. They trudged up the exterior stairs of their shingled townhouse, chattering all the while.

"Yeah? I saw a guy outside of Murphy's Pub on the corner by the Metro station. Red snuggy hat? Black coat, boots? Yeah, I saw him."

Her laugh cut off. She jabbed the key into the front door lock. "Damn."

"So who would want to follow you? I mean, is this the same guy from work you said you're not dating anymore? Did you dump him and now he's sore?"

"No, not him. Someone else."

"An art student-stalker type?"

"No, I've never seen him before. Don't say anything to Mum, okay? She'll only worry."

"When're you going to call her Mom, like Americans do?" Chris had adopted American ways and slang like a duckling to water. Having lived all over Europe and the UK, he'd finally found a place that suited his independent nature. Athena thought that meeting the Skoroses had a lot to do with his sense of *fitting in.*

"Like never, Yankee boy. I'm a citizen of the world, and I can speak as I see fit."

Athena, her right hand still trembling a little, asked Chris to punch in their code-key. Finally, they entered their spacious condo—they were middle-class, after all, not rich by any standards—jostling and teasing each other, stomping and shaking off the snow on the rug in the tiled entryway. One look at their mother stopped them in their tracks. Holding her cell phone in one hand, a dishcloth in the other, their mother looked grim. Tilly the part-time cook and maid standing nearby at the stove and looking equally as grim.

"Let's go for a walk. 'Thena, put your jacket back on and bring the umbrella. That was your father. We need to talk."

"Why outside, Mum?"

"I'll explain. Let's go."

There was a large courtyard in the center of their U-shaped complex, a bank of garages serving as the fourth and rear side of the complex. They reminded Athena of the old-fashioned mews one found in London, behind fashionable mansions and townhomes.

They walked there, her mother holding a huge umbrella over their heads as the snow continued to drift gently down.

"This is too serious for evasions or modesty," her mother began, "Your father informed me that all of the attendees from the British Legation in Washington were followed to and from the secret briefing site in London. The important word is *secret,* or should have been. Our enemies, in particular the suspected assassins, had evidently discovered the location of this meeting. Why they weren't attacked, your father isn't certain, but as soon as the British Legation realized this, security details were tripled. It was a miracle there was no attack the day the Prime Minister attended the meeting. Or perhaps the assassins weren't quite ready. Only the closest aides of the foreign ministry's officers were privy to the meeting place."

Athena couldn't help but frown in puzzlement. What did this security breach have to do with her?

"In other words, 'Thena, your father believes our home

has been bugged. This is the only place where security is lax. I know you were dating that young man from the coffee store. What was his name? Tony something?"

Startled, she replied hesitantly. "Tony Grabowski."

"Lorena had a dream, seemed to think he might be involved with this potential assassination plot. We know you were alone that Friday night. Chris came home on Saturday and your father, Sunday, on his stopover between California and London. That night, you had a date with him, with this Tony Grabowski. Did you bring him to our home?"

This was it, the big question. Athena recalled the uneasiness she'd felt that evening, the long visit to the bathroom that Tony had made, his wandering around their downstairs rooms on his self-appointed tour. She'd been busy in the kitchen, making him a sandwich—

She summarized the evening for her mother, up to and including the end when Tony had seemed anxious to leave all of a sudden. He'd accomplished what he'd set out to do. Whatever that was.

"He didn't disturb anything, Mum. I checked. Nothing was taken or out of place."

"Didn't you use your clairvoyance that evening?"

"No—maybe. I should have." How could she explain why she hadn't? It was different with Kas. She'd wanted to see what Kas thought of her. With Tony, she hadn't cared. At least, not that evening. She'd already written him off as a possible boyfriend. Her intuition—not her clairvoyance—had signaled her that he was not for her.

Her mother just nodded. "We'll let your father do what he has to do tomorrow when he comes home. We'll go with his driver and pick him up at the airport. Meanwhile, a security team will sweep our home in search of bugs."

Athena almost laughed, but her mother's angry countenance stopped her. "Bugs?"

"Wireless transmitters. Which probably picked up a conversation that you had with Chris on Saturday or Sunday about your father's secret meeting in London. Your father said he mentioned the location to you and Chris in passing. A lapse in judgment, he says, and blames himself. He thinks someone listening overheard that conversation, and as a result, all the ministry officers' lives were put in danger."

"Father . . . and you . . . think that Tony hid these bugs in our home?"

Her mother's eyes shone fiercely. "What I don't understand, 'Thena, is why you didn't use your clairvoyance to see through this young man. Tony Grabowski is not his real name. In fact, the Embassy's security team ran a background check and discovered that it's an alias. No Tony Grabowski is enrolled at American University, and the only man by that name with a driver's license is a sixty year-old engineer who lives in Georgia. If this young man's working for those Serbian mercenaries, well . . . then you put yourself at great risk. And other people, too."

Tears stung behind Athena's eyes as a lump formed in her throat, but she swallowed it down. How naïve she was. How gullible and desperate for attention she must be. Were Tony's lines all lies, then? He was nice to her just to gain access to her home?

"I read him a couple of times," she tried to explain, "but I wanted to be like the other girls. Normal ones. I guess I wanted the mystery of it, of not knowing exactly who he was."

Her mother nodded. "I understand, believe me. I'm not so old that I don't remember how exciting and romantic it felt to be pursued by a man whom you could fantasize about. I remember, 'Thena. But you can't fantasize about a man whose mind you can read."

Her mother's sympathy helped to ease her hurt feelings.

"I trusted Tony. He seemed sincere. He acted like he really liked me." Her voice caught and she forced an emotional lump down her throat. The pain of Tony's betrayal would serve as a lesson, that was all. She would never trust a man again unless she could read his mind and see the possibly ugly truth behind his words and actions.

Her mother touched her arm with her gloved hand. Athena knew she understood, but that did not negate the real danger that her naivete had created. What if the foreign ministry's officers and Embassy staff had been attacked in London? What if her father had been killed? All because she wanted something she couldn't have?

Normalcy.

Good god, it's time to grow up, Athena. You are who you are. You will never be normal. You will never have the things normal girls have. Never.

Her mother's thoughts echoed hers. *'Thena, you can't escape it. You must accept the gift you have. And for your own protection, Dio mio, use it.*

* * * *

Anna summoned Athena and Chris early Sunday morning after receiving the call that Trevor's driver was downstairs in his Range Rover, ready to take them to Dulles Airport to pick up her husband. She'd already warned them both not to mention their father or their suspicions aloud while in their condo, so as they were leaving, she let in one of the British Embassy's security teams. Three men began bustling around in complete silence, each carrying a small case of electronic equipment, as Anna and her son and daughter quietly left.

With a heavy heart, she took the elevator with Chris and Athena. She felt violated. First, a strange young man whom Athena barely knew had not only *bugged* their home but had put her overly trusting and lonely daughter at risk. They now knew where the Embassy's cultural attaché and his family lived. She felt acutely the presence of danger even though Trevor had assigned a security team to guard their building day and night until the danger had passed for the British Legation in D.C. Which meant until the PM had arrived and then left the U.S. in continued good health.

Lorena was correct in her interpretation of that dream about the Embassy's staff during the Prime Minister's visit in January. She'd seen Athena and a dark-haired young man on the *fringes* of this plot, in her own words. The young man had duped Athena into allowing him into their home. Her daughter! With all of her skills at seeing beneath the surface of people, her own daughter had refused to use her powers.

Perhaps Athena would learn from this experience. She hoped and prayed so.

Two hours later, as scheduled, she re-entered their condo with her family. Chris carried his father's suitcase, Athena his briefcase, while Trevor, looking wan and haggard from his red-eye flight from London, entered the kitchen where the three security men waited at the table. Anna had prepared a pot of tea for them before leaving, and now they were down to the dregs in their cups. It hadn't taken them as long as they thought. The family gathered around the three men, all wearing blue jumpsuits with fake *Ajax Electrical Services* decals on their fronts.

The oldest of the three, a gray-haired man of medium-height and florid complexion, stood up and went over to the kitchen bar counter. On the speckled granite countertop were three electronic devices. One was different in appearance than the other two. It was larger, boxy and had a switch and button on top.

"We found two bugs. These." The security tech held up the two smaller devices. "Radio frequency transmitters with a range of about two kilometers. About one mile. There must be a monitor in the area or a receiver that's receiving, converting and sending the signal somewhere else. One was under a shelf in your study, Mr. Butler, the other under the cocktail table in your great room."

"Our living room?" Athena asked. "I remember his walking around in there, Father. Later, he took a long time in the bathroom while I was in the kitchen. Did you check there as well?"

"Yes, miss. We checked all over, every nook and cranny, we did. These were the only two."

Trevor rubbed the blond stubble on his cheeks and chin. Anna knew how weary he was after all the travel he'd done these past two weeks, the additional worry and stress. She reached out and touched his shoulder. He looked at her, blearyeyed, and smiled. *At least we now know where we stand, and we're on top of it.*

"What's that?" Chris asked, pointing to the third device, larger than the other two with a toggle switch on top and a button that pulsed a red light.

"That is our radio frequency jammer. By moving the lever, we jam the signal—you see the red light there. On the other end, they hear only static, probably think it's a local cell tower or power line interrupting the signals. If we move it the other way, the light on top flashes green, and the signals from the two bugs continue transmitting."

Trevor turned to Chris and explained, "We're putting the bugs back in place."

"Why?" Athena asked.

The guilt was so apparent on her face that Anna felt sorry for her. All the way back from the airport, she'd apologized to her family in a dozen different ways.

To her husband's credit, Trevor gave Athena a warm, forgiving look. "We'll feed them, whoever the buggers are, misinformation. Only what we want them to know. We'll control the stream of information. We don't know how long it'll be before they figure out something is off, but until then we'll give them false intelligence. My meeting tomorrow with the ambassador and the other officers will determine exactly what that false intelligence will be."

The older security man interjected, "To prolong this misinformation, I advise keeping the green button on as much as possible. Just be aware of what you say down here in the living room and in the study. These are two of the most advanced transmitters I've seen, so if you have to speak in confidence, jam the signal for no longer than two or three minutes. Any longer or more frequently than once or twice a day and they'll get suspicious. They'll know we're on to them. Or, to be discreet, go upstairs and keep your voices low. They might have directional mikes focused on the upper rooms. But that, we can't control."

Her father nodded, and both he and Anna saw them to the entryway. "A huge thanks to you, mates. Let me know if you find out any more about this young man who calls himself Tony Grabowski. If you can find him, you might have a direct link to the Serbs."

When they'd left, Athena approached her father. "I was followed home from work yesterday. A man with a red cap and black coat."

Her father grinned crookedly. "One of our security men, Athena. Don't concern yourself. He wanted to stand out. Like an amateur would, he wore something that would make him noticeable, so you'd see him and let me know that they were on the job."

"Oh," was all Athena could manage before continuing, "Tony left work at Starbucks, you know, with no forwarding address or number. The Saturday before yesterday. Just all of a sudden quit. I called his cell phone number but it was discontinued, and no one at work has heard from him. He said he lived near campus—the U of V. But that's probably a lie, too . . ."

Anna and Trevor stared at Athena. Clearly, she yearned deeply to redeem herself in their eyes. They waited.

"If he contacts me . . . and that's a big if . . . but if he does, what shall I do? Besides let you know, of course?"

Trevor glanced at Anna, then down at the floor as he wearily passed a hand over his forehead. "Let me pose this very question with the ambassador, Sir Peter. My first reaction as a father is to tell you to stay as far the bloody hell away from him as possible, if he does contact you and wants to arrange a meeting. But considering the assassination plot and the danger on our very doorstep, so to speak, I don't know. The Embassy could enlist the FBI and set up a trap."

Fear rushed through Anna as horrible images swirled in her mind. "One thing we'll *not* do is use Athena as bait," Anna said vehemently. Insane, to even entertain the possibility of using their daughter to lure a member of the assassination team out in the open. She wouldn't allow it!

Trevor stared first at her, then at Athena. His face crumpled. "Of course, my darling Anna, I won't even consider it. Now, I'm going upstairs to lie down. Busy day tomorrow."

Greatly relieved, Anna felt her pulse slow down. She looked over at Athena, who just nodded solemnly and walked away. Making sure her mother couldn't touch her and read her mind?

Did all mothers have to go through this with their daughters? Her own mother—Nonna, as 'Thena called her—had complained often of Anna's rebellious ways. Hadn't she left Italy to attend school in Britain and then married an Englishman? What was certain, she had herself learned of late, was that her lovely daughter was more like her than not. Clairvoyance wasn't their only common trait.

Athena had her own stubborn, secretive ways.

Dio mio, the joys of motherhood.

CHAPTER FIFTEEN

Athena was happily distracted by her afternoon painting class the following week. Applying techniques she'd studied and copied from the great painters of the Romantic Period and the early Impressionists in Europe, she was putting on the finishing shadowing touches on Martin Larsen's upper body. Whereas her interpretation was strictly representational, Mikela had decided to render their model's exquisite male form in an abstract style.

"Come take a look, Athena," she said, standing back and allowing her to look around her easel. Although Martin was at the moment inclining on a chaise lounge, his long arms at his side, hands clasped on top of his firm belly, his long legs jutting out in repose, Mikela had one leg cocked to the right as if it were bent upwards. About to kick a wayward soccer ball? Thrust out in an ecstatic spasm? Martin's hands, blocked and angled at his groin, looked as if he were holding his genitals. *His balls and bat,* as Chris would put it.

Athena had to chuckle. At the very least, Mikela's version was humorous and satirical. Modern abstract art was never a favorite style of Athena's, but it could effectively convey the painter's inner feelings about his or her topic. Picasso was a master at hidden emotional messages. Besides, Athena couldn't very well censor or deny her friend's freedom to paint their handsome well-formed model in any fashion she chose.

"Hmm," Athena murmured, "I like the flesh color you chose, kinda peachy with violet-mauve shadows." There was nothing more flattering she could add. What would Doctor White have to say? Did it matter? Mikela was having fun satirizing their hunky male model. Maybe she thought he was too perfect.

"Thanks," Mikela said, pleased. She leaned in Athena's direction and lowered her voice. "Hey, girlfriend, so share. You haven't said more than ten words about the guy in California, the sheriff's deputy. Did you get his junk in your trunk? Or at least give him a hand job? Please tell me you at least did that."

Mikela had a crude way of referring to sex that made Athena laugh.

"No junk, no trunk, no hand job," she whispered back. She put her brush down and took a break, then carried her stabilizing stick with her over to one of the windows, Mikela following her. "We came close, but his father's heart attack interrupted us."

Her friend gasped melodramatically. "No shit! How freaky is that? Did that wig you out?"

"No, it just splashed ice water on us—"

"Literally? Who did that?"

"No, figuratively." Athena shrugged and absently tapped her stick on the window pane. It was snowing outside, all the more reason to dream of sunny California and the ride on Kas' jet ski. She wondered if Kas' dog, Spartacus, missed her more than his owner.

Mikela was persistent. "Hmm, too bad. So? Any plans to meet up again?"

"No. I guess Kas will call or text me if he wants to come to Washington," Athena said and was about to sigh but caught herself. "Really, it was just a—a kind of . . . fling. He was fun to talk to, but"—she shrugged and elbowed her friend as Professor White came their way—"back to the salt mines."

Mikela shot her a look of astonishment. "Fling, huh? Now

hunky Martin looks 'bout as hot as a slab of codfish. Girl, you've sure changed your tune after a one-week fling." She giggled all the way back to her easel.

A half-hour later, Martin took another five-minute break in his velveteen robe, his flip-flops slapping on the hardwood floor as he made his rounds of the large room, warming up his naked body. When he stopped in front of her easel, Athena greeted him with a smile. He no longer made her pulse race, but she was genuinely interested, having heard that he was the assistant manager of a Georgetown gallery. Modeling for art students was his freelance moonlighting—or afternoon job, in this case. Strange, for he could have made so much more money modeling for fashion photographers.

"What do you think, Martin?"

He took his time, all the while shaking his head. Maybe he hated her rather traditional representational rendering.

"Remarkable, your play of color and light on the body. Reminds me of an Ingres, a Camille Corot or Edouard Manet. Realism with a hint of romanticism. Love it, absolutely love it." His voice was quiet and calm, but the look he then gave her was fierce and intense. "Listen, I have a business proposition for you. Meet me afterwards. I'll buy you an early dinner. I don't have to be at the gallery until seven. Please, this is important."

Apparently, Martin knew his art history, for that was exactly the style Athena was trying to emulate. She'd been a Corot and Manet lover since high school art class when, on a field trip to the Metropolitan Museum in New York, she'd bought a poster copy of Manet's masterpiece, *The Bar at the Folies Bergeres*. She'd read about Corot's influence on some of the Impressionists and had studied his techniques.

Intrigued but gun-shy, she touched Martin's arm and leaned towards him. His thoughts and images convinced her that he was serious. She'd seen in his mind a gallery book of photos of Manet's paintings.

"Business proposition?"

"I hear you work part-time at a Starbucks," he whispered, his head inches from hers. "How would you like to earn five to twenty thousand per painting?"

She dropped her hand, incredulous, forgetting to read him. "Why would someone pay that much for an unknown artist?"

His gaze traveled back to the painting. "You'll have to meet me to find out. I can't go into it here and now. Meet me in front fifteen minutes after the end of class, okay?"

Her curiosity piqued, she finally nodded. Martin didn't want *her*. He wanted her skills as a painter of romantic realism, and if what he said was true, she was definitely interested. She could earn more in one month than she could earn as a barista in three or four months. Okay with her.

She could just hear her father. *If it sounds too good to be true, it most likely is.*

When she exited the front double doors of the Institute, Martin was already there, stamping his feet and blowing on his gloveless hands. So unaccustomed to seeing him in clothes, it took her a second or two before she recognized him. His cropped-short blond hair was covered in a black wool cap, snug to his head. He was all in black wool, jacket and muffler over black jeans and black boots. In clothes, he looked taller and stockier, the bulkiness concealing his slim core, his well-defined muscles and sinewy arms and legs. Unmistakeable, Martin Larsen was a guy who could make a girl dizzy with desire or longing. Why was he having such a clinical effect on her, when two weeks ago, he'd sent her heart palpitating?

The vagaries of the human heart. Who said that? No one, just the effects of Kas Skoros.

She was hauling her hobo bag and big case of paints and brushes, having determined already that she'd start on Alex Skoros' portrait that evening. Martin took it from her and motioned her over to his car. A new model Ford Explorer waited in the nearest parking lot in one of the guest stalls.

"Look, I know a nice Italian place about a mile from here. It's too cold to walk, and I'll drive you home afterwards. Where do you live?"

She started to tell him, then remembered her mistake with Tony Grabowski. "That's not necessary, Martin. Actually, I have an evening class tonight, then a friend's picking me up." Actually, one of her father's security details, the same man in the red knit-hat who'd followed her home on Saturday.

"Okay, I'll have you back in time for your class."

Twenty minutes later, they were sitting down at a red-and-white checkered table, lit by a quaint candle fixed in an empty Chianti bottle. An Italian flag was draped in one corner, an American flag in the other. Framed photos on the walls showed family members, she assumed the owners of the restaurant.

"Doesn't look like much," Martin said, "but the food—the lasagne and ravioli, especially—is sublime. Are you old enough to drink wine?"

"I'll be twenty tomorrow. My parents have served me wine at dinner since I was thirteen."

"Well, you look old enough, so Giovanni won't ask for your ID. How about a Syrah?"

They ordered, then chatted a little about their backgrounds. Martin had a master's in fine arts from Columbia, sculpted a little and painted a little, but his primary interest was the business of artwork—buying and selling to art collectors, provenance validation and authentication, preparing a piece for auction, discovering new artists and promoting them. His uncle owned the Visions Gallery in Georgetown, near town center—a great location, he said, for catering to high-minded and deep-pocketed art collectors. He'd never met a diplomat, politician or lobbyist who didn't want to collect art. Most knew nothing about the art world, but it was fashionable to pretend an interest, and even more prestigious to boast about a deal made with an up-and-coming artist on the cusp of fame.

By the time their plates of butternut squash-filled ravioli and an eggplant-and-zucchini lasagne were placed in front of them, Athena was captivated. For a few minutes, they ate in silence and she relished every forkful.

Then Martin took a sip of wine and launched into his pitch.

"Have you heard of pastiches?" She had.

"There's a lot of money to be made in the field of genuine fakes, or pastiches. It's a perfectly legal business, as long as you declare it a hand painted pastiche, fake, imitation, copy—whatever you choose to call it. People are willing to pay up to twenty-thousand or more for a well-done pastiche of one of their favorite artists. The French Impressionists, of course, are always top of the list for Americans, but there's a demand for Post-modern paintings, too. The Peter Maxes, Kaminsky, Tricot, Pino, Shvaiko, Warhol, even the early Kinkades. It's impossible to find anyone who can do justice to a Rembrandt or Vermeer or convincingly enough for a top-quality pastiche. We don't even try the masters of the Italian Renaissance, Michaelangelo, Tintoretto, Da Vinci. We stick to the famous but do-ables. The originals of those nineteenth and twentieth-century masters are out of sight even for the wealthy, but a good pastiche is a conversation piece. An ice-breaker at a social gathering. They'll exhibit it for their guests and then wait for one of them to finally figure it out." He smirked before taking in another mouthful of lasagne.

She was stunned. "That's a very expensive ice-breaker." The wine was making her a little drowsy. *Better stop with one glass if I want to stay awake during European Civ class tonight.*

"A trifling amount when you've got millions to burn," he said, shrugging. "Which brings me to you, Athena, and your extraordinary skill at painting the human figure. I'd like to hire you on a commission basis to paint Manet pastiches. Maybe later a Modigliani or Renoir if you think you're up to it. Do you have the time? I know you're three credits short of full-time status at the Institute. I've checked you out."

That got her attention. She put her fork down.

"Really? How?"

His handsome face broke into a wide grin. "Doctor White. She works for me. Her specialty is Cezanne."

Athena's jaw dropped. This was news, as was the revelation that legal art fakes were such big business. "Are you sure this—painting pastiches—is legal? I mean, I would have to sign my own name for it not to be a forgery. Right?"

"Of course. You sign your name under the master's fake signature. My business partner and I—we call our business Genuine Pastiches of the World's Greatest Painters. GPWGP. Here's our card. We attract customers through our website, through the gallery, word-of-mouth, what-have-you. The demand for high-quality pastiches is huge. We can't keep up with it. So, Athena, are you interested?"

Five thousand dollars was a lot of money. For maybe two weeks or a month of work in the evenings? Maybe thirty to forty hours of highly concentrated painting? She could accelerate her courses of study if she had her mornings free. Perhaps even graduate in less time. That would save her parents a lot of tuition costs.

"Let me do a little research first, okay?" She was going to ask her father to inquire with one of his contacts in the FBI or InterPol or Embassy security. It had to be legitimate and legal, for Doctor White was involved. The idea appealed to her. Not only would it be a challenge for Athena in developing her painting skills, but she might be able to make a career of it. After all, she couldn't depend financially on her parents forever. "It sounds like something I'd love to do. How long would I have to complete a pastiche?"

"As long as a month. We'll try it out, see if your work measures up to a high enough quality. Or if you can turn one out in a month's time. The imitation has to be convincing. All oils, of course. Brushstrokes have to be as accurate as possible. Color, tone, composition all must be accurate. If it's not, I'll pay you the full amount, five thousand, and we'll call it a day. There will be no more commissions. Sound good?"

She nodded vigorously and held out her hand. "We'll give it a try, and I'll do my best. Which of Edouard Manet's works would you like me to try to copy?"

His wide mouth curled up on one side. "*The Bar at the Folies Bergeres*? It's his masterpiece."

She groaned. "That's so difficult. Can I start with something easier? The Balcony? Breakfast? The Waitress?"

"Sure, why not? Let's try *The Waitress*. If you need a place to paint, come to my gallery. I've got a well-lighted back room where some of my painters work."

The gallery in Georgetown? Too far to go. She'd use the Institute's studio in the morning hours. It was open to all students on a first-come basis. "No, that's okay. I've got a place."

"Come Sunday afternoon on December sixteenth. We're launching our new line of Genuine Pastiches to the public with a gallery soiree. Four to eight. Champagne, hors-d'oeuvres. Our painters will be there to greet the public and put live faces to our famous fakes. Our collectors like to meet the pastiche painters. You have my card. So, shall we try each other out?"

Athena nodded. They shook hands while she *read* him. He was envisioning already her handing over Manet's painting, and another pastiche of Gauguin's *Tahitian Idyll* – she recognized the painting – by another new painter in his stable of artists-for-hire. This artist's name was Dan. Another young painter he'd recruited. A Gauguin copier. Another image flickered in his mind. After a long day followed by tonight's close of the gallery, he'd welcome into his arms his lover, Mark. M & M was embroidered on all of their towels, even on the sheets of their king-size bed. She shut off the image.

Not even a trifle disappointed, Athena let go of his hand and smiled at him.

Wouldn't you know . . .

Family birthday celebrations at a restaurant was a Butler tradition. And so Saturday evening, Athena had the spotlight and the full attention of her busy parents. Even Chris had come home to join in on the celebration, no doubt at her mother's insistence. Each member was celebrating a personal triumph in addition to Athena's birthday. Her mother had just finished a translation from English into Italian and French of a New York Times bestselling novel. Her father was celebrating a kind of respite from the worry and confusion of what to do to ward off the terrorists' upcoming attack. As he explained, the Embassy and its security team had finally developed a strategy, one prong of which was the misinformation spearheaded by cultural attaché Butler. That was as far as he could go, of course, the details being classified.

Chris was celebrating his soccer team's win over their rival academy's team. And so they raised their glasses of wine and one of fizzy Coca-Cola, toasting their continued good health and Athena's twentieth birthday.

She'd saved up her cards and gifts for this moment, wanting to open up each present in front of her family. One by one, she read the cards, showed the gift card or opened the box. Always practical, Mikela had given her a card and gift card to an art supply store near the Institute, which Athena appreciated to no end. Art supplies were constantly going up in price, and the costs were mounting each year. Especially oil paints.

The Skoroses had sent a card. Athena's mouth dropped open, and her eyes widened when she read the check they'd sent. "Nooo . . ." She showed the check to her mother, who had the same reaction. Her father stiffened and scowled.

"We cannot accept this. It's outrageous."

"We cannot?" Athena retorted, "I certainly can, Father. Do you realize how helpful this will be? I can finish my bachelor's degree in one more year instead of two."

Her mother looked uncertain. "I had no idea. It's outrageous, but outrageously generous." She confronted Trevor with a typical Italian gesture, as in *Why not, for heaven's sake?* "For them, this is not a lot of money. Well, it's a lot, maybe, but not over the top."

Ten thousand dollars! Her tuition for an entire year. Along with painting pastiches, she could quit her morning job at Starbucks and take more classes.

"How can I ever thank them, Mum? Father?"

Her mother's quick reply overrode her father's recalcitrance. "Send them a hearty Thank-You letter, a nicely framed photo of yourself and keep in touch with them. I think that's all they want, 'Thena. They want you to stay in touch with them. You're in the bloodline, and they take our bloodline very seriously. As seriously as your Nonna does."

Her mother's look, as she glanced discreetly at her husband, said to Athena so much more. *More so than our English relatives. Who don't believe we have special abilities. They think we make it all up.*

Her father's gaze met Athena's. This topic had long been a sore subject for them.

"Don't get the wrong end of the stick, Athena. You know we—I'm proud of your . . . gift. However, our education, our scientific background makes it difficult for us, the Butlers, to accept this . . . this second sight that you and your mother have. Don't take it personally."

Athena did take it personally. "Someday it will be scientific fact, Father, when science has the right measurement tools. Some governments take it seriously enough. Look at the CIA's Stargate project. I read a book about it, but most of it's still classified." Athena noticed Chris' eye-rolling before carefully putting the Skoros's magnanimous check into her wallet. "I'll deposit this tomorrow at the bank."

She hadn't informed her family yet of her other job offer, painting fakes for Martin Larsen's Genuine Pastiches of the World's Greatest Paintings. Her father's constant forehead furrows were a sign that his stress level was still high. When she *read* him occasionally, his worries crowded out his other, more routine thoughts. Not the least was the constant reminder that they were all in danger, as evidenced by the two Embassy security men who sat at the table next to them and kept a vigilant watch while trying to look unobtrusive. All the other Embassy diplomats were enduring such surveillance. As Chris put it, *like white on rice.*

As they were getting ready to leave an hour later, her mother seized her arm. Her pointed look told Athena to turn on her clairvoyance. Indeed, she didn't need to be reminded, for her mother's ability to transmit telepathically was so powerful. It was impossible for Athena to block her, once they were in physical contact.

Detective Palomino would like to see us both on Monday morning if possible. There's been a breakthrough in their serial killer case, but they still need our help. The sooner, the better, he said.

Okay, but at the end of my morning shift at Starbucks. So elev-

en-thirty?

I'll call the detective tomorrow and set it up. Are you certain you're fine with this? You don't have to feel obligated, 'Thena, but the detective has confidence in your abilities. They're desperate to find this monster and get him off the streets.

Athena inwardly sighed. Her feelings were definitely mixed.

Yes, I want to help.

You're no longer a girl, a teenager, figlia mia. I'm very proud of you. You're a grownup in every sense of the word.

Athena shot her mother a dubious smile and withdrew her arm.

All she'd received from Kas personally was a brief text, *Happy Birthday*. The Skoros' generous gift notwithstanding, she was disappointed.

Now this with the cops. More ugliness.

Yeah, adulthood was overrated.

CHAPTER SIXTEEN

Detective Juan-Pablo Ochoa picked up Athena Monday morning at exactly eleven-thirty, her mother already in the back seat of his unmarked police car. As she left and waved goodbye, Fergy was smiling again, having hired four more part-timers at the coffee store. These came from a plentiful supply, the Art Institute and two other universities within a few Metro stops. He'd asked again if she'd heard from Tony Grabowski. She'd said no, but did not reveal what her father's security team had learned about his false identity and what they suspected about him. Until her Manet pastiche passed muster with Martin Larsen and his partner, she wasn't going to quit this job.

Again, in a similar conference room at the police precinct on the Homicide Division's floor, the young Hispanic detective got them seated and served hot teas for both Anna and Athena. Legal yellow pads and pens were already on the table for their use. Before they'd finished half their cups, he brought them up to date on the case. This time, he was willing to reveal much more about the suspects.

"We've had this Person of Interest under surveillance since our lineup and Athena's help in getting information from his jacket. Unfortunately, our eyewitness quickly recanted his testimony one week after the lineup, saying he wasn't sure about the color of the van, the decal, etcetera. Maybe someone got to him—we don't know, but there we were. We couldn't hold the older brother, but we did check out his younger brother, their parents and the family's CPS history—Child Protective Services, I mean. Looks like the older brother served as a punching bag for two out-of-control parents, but the children were never taken away. The parents were middle-class professionals who managed to convince the CPS workers that their oldest son was accident prone." Ochoa paused to smirk and harrumph his disapproval.

Athena liked him even more for that small lapse of professionalism.

"The older brother learned the electrical business at his father's company, left home at eighteen and took his younger brother with him, who was sixteen at the time. Strangely enough, a week later a defective electrical outlet caused a fire in the family home that was so intense, both parents perished. Their bodies were so severely burned that the coroner couldn't find any other COD, uh, cause of death. Looking back, that fire might've been a revenge killing."

"Hmm, I'd call that poetic justice," said Athena. She could see her glib remark displeased her mother, whose spiritual faith ran deep. All life was sacred in her mind, no matter how horribly someone behaved. Athena disagreed.

Ochoa nodded. "The brothers inherited the electrical business and the older brother is running it today. His company has a fleet of six black vans. We impounded all six vans for a week and found no trace evidence of foul play inside. They Luminoled all of them, no blood splatter or patterns of drops. No seminal fluids."

Anna glanced over at Athena and frowned.

What? Like Athena didn't know what *that* meant. *Please, Mum. I wasn't born yesterday.*

Ochoa was far from finished. "There was a fragment of a plastic grommet in one of the vans, alongside the top inside ridge. What you'd find on a shower curtain to hold it to the rod. But that was it. We've formed our own theories about that, but our suspect explained it off as belonging to a plastic tarp he'd used once to transport a dead dog he'd found on the edge of the Beltway. He'd taken it to the city dump and threw away the tarp with the dog's body. Anyway, when we brought him in a third time for interrogation, he insisted on a lawyer and threatened a harassment lawsuit."

"What has he said about his younger brother?" Anna asked. Athena could imagine her mother's mental gears turning frantically.

Ochoa shrugged. "Not much. He's protected him all his life, taking the brunt of their psycho parents' abuse all those years. He says he comes and goes, stays with him when he's in town but the guy travels about. Won't say what he does and where. Then he clammed up. We got nothing else from him. His lawyer said charge him and let's see the evidence. Or let him walk. He walked."

"What's your theory, Detective?" her mother asked.

"I like the younger brother for these attacks on the little girls in these poor neighborhoods. They're weak, vulnerable, unprotected for the most part. We think the killer has a deep hatred towards females, maybe getting revenge on a mother who refused to protect them when they were young. Maybe something else is going on. Maybe both brothers are the perps, taking turns, maybe practicing on the young girls, building up for something more challenging and risky."

"Like older girls? Teenagers? Women?" Athena asked.

This time, Ochoa nodded. "A week ago, a fifteen-year-old from that same neighborhood disappeared. She was found the next day in an alley, the same one where the last young victim was found, her body, raped, strangled and beaten. Almost taunting us, like he's making it easy for us and we still can't get him. Again, there's no trace evidence from the killer. The rapist used a condom, and the body was cleaned up. Someone saw a black van with a decal in the neighborhood that same day, but our primary suspect, the older brother, has an alibi. And supposedly, all six of the company's vans were out on calls. He showed us the call ledger. Not one of their vans was near that neighborhood. If the ledger is correct, that is. Could be doctored up, for all we know. And, as the guy's lawyer says, there are tens of thousands of black utility vans in this city. We're concentrating on these two brothers because of what Athena saw in that jacket."

That hit Athena hard. What if she'd made a mistake and saw something out of context or saw jumbled, mixed images. She swallowed the lump in her throat and stared at the yellow pad on the table. A man's life was at stake. She had to be certain.

"The killer's clever at covering his tracks, isn't he?" her mother said suddenly.

"So you think only one of them is committing these crimes?" Athena asked her.

She nodded. "But they're complicit, I think. The older brother is still protecting the younger one. That's his emotional grounding. He has nothing else to live for."

"We agree," broke in Detective Palomino as he entered the room. The older, taller detective carried a box containing several paper evidence bags, all labeled with a white *chain of custody* log attached to each bag's front.

"Sorry, Mrs. Butler, Miss Butler, I was interrogating someone, and it ran over. Bosco and Rosen took over so I could bring this to you." The two women stared at the box of evidence bags. "As Ochoa probably told you, we've had our prime suspect's place of business and residence under almost constant surveillance for the past two weeks. The younger brother has never been seen in either place. We've had BOLOs out—Be-On-The-Look-Out—for the younger brother. We have his DMV photo from ten years ago. Our lab techs aged him but we got nothing. Nothing. When the older brother put a garbage bag in his dumpster, one of our officers recovered it. Old clothes were inside, several items in a larger size—we believe, the younger brother's size. Our lab has analyzed all the items, which were washed and cleaned before thrown away."

"That didn't make sense to us," cut in Ochoa. "Who cleans something before throwing it away?"

So far, Athena was following their update and the logical theory they were posing. The cops had hoped they'd finally gotten a break in the case. Physical evidence which would justify arrest warrants.

Palomino perched on the edge of the conference table and sighed. His eyes were puffy and red, his forehead creased with deep lines. This case had taken its toll on him, apparently. The new victim, the teenaged girl, obviously weighed on his conscience. After a month or two, the case was unsolved.

And the killer walks among us.

Palomino looked first at Anna, then at Athena. "Rather than tell you what conclusions our lab came up with, I'd like you both to handle each item and tell me what you see, what you think. You can write your impressions down on those yellow pads. Are you both willing to do that?"

Athena glanced over at her mother, who nodded her assent immediately.

"Me, too," she finally added.

One at a time, Palomino opened the bags. He had each woman sign her name to each bag and put on a different pair of latex gloves with each item before touching it. They did so, the whole process dragging out as they removed the gloves, signed a new bag, and then put on new gloves for each new item. Most of the items were shirts, not very old but worn and faded, cotton flannel, long-sleeved shirts, some with half the buttons missing. One item was a pair of white athletic socks, stained and soiled, not cleaned beforehand. This stood out, as though the killer or older brother were volunteering a clue, challenging the cops. At first Athena thought it might be a trap set by the detectives just to test them. Then she began to focus on handling each item, turning away from her mother in order not to be influenced by her countenance or body language.

All of this was done in total silence, except for occasional reminders by Palomino to sign the *chain of custody* log sheet. Ochoa went out once and came back ten minutes later to continue observing the whole process. Athena suspected he was videotaping their examination of these items, for what purpose she had no idea.

One item, the socks, captured her full attention. She wrinkled up her nose and smelled them but could only detect a mixture of sweat and dirt. The flow of images began almost as soon as she did this. The scent of the sea, brine, salt air and sweat flowed into her mind. Followed by a heaving boat—no, ship. A large container ship. Its dark underbelly, the confined spaces, narrow passageways. It had a smelly head for men only, a lighted galley with a large stainless steel sink. A small mess hall, trays of heaping portions of hearty food, hardworking men's meals. She saw a man's hands working at electrical panels, long fingers manipulating the various colored wires. His knuckles were scuffed and swollen.

So the younger brother was an electrician, too. On the crew of a big freighter.

Wait . . . wait . . . don't blurt it out . . . be patient . . . here it comes . . . She recognized the octagon tower . . . the pentagon-shaped Fort McHenry . . . the port beyond the buildings. She'd been there several times in the past few years. Baltimore.

Athena dropped the socks and gazed over at Detectives Ochoa and Palomino. Her mother glanced at her, exchanged a look over the socks on the table and nodded soberly.

They'd both seen the same thing.

"Go ahead, 'Thena," urged her mother, peeling off her gloves and sitting back.

"Well, here's what I saw," she began hesitantly, "My mother can verify or not. It's just what I saw."

"It's okay," said Palomino, "just tell us."

"He goes by an alias, but I couldn't see it," said Athena, and launched into a description of what she had seen, the various smells and images, ending with the name of the port city.

Ochoa sat and took notes, every so often glancing up at the hovering Palomino. The lab analyst, Athena guessed, had found traces of sea salt, but all the rest was new to them.

When she finished, Anna verified it all before adding, "I kept seeing the letters B-U-L-L-W-O-R-T-H. I don't know if that's the name of the ship or the ship's captain or this young man's alias. Everything else was as 'Thena described it. I had the same vision."

Ochoa was out of the door before they could say anything else.

"Nothing more?" Palomino asked. When they shook their heads apologetically, he stood up, ebullient and smiling. "Thank you so much. We'll check this out and get back to you." He kept shaking his head and muttering to himself.

He went to the door that Ochoa had just hurried through and called someone in.

"Captain, I'd like you to meet our two volunteer consultants, Mrs. Butler and her daughter, Athena Butler."

The supervising officer, a big African-American man with a military bearing, bald and dressed nattily in a dark suit and red silk tie, nodded his head in greeting, looked the two women over and said little except, "Thanks for your help." Then he was gone.

After his hasty departure, Palomino chuckled under a

raised hand, as if he were stifling a cough. "He absolutely *hates* our use of psychics. Thinks they're all self-serving shysters. Before you two came along, we had several who proved worthless and ate up our time and energy. Wait till we show him how we tracked down the person who's now become our primary suspect. He'll want to boast to the D.A. that it was *his* idea."

Her mother stood, her back arched, her chin up. Athena knew she was slightly annoyed and preparing to make a point.

"Remember our agreement, Detective Palomino. Our involvement in this case, our helping your team of homicide detectives, must remain a secret. I don't want the press to hear of this. If our identities were made known, my family's safety, my husband's career, our peace of mind would be compromised."

Palomino swiftly sobered, approached her and shook her hand. "Of course, Mrs. Butler. I don't want this to leak out any more than you do. Nor does my captain. He's afraid he'll become the laughingstock of the entire division. We'll keep this on the Q.T. We're still a long way from solving this case. We still need physical evidence that ties this younger brother to those victims. When we bring him in, we'll ask you back. If that's okay with you."

Her mother nodded. Athena had an idea. "Detective, if there's a way you can allow me to touch the man . . . without his seeing me or finding out who I am." She shrugged. "Just a thought."

Anna shot her a warning look, her dark eyes glittering like onyx. "Absolutely not, 'Thena. It's too dangerous." Palomino just nodded in agreement.

Later, as Detective Ochoa escorted them down in the elevator, Anna leaned over and whispered, "What does Q.T. mean?"

"I don't know, Mum. American slang."

She turned to Ochoa and asked him.

"On the quiet. Like, secret," he said.

"Do you think we helped?" Athena asked.

He looked pleased with them. "Oh, I think so. We'll find that SOB now. Once we have him in custody and lean on him, get him to confess . . ."

Her mother turned to the detective, her eyes hooded and dark.

"That's not likely. He's too clever, feels no guilt. Not by a long shot. And that's American slang, too."

Ochoa dropped Athena off at the Art Institute, retrieved her art supplies from the trunk of his car, and shook her hand. She watched him drive off, her mother waving from the back seat. The unmarked police sedan passed a brown Toyota SUV, parked along the curb. Filled with men, from what she could see from her vantage point. Something drew her notice. A male face stared at her from the back seat.

She squinted into the weak sunlight, automatically shaded her eyes and stared back. What she saw made her drop her case of supplies on the pavement. It sprang open, scattering tubes of paint, brushes, and plastic jars of varnish. A young man about to go up the steps stopped to help her pick them all up. Her heart pounding, she dashed up after him and hurried through the front doors.

Inside, she hid behind a wall and stopped to catch her breath.

Tony Grabowski! Was he stalking her?

She punched in her father's personal number at the Embassy and left a message, ending with, "What do I do?"

Chapter Seventeen

While she waited for her father's return call, she continued upstairs to painting class. It seemed that she was forever late to her painting class. Bizarre, for that was her favorite one at the Institute, but these visits to the Metro police always made her miss lunch and the first fifteen minutes of class. Doctor White wasn't going to be happy. Grrr!

Along one wall, a bank of tall, wide windows welcomed whatever natural light was available to the twenty-odd student painters already gathered and busy at work. The windows overlooked the street and ended midway to the floor, where a long counter ran to accommodate student supplies. Underneath, there were slats labeled with students' names, storage for canvases and portfolios. As Athena pulled out her work-in-progress canvas, she peeked out of one window. The brown car was gone.

Her heartbeat immediately slowing, she wondered if she'd hallucinated. Was she so creeped out by her visit to the cops that she was seeing bogeymen who weren't there? Mentally shaking herself, she took her canvas over to her usual easel and set it up. Mikela was already there and turned around on her stool to wave a few fingers in greeting. She had buds in her ears, something that Doctor White allowed. *Music feeds the soul and the creative muse, and all that.*

Just as well. Athena didn't feel like talking. A trip to the homicide detectives always put her in a sad, contemplative mood. It was a real bummer to help the cops find the bad guys—the really bad guys. The dark side of humanity depressed her and filled her with a sense of collective doom. It was hard to shake off.

Their model for the week was a woman, young and curvaceous in her renaissance plump and bosomy flesh. She held a red velvet cloth draped over one arm and posed on her plinth like Botticelli's *Birth of Venus*. Instead of a cascade of strawberry blond locks, her brunette waterfall fell in curls down her naked breasts. Unlike Venus, too, she was olive-skinned and held a swatch of red cloth over her pubes instead of a lock of hair. But the woman's face reminded her of a Titian or Tintoretto, the Venetian Renaissance painters whose treatment of the female figure resulted in a softer, more romanticized style. Their portrayal of feminine faces was idealized, too, cherubic and pretty. She would try to emulate them as she painted this model.

Because of the classic pose, she was a nice substitute, but darn! Martin was a more enjoyable model to gaze at, especially for the female painters. The guys in the class, however, appeared more alert than usual. Doctor White was making her rounds, and Athena hadn't even sketched her Venus out in pencil. Making herself focus to not dwell on her visit with Palomino's team or on her possible sighting of Tony, she got to work. Soon the sensation of dread faded as she transported herself into fifteenth century Italy.

An hour later, her cell phone buzzed in her jeans pocket. She'd drawn out Venus, every detail of her face and body, her hair, her draped cloth, and had painted the background with a base color—a pale mixture of cadmium yellow, ochre and titanium white this time—which she preferred to do before tackling the subject. Doctor White had approved and had said nothing about Martin's business, Genuine Pastiches of the World's Greatest Painters. Perhaps her instructor didn't know that Athena might become the Manet to her Cezanne.

If she passed the pastiche test, that was. She'd followed the photograph of *The Waitress* but had only just outlined the figures and background. Hadn't yet put brush to canvas. There weren't enough hours in the day, it seemed. She was always playing catch up.

The buzz on her phone persisted like a swarm of angry bees, so she withdrew to a far corner of the vast room and turned her back on everyone. It was her father calling back. In a jolt, the present yanked her back.

"What's this, Athena? You saw the chap who bugged our home? When? Where?"

Her father's strained voice made her wince with guilt.

"I think I saw him, Father. Maybe I'm just seeing ghosts, I don't know. I was in front of the school, about to go in. He was in an SUV with three or four other men. They drove off, so maybe I was wrong."

"Did you get the car's license plate?"

"No, I-I," she mentally slapped herself, "I was so startled. If it *is* him and he comes back, what should I do?"

"Stay in class. Have supper in the cafeteria, don't go outside. I'll send Max—by the by, what happened today? Max said he lost you when you got in a car with a man and your mother. He was very upset. What's going on there? You can't just take off and ditch your protection detail, Athena. And your mother, what were you and she doing, running off like that? I can't abide that, not now. Not when we're all under alert."

Uh-oh. Her mother hadn't informed her father about their appointment with Palomino's homicide team.

"Father, tell Max I'm very sorry," she said, trying to grovel for forgiveness, "I'll tell him in advance next time—"

"Next time? What do you mean?" She could hear her father losing control on his end. He'd raised his voice, something he rarely did. He was so proper English, after all. But there were times she wished he'd lose his composure and scream bloody murder, like Nonna and Giancarlo, her mother's family, typical Italians who knew how to let off steam. They let it blow like a volcano, and then it was over and everyone calmed down. It would probably be healthy for her father if he could be more like her Italian family. Or even like the rambunctious Skoroses, all hearty bluster and bonhomie.

"Father, you have to talk to Mum about this. I promised her I wouldn't say anything."

"Well, bloody hell," growled Trevor Butler, "You stay put so Max can catch up with you. He'll bring reinforcements. If that villain shows up and wants to talk to you, ignore him. The bugs are still working, and as far as he knows, we don't suspect a thing. Don't get into a car with him, Athena, even if he's alone. His Serbian mates might be right behind him. I don't know what Max and his team are planning, but I'll let them know where you are." His voice cracked a little, a sign that her father was getting emotional. "Whatever you do, Athena, don't get into a car with that culprit."

"No, Father, I won't." *Gosh, I'm not totally brainless.*

She sighed and returned to her work.

That evening her Western Civilizations class dragged, the professor droning on about the consequences of Alexander the Great's attempt to conquer the world as he knew it. Dutiful, however, she took copious notes in her iPad, letting her fingers click automatically on the keyboard to the spoken words while her mind went numb. Later, she'd read her notes and memorize the salient points for their mid-term exam.

At the end of class, she collected her art case and hobo bag, which held her notebook, iPad and sundry necessities, including her canister of pepper spray. On impulse, she tucked the canister in one of her parka's front pockets. One of the male students, a nice guy called Jeremy, teased her about it as he walked her down the stairs and outside. The snowfall earlier that day had long since melted, and the nighttime sky was clear and starry. On the negative side, because of the cold weather, the sidewalks were slick with icy patches.

"Watch out for the ice," Jeremy warned.

She nodded and waved goodbye as he met his girlfriend in front and took off down the street. The school's entrance disgorged a flow of evening students under its bright mercury-vapor lamps. Nervously, she waited at the bottom of the steps and watched several students slip and slide on black, invisible ice, squealing or swearing up a storm. Max, her bodyguard with the red knit cap, should be along soon. Would she recognize him? He changed disguises every other day.

"Hi, Athena."

She froze, recognizing the voice. Pulling herself together, she fixed a smile and whipped around to face the young man approaching her.

"Tony! What brings you here?"

His hair dark and curly as always, he still cut a tall, handsome figure in a brown bomber-style leather jacket, jeans and boots. But there was a haunted look about the eyes and a tense hardness to his features. His hands emerged from his pockets to clasp her shoulders in a kind of loose hug. Instantly, she hugged him back, shocked to realize that a part of her was still drawn to him. Nevertheless, her clairvoyance honed in like a swiveling satellite dish.

Play the part. Check on the bugs. They're nearby, watching me. Watching us. The assholes don't trust me. Gotta show 'em I know what I'm doing.

"I was passing through, thought of you, remembered that

you had night class on Tuesdays and Thursdays. I can drive you home. My car's over there." He pointed to the older model BMW he'd driven on their last date. It was parked across the street in front of an all-night diner. She glanced around, looking for the brown SUV she'd spotted earlier, and thought she saw something resembling it a block away, facing in the same direction as Tony's BMW. Towards the Three-Ninety-Five highway.

Athena didn't move from her spot on the treacherous sidewalk as she disengaged herself. "I'm waiting for my . . . my older brother. He's going to pick me up. Was that you I saw in the brown SUV?"

"Yes, a bunch of guys I know. You looked frightened before. Why did you bolt like that?"

Her heartbeat raced as she tried to think of an excuse. She shrugged and smiled sheepishly. "Seeing you like that, out of context, it startled me. Then I realized how late I was for class . . ."

He seemed placated. "You're always late for class."

"Don't I know it. What happened to you, Tony? Why did you quit work all of a sudden? No notice, nothing. Fergy was fit to be tied, said you aged him ten years. Why didn't you let me and the others know you were changing jobs?" She sharpened her voice a little in challenge.

He looked down at the ground, feigning—she knew—genuine apology or embarrassment.

"I know, I know," he said, "I should've said something, but I got the word from my new bosses early that morning. Had to leap at the chance."

"Oh yeah? What're you doing now?" She pretended to slip a little so that she could grab onto his arm. Chortling under his breath, he held her around the waist and said, "Whoa, there." His features had relaxed considerably.

"Research for a lobbyist firm that works for several House

Reps. Pays well, and it's in my line of study. Pre Law."

She felt his fear, as palpable as twanging guitar strings. Her own nerve endings were twanging, also, making her want to jump out of her skin.

Research for a bunch of Serbian thugs. Her father called it groundwork in preparation for a terrorist attack on the British Embassy. How had they convinced Tony to help them? What else was at stake? Besides the lives of hundreds of British subjects?

She continued to interpret Tony's thoughts and feelings, transmitting to her mind like instantaneous tweets. Deep regret coursed through him, fed his fear. He was paid well, very well. Fifty-thousand dollars! But if he failed, they'd cut him up in a hundred pieces and dump him in the Potomac. Fish food, they'd said. And they'd laughed.

"That's good. I don't blame you for moving on." She smiled and let go of his arm. How on earth had he gotten involved with them? Was he just another con man for hire?

"Wanta get some coffee at the diner?" His quick glance over to his car, parked across the street in front of the diner, was a *tell,* in Detective Palomino's parlance. His endgame. Get her in his car somehow. She slipped a hand up his arm and rested it on his shoulder. In one of his pockets there was a vial of chlorohydrate, a knockout drug. He'd dose her coffee and as she was konking out, he'd help her to his car and whisk her off. For what purpose? To blackmail her father into revealing classified details about the PM's visit? What else did they want? Insider information that could—

That meant the thugs knew their bugs in the Butler household were useless to them. The thugs were being fed nonsense.

"Sorry, I can't. My older brother—"

A hard, flinty look came back into his countenance. "I don't remember your saying you had an older brother. Just the younger one, Chris, I think his name was. What high school did you say he was going to?"

If we can't get the daughter, we'll get the son.

She bristled at the mention of Chris' name, never having told "Tony" the academy's name. Her father's occupation in a variety of countries had taught the family to keep circumspect about certain family details. Her nerves kept vibrating. She stiffened and backed up a couple of steps. Deep in her parka pocket, her fingers pried open the lid on the pepper spray canister.

"Yes, I might not've mentioned Max. He lives in England. He's in the military. We don't see him that often. He's here on a visit."

A man approached, wearing a dark blue wool jacket in the style of a peacoat, a sporting cap covering his head. This time, he was clean-shaven and looking younger than he had the last time she'd seen him, which was early that morning on her way to work. To her relief, she sagged a little and let go of the canister in her pocket.

"Speaking of the devil, here he is. And not too soon, Max. I was beginning to freeze out here. I've still got homework to do tonight."

Max came abreast, smiling affably, and shook Tony's hand upon her introductions. To her amazement, Max appeared completely relaxed. She was a bundle of nerves.

"You ready to go, Athena? My car's in the lot over there." Max bent down and bussed her cheek. "I was just chatting up a couple of students. Where's your car, Tony? Need a lift somewhere?"

Recovering, Athena pointed to Tony's BMW across the street. If others in the Embassy security details were around, maybe they could follow him. Maybe ferret out the Serbians.

Tony looked like he'd lost his best friend. Anxiety etched his face, but he was quick to smooth over his emotions.

Something about Max's military bearing had discouraged the scoundrel from any further attempt at kidnapping her. He cleared his throat before speaking, as if bringing his voice under control.

"I'll be calling you, Athena. Maybe get together sometime when you're not busy," Tony said before turning towards the street.

"Okay, call me, Tony."

Like many students who were about to cross the two-lane street to get to the side of the subway station, he hustled over to the meridian and then merged with the crowd. In seconds he was well out of earshot.

"So that's the bastard who planted the bugs," Max said as he took her arm, "I hung back, waiting to see what his line would be. With so many people milling around, I knew you'd only be in danger if you went to his car or if another car came up beside you. That couple over there, they were ready for anything."

Feeling numb, she nodded, her smile fixed like a puppet's. Tony had glanced back a couple of times before getting into the BMW. As Athena walked to the parking lot with Max beside her, picking their way around the ice, Tony looked at them one more time and waved while driving off.

"Max, he was planning to drug me and kidnap me. They know we know about the bugs."

Instantly, instead of asking her how she knew this, Max made a circling gesture with his right forefinger and stared after Tony's BMW as though memorizing the car's license plate number. Unfortunately, the plate had been muddied over. Behind her, she heard an engine rumbling, the throttle spurring it to life. The male-female couple Max just referred to had jumped on a motorcycle and were now speeding off after Tony's car. The woman's white wool scarf trailed behind her in the wind.

"There's another car, a secondary, right around the corner. They'll move in position when the time is right. Maybe we'll get lucky and he'll lead us straightaway to those Serbs. So how do you know he was planning to drug and kidnap you?"

She knew her father hadn't revealed his wife's and daughter's special powers to any of the security teams. As a reply, she shrugged and pointed to the diner.

"He wanted to buy me coffee at the diner. Isn't that how someone's drugged? They go off with someone they trust, don't pay attention to their drinks. Next thing they know, they wake up in some strange place. Tied up, at some sadist's mercy."

Max looked at her pointedly. "You sure you don't want a career at MI-5 or MI-6? You could also fit in with the FBI or CIA." He laughed at her shocked reaction. "Well, miss, let's get you home safe and sound. And the next time you go off with your mother on some mysterious errand, do have the courtesy to give me a hail and fare-thee-well."

His reassuring voice and solid presence—all in a day's work, after all—made her teary-eyed. The evening still crackled with surprises. Her insides were no longer trembling, her hands were no longer shaking, and her voice sounded calm to her own ears.

"Yes, Max. I promise. I won't ditch you again."

"Whatever was that about, anyway? You and your mother going shopping with a friend? Who just happened to be driving an unmarked police detective's car?"

You can't pull the wool over this guy. Mum should've known better. We have to tell Father what we've been doing to help Detective Palomino's case.

She wondered what Max would think, a British security officer, about her mother's and her secret gift. Her father would die of shame. All the jesting directed at her father at Embassy meetings—would he ever live it down? Would his career, that he'd worked so hard at and sacrificed so much for over the years, survive such ridicule?

Sorcerers in a proper English diplomat's family? What, you say? Do they conjure up spirits as well? I daresay, I've never heard of anything more preposterous! We can't tolerate such nonsense in the diplomatic service.

"Sorry, Max. It's a secret."

Max cast her a feral grin in the harsh lighting of the parking lot.

"Blimey, what do you know, like everything else in this bloody job, you've got a secret. Join the club, Athena. It goes with the territory."

CHAPTER EIGHTEEN

A week and a half later, Athena found herself with Max again, this time as her driver. They'd just pulled up to Visions Gallery on Wisconsin Avenue in Georgetown, a block from the Ritz Carlton, and he'd dropped her off. If someone was watching her, they'd think he'd driven off and would come back later to pick her up. However, she and Max had formed a plan, but it was up to her to carry it off.

The gallery that Martin Larsen helped manage in this upscale neighborhood was modern, spacious and well lighted, in counterpoint to the gloom outside on this cloudy winter's afternoon. A big gilded and framed sign on an easel promoted the event. *Genuine Pastiches of the World's Greatest Painters.* Underneath the heading ran two columns of names, fourteen artists in all. She located Doctor White's name and next to it, in parentheses, Paul Cezanne's, indicating her specialty. All the other contemporary painters of pastiches were publicized in the same way, making the whole business idea look quite legitimate. That eased her skepticism more than a bit.

Because she'd arrived two hours later than its official starting time, the receiving line had scattered. Only Martin and his gallery partner, his uncle Lars, approached and greeted her. He called over his other partner, Mark Cochinelli, and introduced her. A flashback vision. *The Mark of the M & M sheets.*

"This is Athena Butler, our potential Edouard Manet specialist."

Both men, Martin's Uncle Lars and Martin's partner-lover, Mark, appeared surprised.

"So young?" They looked askance at Martin after shaking her hand and smiling effusively. There was doubt underlying their charm.

"Ah yes, but I can spot talent when I see it. Why else would I endure those tedious hours modeling? One of the fastest ways to spot an up-and-coming painter."

Mark hung a loose, proprietary arm over Martin's shoulder. "It bothers me no end that he exposes himself in such a way. But"—he shrugged philosophically—"it's true that he's made several remarkable discoveries that way. Our business is simply booming. Look around you."

"Mix and mingle, Athena, have some champagne, some tasty hors d'oeuvres. Oh, here's my Gauguin specialist. His *Tahitian Idyll* is generating a lot of interest. So is Francine White's *The Card Players*. We've just sold it. At a higher than expected price, I might add."

The three men moved on and so did she, but she was waylaid as she headed for Doctor White, standing proudly beside her pastiche and answering questions of, Athena thought, a reporter for the Washington Post's variety pages. A young man had stepped in front of her, blocking her progress.

"Hello, Martin said I should meet you."

"Really? Why would he say that?" she asked.

The young man, not much older than Athena, looked down at her—yes, he was taller than she was—and extended his hand. Not so much handsome as cute, with wavy brown hair falling over his forehead carelessly in a manner that matched his dress, faded blue jeans over which flapped a white oxford-style shirt. He wore sockless loafers, apparently heedless of the wintry day outside. Intense green eyes fixed her with a slightly competitive stare, as though he were checking out a possible rival in the world of painting.

"He said you're a potential recruit. Manet?"

"Yes, and you're Paul Gauguin." It seemed odd that they'd already taken on the monikers of the masters whom they were attempting to rip off. Rather, imitate legally.

They shook hands. *He's attracted to me, thinks I'm pretty. Likes my hair, face, figure. Even my height. And he's curious to see what I can do, what kind of painter I am.*

All of a sudden, she was glad she'd taken extra care—all of fifteen minutes' worth—with her makeup, having put on eyeliner and mascara, blush and lipstick. Her outfit was a little dressy, a glittery green and gold tunic over matching green velveteen leggings, three-inch black heels and a black-velvet clutch purse. She'd even worn gold hoop earrings and a gold-plated bangle to accessorize the ensemble. Her hair, brushed to a wavy sheen, was drawn away from her face and fell down her back in a plain hairdo.

"I'm Athena Butler. And you're . . ."

"Dan Grantham. I graduated from the Art Institute two years ago. Martin says you're a student there."

She nodded, reluctant to show the full extent of her interest in this young man, doubtful that he was another Tony but still gun-shy of making a serious mistake in judgment.

"Second year, but I've studied art since the age of six. My parents indulged me with lessons, and when they couldn't, I taught myself."

He chuckled, and when a server passed by, grabbed her a flute of champagne.

"I know how that is. I had the worst art teacher in high school, and my parents never took my interest in painting seriously. Said I needed to learn a practical skill like engineering, computer science or the like. I satisfied them by learning how to fly like my father, an airline pilot. Took lessons in high school and did airplane mechanics, mostly prop jobs, while attending the Art Institute. I still do airplane mechanics on the side, but now I fly charters for a local commercial service, sightseeing flights around the D.C. area, that sort of thing, as a day job. The rest of the time, I paint. This is my first real paying art job."

She listened, intrigued by his friendly, outgoing personality but wanting to touch him to *see* how truthful this personal history really was. The moment arrived when an elderly woman and man needed to pass by them. She took his arm and steered him out of the way.

He's nervous. Wants to impress me but he thinks he's talking too much. Everything he says is true.

"Can we walk around, Dan? I'd like to see all of the pastiches." He agreed heartily, and when they approached Doctor White's painting of *The Card Players*. Athena pulled him aside, kept him far out of earshot of White and the reporter.

"Did you ever have Doctor White for painting class?"

"Yeah, she's the one who suggested my name to Martin. She knew I loved Gauguin, his subjects, colors, style."

They studied the professor's rendition of Cezanne's famous painting.

"What do you think? Think it's a good fake?" she asked him.

Dan emptied his flute and set it down, obviously not there to get plastered. She did the same, needing her wits about her for another reason. He leaned in close to her and touched her shoulder. His well-formed, masculine lips hovered inches over her face, so close that she could feel the brush of his champagne breath upon her cheek. She caught a whiff of citrusy cologne and delicious male musk. She fought down a ripple of desire.

"Don't let Martin hear you call them fakes. He's proud of this business of his, and I think he's proud of the stable of talented painters he's collected, too. He doesn't call us forgers, although that's what we'd be if our names weren't on those paintings."

"So what do you think?" she repeated, indicating White's

Cezanne.

"Very good in composition and color. Can't see the brushstrokes, so don't know about that. I'd have to hold the original next to it to judge the accuracy of her shading. But it's very close. It just sold, according to Martin, for sixty-five thousand dollars. My Gauguin's on sale for fifty-five."

"And we're getting five thousand per painting?" Ten percent for doing all the work? It didn't seem fair.

"Who told you that? Martin?" Dan harrumphed softly. "I wouldn't get my brushes wet for less than fifty percent. The gallery still makes out like a bandit. But they've got, y'know, overhead, publicity costs, patent fees. It's a kind of consignment business, but they control the patents."

She turned to stare at him. "Fifty percent? You're not joking, are you?"

"Hell, no."

They walked around and looked at all of the pastiches, all thirty-one of them, painted by fourteen artists, and stopped at several to meet the painter and shake hands. Dan introduced Athena to them all, having met them before, evidently. She appeared to be the youngest recruit so far, if she passed the test.

As she toured the gallery and noted the prices of all the pastiches—about half already posted with SOLD tags—numbers tumbled through her mind. If all of them sold for the price of the Cezanne, or even close to it, Martin and his partner stood to gain one point five million dollars, minus fifty percent. Most of the guests were obviously well-heeled, and she recognized several from appearances on TV news programs. These were the movers and shakers of the *powers that be inside The Beltway,* as her father called them. And they represented millionaires from all over the globe, not just American politicians and lobbyists.

Athena ruminated over the numbers. Martin had told her

five thousand for her Manet. Was he not expecting her to do an adequate job? Was the five thousand just a payoff for a tryout that he doubted would succeed? By the end of their rounds, Dan hovering by her side the entire time, Athena was boiling mad, and determined to show Martin a thing or two.

She looked at her watch. Time to go. Although it was an hour before the exhibition was scheduled to close, she had agreed to Max's plan. Without her father's knowledge, for the tail on Tony that night had ended at his apartment. Since then, as far as they knew—for Tony was now using burner phones, that couldn't be tracked, probably a new one every other day—there was no apparent evidence of his contact with the Serbian thugs. No dead drops, no handoffs, no face-to-face communication. Tony was clever and well enough trained to conceal whatever he was doing. Max and his team were stymied and desperate to try something else, for they assumed that Athena was still being followed.

"I've got to go, Dan." She realized that he wanted to walk her out. "No need to escort me. Somebody's going to pick me up in a few minutes."

He wouldn't take no for an answer, so she allowed him to accompany her as far as the front door of the gallery.

"Please stay. You should be there when your painting sells. It looked like you had two potential buyers."

"You trying to get rid of me, Athena?" he asked, grinning, "If it's not your boyfriend who's picking you up, I'd like to see you again."

"It's not my boyfriend." He followed her out the door and onto the sidewalk in front. At six o'clock, dusk had fallen to darkness. Although the street was well lit, the sky looked like a giant kettle lid had blotted out the stars. And the cold, despite her wool coat, settled into her bones. She looked squarely at her new friend, Dan, who hadn't bothered to pick up his jacket when he followed her outside. She liked him and wanted to see him again, but how could she explain what might happen in the next few minutes?

"You really need to go back, Dan. Some potential buyer might want to meet you."

Half of his mouth turned up in what she had found to be an irrepressible, sly grin. Now, the grin caused her real fear. He wasn't taking her gentle brushoff seriously.

"I'd like to see you off first, make sure you're not just blowing me off."

Athena glanced up and down the street. Too late! There it was, that brown SUV, pulling out from the curb on the opposite side. In terror, she watched it make a screeching U-turn a little past the gallery. When it halted in front of them, four men wearing black hoods—balaclavas—jumped out.

They pointed pistols at their heads.

Chapter Nineteen

What happened next was like a movie tape on fast-forward. Shouts rang out, "Get in the car! You, not him!" "If he moves, shoot the fuck!" "What's going on—"

"No, don't hurt him!" "Get her inside! Now!" A hand grabbed her, thrust her against the side of the open car door. Dan tried to seize her. She screamed at him, "No!" The thug trying to push her into the car took aim at Dan but was whipped around violently. He lurched onto the sidewalk, blood pooling under his head. Dan fell over on his back. Heads under hoods looked up and around. A sniper's bullet had come from out of the darkness. More shouts, this time with renewed urgency and fear.

Brakes screeched. A black Range Rover halted in front, its front bucking down, then back up, reminding Athena of a motorboat in rough currents. Another one pulled up behind, nearly ramming the Serbians' SUV. Men jumped out and yelled at the would-be kidnappers. These men wore navy blue jackets with white letters that read FBI. More shots fired.

Athena felt a stab in her left arm, like a needle jammed in hard. A streak of fire shot up and down her arm. She lost her balance and swayed a little. The two Serbs left standing dropped their pistols, held up their arms, and clasped their hands behind their heads. The beginning of a thought formed but broke away. She felt herself pitching forwards onto the sidewalk as blackness closed in.

She drifted in and out of consciousness for a while. Felt her head cushioned on Dan's blue-jeanned lap. Saw a fragment of Max's angry face. Then was lifted up on a . . . bed? Gurney . . . siren going, reminding her of the police klaxons in Europe, two-toned squeal . . . moving fast . . . ambulance rocking a little . . . a surge of nausea made her moan aloud, then a prick on her right arm . . . blackness closing in again.

When she awoke hours later—many hours later—all she heard was buzzing. Voices from far away filtered in. Thank god! She wasn't dead. Relieved, she ventured to open her eyes even as both leaked tears of joy. Everything was in shades of white around her. The trappings of a hospital room registered in her mind. There was another person—no, several in the room. Her mother's voice, then her father's—hard-edged, stifling raw emotion. Another one, brittle and angry—Max! He'd stopped the kidnapping, captured the Serbian thugs—she wanted to shout *hurrah!* She thought of Dan . . . her new friend and fellow artist. Was he okay? *Oh god, if anything happened to him – it'd be my fault!*

Her voice failed her. Her left arm hurt like the dickens, but she couldn't move it, couldn't move any part of her body, didn't really want to . . . her head was pounding . . . she cried out . . . voices came closer and surrounded her. Then a warmth flowed through her veins, engulfing her completely, and she was out again.

The next day, she discovered her arm in a cast from her left shoulder and curving down at the elbow to encompass her forearm. Her wrist and hand were free but largely immobile inside the cloth sling that crossed her chest and Velcroed behind her neck. She said another prayer of thanks—her right arm was unharmed and ready to go back to work. She couldn't miss too many days of school.

Her mother walked into the room and placed a vase of flowers on the ledge by the window. Gray light streamed in, so Athena assumed she'd been in the hospital for less than twenty-four hours.

"Mum." That one word summed up all of her emotions.

Anna Butler came over to her bed and kissed her forehead, then in Italian fashion both of her cheeks. She took a seat on Athena's bed.

"How do you feel, *figlia mia*?"

"Fine," she said drowsily. Looking at the various lines trailing from her right arm up to the bedside dolly-contraption made her weary, but she strove to summon the energy to ask her questions. She needed to know. "The arm aches like, uh, like the devil but at least it's not my right arm. I'd lose months of school work . . ." She sighed deeply. "Mum, tell me what happened after I conked out. Was Dan hurt?"

"Dan?"

"The guy I was with. He's a pastiche painter. We met at the gallery. He came outside with me even though I told him not to. He was being a gentleman, a guy . . ."

"As far as I know, he wasn't hurt. Max said—by the way, he'll be coming later today for your statement. Your version of what happened. He needs it for his report. Your father is very upset with Max and his security team, but the Ambassador was happy. Still, your father would never have approved of this operation, this luring those Serbian thugs into the open. In theory, it sounded good and it appeared he took every precaution. But anything could go wrong. And it did. However, it could have been worse. You and that young man could have been killed." She broke off, her voice catching as she, too, suppressed her emotions.

Athena realized she'd held her breath for over a minute. She exhaled and continued to breathe deeply until her heart rate settled. A spurt of genuine pleasure darted through her. There was something about Dan that she liked very much. Much like the instant attraction she'd felt with Kas Skoros.

In addition to the growing sense that both men were going to change her life in some way.

"Thank god! For Dan, I mean. Did you see him or speak to him?"

Anna shrugged with one shoulder, not so elegant, she'd said once, but it was the Italian way. It seemed to Athena that anything her mother did differently from the English or the Americans was *the Italian way*. The pride in her heritage always seeped through.

"See him, no. We got a call to come to the hospital. That young man wasn't here, but he did call us this morning."

"I'm so glad he wasn't hurt—I'd never forgive myself. This arm—I can't lose school time. I have a Western Civ mid-term on Friday, and my painting of Venus is due right after Christmas break. And I need to start Alex Skoros' portrait." She didn't mention her pastiche painting of Manet's *The Waitress*. "Max said no one would get hurt. Wishful thinking, huh?"

Her mother's eyes blazed her own brand of fury. "I knew you were planning something with Max and his team, but I didn't know exactly what. Don't ever do this again, 'Thena. These ops, as Max calls them, never go according to plan. Someone always gets hurt."

"I was surprised—" Athena began, "No one fired a gun at me. So how did this happen?"

"Max said one of the fired bullets ricocheted off the sidewalk. A bullet one of the thugs fired." Her mother sighed audibly and swallowed, then smiled warmly as if to erase the image in her mind of how close the bullet came to ending Athena's life. "Don't worry, the bone will heal, and there shouldn't be any nerve damage, according to the surgeon.

You'll have some physical therapy, but in time, all should be well. You can take your mid-term, dear, but everything else will have to wait."

She stood up and walked to the vase of yellow roses which she'd set on the window sill. With one hand, she spread the long stems apart.

"Which reminds me, the Skoroses sent their best wishes for a full recovery. And this bouquet of flowers. Athena, you don't worry about school. The surgeon said you could leave the hospital tomorrow or the next day and resume your schedule. Only just slow down a little. Of course, your work at Starbucks is finished for the time being. At least for two months. You are not to worry about tuition costs or anything else."

Athena's mouth fell open. She'd forgotten all about her part-time job, partly because she'd focused so much on winning the pastiche painting assignment. She wanted badly to join Martin Larsen's team of talented painters who earned a fifty percent commission. And she wanted to see Dan Grantham again. After last night's attack, would he ever want anything more to do with her?

"Athena, I called your boss, the manager of the store to let him know. I told him you'd fallen on some ice and broke your arm. Poor man, I think he's had a run of bad luck of late with his employees." She broke off when a nurse came in to adjust one of the IV lines and shoot a hypodermic of clear liquid into it. Painkiller, the nurse explained, then left abruptly.

Good thing, Athena thought, and not too soon.

"Mum, what about Christmas in London? We're still going, aren't we?"

"Of course. We wouldn't miss Christmas with the Butlers. And Nonna and Giancarlo are looking forward to seeing us, too, in Como. Our flight leaves Saturday evening. All of the

Embassy staff and their families have been ordered to fly on separate flights. As a precaution." Her mother looked sad for a moment, then suddenly brightened. "You'll be on orders, 'Thena, to take it easy, but the doctor said flying shouldn't be a problem."

The implied significance of taking separate flights weighed on Athena's mind. The Foreign Office wasn't convinced the danger was over for diplomats assigned to the U.S.

"What about Tony, or whoever he was? Did they arrest him, too?"

Her mother came over, stroked Athena's right hand, and remained silent.

"Tell me, Mum. They must've arrested him. They followed him that night after my class and discovered where he lived."

Anna locked gazes with her daughter and removed her hand. "Max said they didn't arrest him sooner for fear they'd tip off the Serbians. When a security detail and two FBI agents arrived at his apartment last night—about the same time as the ambush—they found him dead. The Serbians were evidently disappointed in him."

"They shot and killed him?" The awful truth was slowly sinking in. Did her actions that night, when she refused to go along with Tony's plans, prompt the thugs into punishing him?

Her mother's eyes wavered, then returned. "Something like that. The less you know, the better."

She was right. Athena didn't want to know the full truth. The image would sear her brain for the rest of her life. It was better not knowing what really happened to *Tony Grabowski,* but she was still sorry that they'd killed him. She would never know the kind of life he'd endured that propelled him into the criminal camp.

Athena said nothing for a while. Thankfully, Anna steered the conversation away to another topic.

"This young man, this Dan Grantham, wants to visit you. I told him to wait a few days. You need to rest now."

A bubble of pleasure rose inside her at the thought that Dan still wanted to see her. He obviously didn't blame her for what happened.

"Rest? If only my mind would let me . . . I have so much to do . . . study for my mid-term . . ." Her eyes grew heavy before she remembered the painkiller in her IV. No use fighting it.

Powerful stuff.

She flushed the toilet and washed her hands at the sink. Thankful for having some use of her left hand, she noticed how swollen her palm and fingers were. The doctor told her the swelling would go down in a couple of days. Though showering with a plastic bag covering her cast was going to be jacked, she'd manage somehow. Two days after the big operation, she'd weaned herself off most of the painkillers.

She let out a gasp. Emerging from the bathroom, she was startled to see Max standing by her bed. He held a box of Sees chocolates.

"Brought you a change from hospital food, decadence in a box." He gave her a rueful grin. "And an apology for how things went. Not bloody perfect, as we'd planned, was it?"

Embarrassed at her exposure in her open-backed gown, she backed up to the bed and climbed in as demurely as she could manage with one arm. Max, dressed in another one of his disguises—a dark suit and tie and slicked down crew-cut—helped her with the blankets. He looked like any proper attorney or insurance person.

"Thanks, Max," she said, accepting his gift.

"Your mother said you were feeling much better. I spoke to her in the hallway just now." He produced an iPad out of his attaché case and set it on his lap after sitting down. "I need to take your formal statement for my report, Athena. Especially an explanation as to the presence of the young man. We took his statement at the scene but, as you can imagine, he was fairly shaken up."

"I can imagine," she quipped, "Yes, I'll give you my statement, but only after you answer some questions of mine."

He looked surprised but closed the iPad. "Go ahead."

"I didn't see everything that happened. I was kinda busy trying not to get shot and distracted by Dan being there." She darted him a wry shrug. "Guess you can't assume anything, can you? Those thugs, Max, did you get them to talk? Did they tell you everything you needed to know?"

"I'm afraid not. The three that survived, all in FBI custody, have clammed up tighter than a witch's a—uh, well, let's say the only thing we've learned is not what we hoped to hear." He looked down, as if contemplating how much he should reveal. "As I told his Lordship, the Ambassador, and the others at the de-briefing meeting yesterday, all the Serbians would say is that there are others, another backup team is already in the country. Sheer bravado and bluster, we don't know. Needless to say, we're still on full alert."

Her stomach had dropped to her knees, and she felt the blood drain from her face. The required separate flights back to England for the holidays now made further sense.

"So this," she held up her casted arm, "was for nothing?"

When Max saw her reaction, he said, "Not entirely. The Embassy is buzzing with the news, how our security team and the FBI, with your assistance, of course, lured these terrorists into the open. Which provoked them to make a serious mistake. I have no doubt that you and your family will be receiving an invitation shortly to his Lordship's residence for an unofficial dinner. He aims to honor your and your father's roles in this whole counter-intelligence operation."

Athena nodded. Grateful for that bit of news, not the least knowing that the honor would lessen her father's fury over her role in Max's operation. Still, the Embassy was in grave danger if there was indeed a backup team in place. An idea crept into her mind.

"Max, do you think—if there is a backup team of assassins—the Serbians were put in to do a dry run, a kind of dress rehearsal? I'm thinking maybe they weren't meant to succeed all along."

Max's blue eyes narrowed as he stared at her. Her gaze didn't waver, either.

"This is exactly what our best counter-terrorist analysts are theorizing," he admitted, "What makes you draw that conclusion?"

She recalled a fleeting emotion, a sense of outrage and understanding, that had passed into her mind when one of the hooded Serbs grabbed her. The man, who'd aimed at Dan and was shot and killed a second later by one of Max's snipers, was skeptical and already suspecting they'd been set up as test-runners, sacrificed to a second team's better plan.

"Just the way things turned out. When we get back after the holidays, Max, I'd like to help."

He shook his head and stood up. "Absolutely not, you and your family have done enough. More than enough. Your parents forbid it and so do I. We'll do our job, and this time, the Americans will be involved every step of the way. They've got eyes in the sky and ears in the wind—"

"Yes, I know," she said abruptly, "they've got the NSA." She took a deep breath. "What if there's an insider in the Embassy? Can't you get the FBI to subpoena phone records?" She recalled something Detective Ochoa had taught her during their last drive from the police precinct. "I think American cops call them LUDs. Local Usage Details. Telephone companies keep tabs of all calls made in or out. If someone in the Embassy has made unusual calls, can't you zero in on them? Keep them under surveillance? That person would have to make contact with someone on the terrorist team, wouldn't they?"

He studied her face a moment longer, then opened up his iPad. "I think you've been watching too many cop dramas on TV. The LUDs don't work on burner cell phones. Now let's get down to brass tacks, Athena. I need your statement."

She exhaled her breath. *Oh well, it was worth a try.* She absently tapped a finger against her hard cast, reminding her how far she'd come and how much she'd given up in this case.

"Okay, but let me just say, I know I can help. When we get back from England, let me help."

"How?"

Her secret. She'd promised her father.

"I can't exactly tell you—"

Max rudely tapped his wristwatch. "Haven't got time for this. Now tell me in sequential order what happened that night, beginning from the moment I dropped you off at the gallery. Go slow. I'm not the world's fastest typist."

With a show of impatience, she huffed her assent and recounted every detail she could recollect from that eventful evening.

Meanwhile, her mind churned. Max would see. She wasn't giving up on exposing those terrorists and their plot. If there was a way to help, she'd find it. And keep her secret in the bargain.

CHAPTER TWENTY

Athena's mother found her in the attic, painting by the dormer window. It was the day after Christmas, and the house was quiet. Trevor had taken Chris to a soccer match in north London, and they had enough leftovers of ham and roast beef to last a week. Trevor's older brother, Terence, was a solicitor and a confirmed bachelor who, while they were roaming the world on Foreign Office postings, lived in the London townhouse and maintained the place. *The place* being a three-story, four bedroom and three bath Edwardian, with a full attic and basement. While they were away, Terence had a woman come in for a few hours each day to cook his dinner and do general housecleaning. Fortunately, the woman had the week off, for Anna didn't like to share household duties with any other woman, not while she was in residence. She had her own fixed way and preferred to be the woman of the house while home in London.

"Take tea with me, Athena. I have some things to share with you."

Her daughter, still in her bathrobe and nightgown, devoid of makeup and her hair disheveled, glanced up and groaned. Athena, the artist, apparently didn't want to be disturbed.

"Mum, I'm in the middle of—"

"'Thena, we need to talk, and with your father out of the house, this is a good time. Let's take some air and walk to the village for tea. Remember the scones at Dorkers?"

Famous all over London for its variety of scones, all made

with fresh fruit, Dorkers had long been their favorite place for mother-daughter tea. The village was actually the urban town center of Kensington, a quarter-mile away south of Portobello Road, a quaint street from which their own street, Lime Court, veered. Their once artsy-craftsy neighborhood had become in their years of globetrotting one of the most gentrified, upscale areas in metropolitan London. Trevor said he couldn't afford to buy the townhouse now, thanks to the inflation of real estate in London.

Athena paused, her brush suspended in air.

"Dorkers? Haven't been there since last summer." Her attention turned back to her painting, the beginning of Alex Skoros' portrait. "I just had the urge, the feeling that I needed to get this portrait done. ASAP, you know?"

Anna focused on a spot on the wall, remembering all too well her cousin Lorena's precognitive dream. Alex would be killed in a car crash while driving in a car with Kas, his younger brother. She'd first had this dream a year ago, and since then had strongly advised—no, nagged incessantly—the two brothers to never be in a car by themselves with Alex at the wheel.

If Athena was sensing impending tragedy, then Anna's own dream—occurring last night—was validated. In the dream, she saw Alex in an open casket, the men of the Skoros family and their Greek-American friends all wearing black armbands. Despite all of Lorena's warnings to her sons, Alex's fate awaited him. Poor soul.

She focused again on her daughter, hesitating over her canvas.

"'Thena, get dressed. We'll walk and talk. I have several important tidbits of information to share with you."

Finally Athena sighed heavily and began wrapping her brushes in foil, keeping them damp and ready for her return.

"I've been going at it since six this morning. I'm so blearyeyed. God, where has the day gone? I've had no problem with his body. It's his face, his expression I can't seem to . . . Oh well, time for a break."

Forty minutes later, Athena was walking beside her, wearing her usual jeans, sweater, one side of her parka on, the left side slung over her shoulder like a cape, her left hand holding it in place. Athena looked like a young teenager instead of a twenty-year-old. A white knit cap holding her blond hair in place as it streamed down her back, reminded Anna of the white-haired four-year-old that her daughter used to be. Athena marched up Portobello Road, now eager to sample Dorkers' latest creations. Anna had to clutch at her sleeve to get her to slow down a little—her legs were so long, her stride so wide.

"Sorry, Mum. How's Father bearing up under all the strain? Is he able to relax a bit?"

"The soccer's a good distraction for him. Good for Chris, too, to spend a day with his father and uncle."

"Yeah, male bonding and all that."

"We've been invited—all of us, in fact—to the Ministers' New Years Eve Ball, but of course we'll be in Como then. There will be a number of social events when the Prime Minister arrives in Washington, including a State Dinner at the White House. Your father and I have been invited to that as well."

Athena looked impressed. "Wow, a dinner at the White House. How did Father pull that off?"

That earned a surprised smile from Anna. "You had a lot to do with that, *figlia mia.* Sir Peter Willcott is including us in the British delegation, his way of rewarding us for having such a brave daughter." She gave her a quick, loose hug, ever mindful of Athena's arm cast and sling. "You're invited, too, and Chris. Isn't that quite an honor?"

Athena looked nonplussed. "But my arm'll still be in a sling! And everyone'll be in formal wear. Oh brother, of all times to have a bum arm."

"Your arm? All the more reason to remind them that the threat hasn't gone away. Your father feels that the ambassador has given the PM false reassurance that all is well, there is no more threat to his safety. There are too many other occasions, like the formal banquet at the Embassy. Your father's in charge of planning and coordinating that one." She sighed audibly. "I daresay, I'm quite worried. Lorena and I have been having terrible dreams, not only about Alex but about the PM's visit. Sir Peter thinks all is well now that those Serbian mercenaries are out of the picture. Quite the contrary."

"Maybe your dreams are just dreams of worry, anxiety. Y'know, like me dreaming I've flunked my Western Civ exam."

Anna remained silent.

Athena added, "So you think the Serbs were telling the truth? There's a second team of terrorists on standby?"

"We believe so," Anna replied solemnly. "Lorena and I, anyway. The security details, also. At least, they're not discounting the idea."

"What can we do to help, Mum?"

Anna gave her Italian shrug. "You and I are doing nothing." She brightened suddenly. "I'm certain Max and the other security officers know what they're doing. With the FBI's assistance, they'll sort it all out."

They stopped at Notting Hill Gate to let a convoy of trucks pass, then crossed over to Kensington Church Street. A couple of blocks to her left, there was Kensington Gardens—and the Palace where Princess Diana once lived. They were veering to their right, however, up Campden Hill to Kensington High Street, where Dorkers reigned supreme. At five o'clock, the pub—with the bakery next door—was filled to overflowing. They were lucky to find a table when a family of four suddenly finished and got up to leave.

They studied the enticing menu. All sorts and types of scones were offered.

"Ooo, here's a new one," cooed Athena, "Apricot and walnut. Doesn't that sound yummy? I'll take two and skip dinner."

"The fig and pistachio sounds good to me," said Anna. When the server departed, she took a card out of her purse, holding it up for Athena to see the expensive cardstock and ornately scrolled calligraphic printing. "We just received this. An announcement of Alex Skoros' upcoming wedding to Nikki Theopoulis."

She handed it to Athena and watched her jaw drop. Was it what she feared, that her daughter actually had a crush on Alex? Curious, she seized her right forearm.

Athena shook it off gently, smiling wryly. "Just ask, Mum. No tricks. And no, I'm not hurt—shocked, yes, that it's happening so soon. Alex is such a playboy. Kas doesn't like her, says she's a GAP, a Greek-American Princess. Wonder what hold she has over free-as-a-bird Alex. When's the wedding?"

Anna withdrew her hand and gave Athena a half-apologetic smile. "In two months. It does seem sudden, doesn't it? He never spoke of her while we were there. Lorena said he was dating a variety of girls, that was all."

Athena said softly, almost wistfully, "Kas told me when we were there. Guess Alex was keeping it a secret, but now it's out. I imagine Kas might be looking to settle down now that his brother's tying the knot. Or maybe not. Kas seems to march to his own drummer. One of the qualities I suppose I like about him."

Anna said nothing, and they both occupied themselves

with their tea and scones. They sampled a bit of each other's and exchanged opinions. Finally Anna smiled, changing to a cheerier topic. "Have you heard from that young man, Dan? The painter?"

"Yes, he's called a few times." Athena shot her a quelling look.

End of story.

Obviously wanting to change the topic, Athena frowned. "Have you heard from Detective Palomino?" The pub's noise level had increased to near shouting volume, so she had to lean towards Anna to be heard.

"Ah, yes, an update on the serial killer—rather, the alleged serial killer," Anna began, sighing, then launched into it. They'd located a container ship with an American registry, the Baltimore Bullworth, that had left the U.S. over three weeks ago, stopped over in several West African ports-of-call, and then continued on its way to Abu Dhabi with half a shipload of small electronic and automobile parts. On its return trip via the Indian Ocean, it was taking on Indian computer parts and textiles at various Indian ports and making a stop in Vietnam for furniture and in Japan for cars and motorcycles.

"According to the detective, if he doesn't jump ship at one of these ports," Anna explained, "this Person of Interest will eventually return to his home port of Baltimore and will be taken into custody. All they can do is question him and try to extract a confession or at least some information that might aid the Assistant District Attorney's office in indicting him for murder. Palomino said he wasn't going to hold his breath, waiting for either one. They've searched the brothers' place of business, that electricians' shop. Nothing's there that could help them."

Athena shook her head. "He's too smart to leave any evidence behind. They should question his shipmates. Oh, and contact the local police at those ports-of-call, see if any girls show up dead. Wouldn't that be too coincidental?"

Her daughter's tone of voice sounded so cynical and pessimistic. Not for the first time, Anna wondered if by exposing her daughter to such human ugliness, she'd succeeded only in making her lose faith in the basic goodness of mankind. *Still, the veil has to come off for everyone at some point in their lives. Doesn't it?*

Was this cynicism an unintended consequence of their God-given gift? Anna looked away.

Or did God mean for some reason that we should be on the alert for the evil among us? So that we can do some good to offset the bad?

Athena was now smiling at someone behind Anna, causing her to turn around in her chair. Max and Trevor's secretary, Winston Blake, had just walked into the pub, their gazes landing immediately on the two women. The two men, about the same age, approached, Max in the lead.

"Fancy meeting up with you two lovely ladies," greeted Max, this time casually dressed like Athena in jeans, leather jacket and boots. "I was just taking Win for a spin on my new Harley, or Hog, as the Americans call it. Athena, you've met your father's new secretary, haven't you? No? Mrs. Butler, you have, I believe." With Anna's brisk nod, he introduced Winston Blake to Athena. They shook hands, his grasp lingering long past propriety, until Max raised his eyebrows. Anna considered him nice enough, but too handsome and vain for his own good. However, Trevor liked him and found him to be a very capable right-hand man.

"Don't be such a sod, Win. She's too young for you, ol' boy." Max laughed and addressed the two women, "Win was with our Embassy in Tripoli, and before that, Riyadh. He's one of my Cambridge mates, so too old for you, Athena. Keep that in mind, Win. My job's protecting her and the rest of the Butlers until this nasty business blows over. And that means protecting her from blokes like you."

Both men laughed. To cover Athena's apparent flustered expression and blank confusion, Anna asked them what brought them to Kensington.

"We stopped to visit some schoolmates of ours who live in South Kensington near Warwick Gardens," Max responded. "Of course, who hasn't heard of Dorkers? We said we'd pick up some scones on our way to meeting them later in Piccadilly. Did you have a good Christmas?"

They said they did and chatted on for a few more minutes before Max and Win left.

As soon as they were out of earshot, Anna turned to Athena. Her face looked as pale as the scone on her plate. "What's the matter, 'Thena?"

Athena looked down at her hand, holding a spoon and stirring an empty cup of tea. "I don't know, maybe nothing, Mum," she murmured breathlessly.

"Listen to your instincts, *figla mia*. What did you see?"

Athena's deep green eyes rose to meet her mother's. They held for several seconds before she spoke.

"Maybe I should talk to Max tomorrow. He'll laugh in my face and think I'm totally blinkered but . . . remember what he said, the danger of an insider, someone inside the Embassy who knows what all the plans are for the PM's visit?" She glanced over at the pub's side door, through which the two men had just exited to enter the bakery. "Well, I think I may've found him."

Anna sat back, stunned.

CHAPTER TWENTY-ONE

Ignoring her mother's warning not to reveal her suspicions to anyone before speaking with her father, Athena used her cell phone to contact Max late that night. Placating her, she felt, Max agreed to meet her for coffee very early the next morning. Before anyone in their household—her parents, Uncle Terence Butler, and Chris—woke up, she was trudging up Portobello Road, her parka clasped around her. The air was chilly and the sky a leaden gray. Dark clouds presaged rain. The air was so moist, she could almost lick the condensation.

A little needle of guilt pricked her. Maybe she should have listened to her mother and described what she saw to her father to get his opinion first, but she had chosen to listen to her own instincts. And they told her to act—now!

In Kensington village, a new Starbucks store had arrived in their absence, and it had become a popular social mecca for locals and tourists alike. At seven that morning, however, only commuters were there. An angry Max fumed in one corner, his back to the wall, watching everyone who entered and left. He'd bought her a latte, so she took her seat quickly. Without preamble, he launched into his tirade.

"Miss Butler, the only reason I came is out of respect for your father. But he doesn't know you're here, does he? Whatever you suspect about Winston Blake, just remember he's a mate of mine and we go way back. I've never seen anything in his behavior or job folder that would make me even consider the possibility that he'd be a traitor to queen and country. So you'd better be sodding well confident that your information is correct." His cheeks flushed and his breathing heavy, Max looked ready to grab and shake her silly.

Athena took stock of herself and decided to proceed slowly and cautiously. "Max, or whatever your real name is, I'm going to tell you something about myself, something you will most assuredly find difficult to believe."

"It better knock my socks off," he said, then sipped his coffee, his dark blue eyes trained on her, looking for any sign that she'd completely gone mad, she knew. Or worse, that she was conniving and dishonest.

"When I was nine years old, I became clairvoyant," she began tenuously. "My mother has this skill, and her mother, also. It runs in the family, Max. We're the modern-day descendants of a long bloodline that we believe goes as far back as ancient Greece. Perhaps even further back, we don't know. When we touch people or things that they've touched, we can *see* things. Read their minds, see into their lives, their emotions, their memories, things that are important to them in some way."

"Bollocks!" He sat back, his lids lowering to half-mast. A humorless smile curled up half his mouth. "I knew there was something strange about you. You're fucking delusional."

Athena shuddered a little, feeling the sting of rejection. This was exactly why her mother tried to protect her by keeping their skills a secret. But when lives were at stake, wasn't it worth the risk of being hurt? She drank some coffee before an idea struck her.

"Okay, not surprising, your reaction. Give me your hand, Max. Think of something that happened to you that no one else on this earth knows about. Please, indulge me. Then if you don't believe me, I'll apologize for taking up your valuable holiday time."

"This is fucking lunacy . . ." Max rolled his eyes and very slowly placed his left hand on the table, his right hand, she noticed, burrowed in his jacket pocket, always gun-ready, always on the alert for danger.

She leaned forwards and grasped his left hand and held it firmly, waiting for the images and emotions to transfer into her consciousness. Not fully prepared for the anger that flooded her, she suppressed her sudden fear and calmed herself down. Certainly, he wouldn't shoot her, would he? She inhaled slowly, exhaled slowly.

Wait for it . . . wait for it . . .

What she saw and felt made her smile on the surface but cringe underneath. What little boys do to protect their mothers . . . was that what propelled Max onto a career in law enforcement? He had a deep need to protect people he cared about, and by extension queen, country and their representatives.

She let go of his hand and watched him smirk. "Astound me with your cheap little parlor tricks, ol' girl."

She took a deep breath and exhaled, calmed herself down. If he didn't believe her, then what?

"Okay, here's what I saw. You were about five or six, I think, sometime after your parents divorced and you were missing your father. Your mother was dating a man who had a dog and a car. A Range Rover. This man seemed to care more about this car than your mother. He was a bully, and your mother let him dominate her. He wouldn't let you ride in his Range Rover unless you sat on a towel. He called you Poop Face. One day you got a rag, dipped it into the toilet and then smeared your . . . uh, poop, uh, feces all over the cargo floor of his Rover. You threw away the rag and then pretended his dog did it. He knew it was you and he never came back. You never told your mother what you did. Your mother was sad, but only for a short time, because she met your stepfather after that, and you two got along fine. All in all, a fairly ingenious way to drive off your mother's wanker of a suitor."

She lifted her gaze to Max's. His jaw had dropped. "How the fuck—"

Shrugging, she drank the rest of her coffee.

Max kept murmuring, "How the fuck—"

Finally, she set her cup down. "Max, I couldn't tell you how this works any more than a child prodigy like Mozart or Michelangelo could explain how their gifts worked. It just does. My mother has a theory—unproven, of course—that it's a gift from God. That God allows us to tap into something like a river of universal human consciousness. An entire history of human experience that goes back into time, since the dawn of mankind. She calls it The Flow. I don't know about that. I can read a dog's conscious mind, also, so maybe it's just an extraordinary mental skill that many people and maybe many animals have, but in varying degrees. Like any skill set, y'know?"

His eyes remained wide and uncomprehending. "Blimey, you'd make the perfect spy. If this is real and not some elaborate trick, girl, you should join MI-6."

Max appeared to calm himself down as he ran his hand over his face, scrubbing the stubble on his cheeks and jaw. "All right, Athena, tell me what you saw when you shook Winston's hand yesterday."

Two minutes later, she finished but added, "I saw the gym locker number, the combination on his lock, but the note that was left inside his locker, I couldn't see. It could be something personal, but I don't think so. I think it has to do with this plot to harm the Prime Minister when he goes to the United States."

He took a small notebook and pen out of his jacket's breast pocket. "Run it by me again, Athena, but this time slow it down."

She did, pausing to replay in her mind slow-motion what had flashed into her brain in a couple of seconds. "The locker number is forty-seven, on the right-hand side as you face a large wall mirror. If you go to the end of the locker row and turn right, that's the men's bathroom. To the left are the showers. A hand put the note through one of the three slats at the top of the locker, then the man glanced at himself in the mirror, making sure all the locker rows were empty and no one saw him. It was in Winston Blake's mind, I think, because he was imagining this man doing this. He knows this man and this is their—what do you call it?"

"Dead drop," supplied Max.

"Yes. I think Mr. Blake has been checking his gym locker every day since coming home to London. He's waiting for something important."

"I know his gym. He told me yesterday he goes there whenever he's back in country." Max stood up abruptly. "C'mon, Athena, I want you to come with me." He thrust the pen and notebook into her right hand. "On the way, you can sketch the man's face. If you can."

Surprised, she sputtered, "O-okay," and followed him outside where he flagged down a taxi. In the back, she began the outline of a man's face, filled in the head hair, receding hairline, the man's mustache and beard but was stymied by the eyes and nose details. When she looked up, the surrounding neighborhood startled her.

"You didn't see this?" Max asked her.

"No, I was just inside the gym." She was nervous all of a sudden, for the taxi was cruising down the main thoroughfare of a Middle Eastern neighborhood, an area called a "No-Go Zone" by local Brits, also known as a Sharia-controlled zone. Her father had told her that there were now over ninety local Sharia courts in Great Britain, where Islamic Sharia laws were acknowledged and held almost as much legal weight as British national laws.

Max told the driver to stop in front of a gym that catered only to men, and from the look of it, mostly Middle Eastern men. He prodded her to the sidewalk.

"I'm going inside to check out Win's locker. If this combination number checks out, I'll take a quick look inside. Meanwhile, I want you to look over any security tapes they might have. If you see the man in your sketch, let me know."

"But Max, I'm not authorized—"

"You're with me, so you're authorized." He looked at her hair, tucked inside the collar of her parka, and unfurled the black scarf he wore around his neck. He wrapped it around her head and tied it under her chin. "So we don't cause a riot. This is Little Kandahar."

The gym was small, consisting of two rooms filled with machines. In one corner, a roped off ring for kickboxing and other close quarters combat dominated. In the rear, a door led to the men's locker room, bathroom and showers. To their immediate left was the manager's office.

Max showed his gold badge to an older, gray-haired, swarthy-complexioned man who sat behind a desk, his focus glued to a computer screen. To the man's side, another monitor sat, its screen divided into quarters, indicating four separate security cameras on the premises. There were no cameras in the locker room or bathroom—for privacy's sake, Athena surmised. When Max requested that the man show Athena, his *partner*, the security tapes for the past twenty-four hours, the man scowled but reluctantly complied. The man, Mohammed something-or-other, turned off his computer and allowed her to sit at his desk while he rewound the security tape back to the day before, and then played it forward. He showed her how she could fast-forward it as needed. As she began to concentrate on her task, the manager closed the door behind him as he accompanied Max to the locker room. She heard him bark at someone, a young bearded man who then entered the office and stood by the door, occasionally sliding angry looks at her.

Obviously, these men did not approve of women invading their turf, no matter how official they appeared. The sooner they accomplished their mission, the better. Minutes passed . . . five . . . ten. The manager's watchdog kept glaring at her, trying to intimidate her, not that his hostile stance didn't make her a little nervous. It did, but she persisted in focusing on her task as well as she could.

She fast-forwarded the tape at several points, slowed down at others. At the tape's time imprint of six o'clock pm, a young man with a mustache and beard entered the gym. She punched the stop button. He looked like the man she saw, the man in Winston Blake's mind. With her cell phone, she took a photo of the screen on pause, added to her sketch and afterwards pressed fast-forward.

Just then, Max re-entered the office with the gray-haired manager in tow. The man looked livid, the outrage clearly erupting from his expression. Although Max reminded the manager that their visit should remain confidential, even Athena knew that was an impossible-to-enforce request. Still, she breathed a sigh of relief that they could leave this very inhospitable place.

Back in their waiting taxi, they exchanged information. Athena showed him her completed sketch and the photo she took. The photo's resolution was poor, but her sketch was as accurate as she could manage.

"I'll have tech run it through our database." Which database it was, he clearly wasn't about to share with her. Her father had mentioned a terrorist watch list, a No-Fly list, and several more, but she hadn't been paying much attention at the time.

"What did you find?" she asked, letting out another deep breath as they left the No-Go Zone. It was then that she realized how tense she'd been when the cab turned down a street onto Euston Road, heading west towards Marylebone Road.

"Your description of the locker room was spot on. I found Win's locker, the combination you saw unlocked it, and here's what I found inside. I took a photo and left it there, of course. Good thing we came early, before Win showed up for his daily workout."

The photo on his smartphone showed a note, black calligraphy and hand-written block letters and numbers on white paper. She couldn't decipher the Arabic, of course, but the letters and numbers were discernible. CNB, followed by ten numbers. Underneath were three sets of numbers beginning with the District of Columbia's area code.

"What does it mean?" she wondered aloud, giving Max his notebook.

"You don't know?" He stared at her for a moment.

"I don't always know how to interpret what I see," she said in explanation. He nodded, seeming to understand.

"The Arabic, I've no clue," he said, "I'll get it translated. The rest, my best guess, Cayman National Bank, a private account number, a contact phone number in D.C. This may be harmless, and I hope to god it is. Win's got some family money, so I don't see him betraying his country for more."

To Athena's mind, Max didn't sound that certain. Yet his first reaction was to suspend judgment in defense of his old schoolmate.

In counterpoint to his words, Max's glum facial expression told it all. She said, "You really don't think so, do you, Max?" He shook his head, a haunted look darkening his deep-set eyes.

The taxi pulled to a stop in front of the Starbucks store in

Kensington. There, parked along the street, stood his motorcycle. Max paid the driver and they slid out. As rain began to steadily fall, they stood huddled together. Despite the nerve-racking experience, she was glad she'd taken the plunge and revealed to Max the truth.

"For the time being, Athena, let's keep this information to ourselves," he told her, "I've got to check out some things first. Don't even tell your father. I don't want to cast aspersions on a pal without more evidence to support it."

She smiled. "Okay. Promise me you'll keep my secret . . . a secret. Father doesn't want anyone in the Foreign Office to know about me. Or about Mum, either."

Max made a sound between a snort and a laugh. "Guess he's afraid MI-Six'll try to recruit you both. Can't blame him. It's dangerous work. When you agreed to come along with me today, I knew you weren't just fucking around. Athena, you've got my word. Your secret's safe with me." He took back his scarf and wrapped it around his neck.

Tucking her head under her parka hood, she watched him mount and ride off. Then she turned and walked down Portobello Road.

Max held his emotions close to his vest, she knew—it was probably part of his job description. She marveled how impassive he'd kept his countenance throughout the whole incident. But she knew what they'd uncovered—ugly truth or harmless note—had truly shaken him.

She wondered what he'd do next.

CHAPTER TWENTY-TWO

Two hours later, as Athena was applying the last mauve tinted shadows to Alex Skoros' face and neck, her mother knocked and then abruptly entered her third story bedroom. Athena was standing by her dormer window, where there was at least some natural light, although it was weak, meanwhile alternating between wishing that she could do *plein air* studies in sunny California to thoughts of Kas Skoros in his bare chest and animal-print briefs.

Her mother came over to have a look at the portrait. "I thought I heard you come back in. Ohh, *va bene. Che bello, figlia mia*!"

"Thanks, Mum," said Athena, pausing and stepping back. "Do you like his pose?" She'd painted Alex standing in front of the family's carved wood mantelpiece, his left arm slung lazily back and resting on the wood as if he were in the middle of regaling his family with a funny story. Alex, the born *raconteur*. Lorena and her family, she felt, would love this interpretation of their most charming male member. "I'm pleased with it. It's turning out well, probably my best portrait so far. Using one hand is making it a little slow going, but it's coming along. What do you think, Mum?"

"Yes, by far, your best. You've captured Alex's winning personality," agreed her mother. Her gaze turned back to the bedroom door. "Where did you go so early this morning?"

Athena lowered her voice in case her father was nearby. "I met with Max and told him what I saw in Winston Blake's mind. Don't tell Father, please. Max wants to do some digging before anyone jumps to the wrong conclusions, and we don't want to jam up Father's relationship with his new secretary, do we?"

Anna agreed with a curt nod and a frown.

"Listen, our plans for visiting Nonna in Como have changed somewhat. Your Uncle Terence is ill, we think the flu, and your father wants to stay and watch over him. But I told him he needs a real vacation. Italy would do him a world of good. He hasn't seen Nonna and Giancarlo in over a year, and so I insisted that he come with Chris and me. They need you to stay, also, to help with meals and cleaning." She stopped as Athena opened her mouth to protest. "I know you'll miss seeing Nonna and Zio Giancarlo, but that can't be helped. I need to see my mother, and Chris missed out on the last visit because of a soccer tournament, so he'll be coming with us. We're flying to Milano this afternoon."

With a show of extreme disappointment mixed with resignation, Athena nodded, then shrugged gallantly. "Oh well, it'll give me a chance to finish this and mail it off."

It appeared her mother was about to say something, but she stopped and nodded instead.

"You know how to make a stew, a pot roast, bangers and mash. The deli has pasties, too, and your uncle's favorite herring salads. I know he likes the herring in mustard and dill sauce, so buy some of that, Athena. I think Uncle Terence would love some comfort food. He can barely hold down chicken broth for now, but he will bounce back. Mrs. Hughes will come over if you need an extra hand—"

Athena made a dismissive gesture. "No need. I can handle domestic duties, Mum. I'm not a child." Another thought occurred to her. Mikela's New Year's Eve party back in D.C. She wondered, also, what Kas would be doing for New Year's.

Her mother stretched on her tiptoes and kissed Athena's

cheek. "I know you're not, *figlia mia,* but you have only one working arm. If all goes well, we'll be back in one week and then on to America." She stopped at the doorway on her way out. "It's important that you finish Alex's portrait."

A lump rose in Athena's throat. She knew what her mother was trying to tell her. Yet, such a horrible premonition—if that was indeed what it was and nothing more—was better left unspoken. She looked around and rapped her knuckles on the wooden window sill.

"Yes, I know."

Lovely aromas wafted from the open crockpot, pleasing Athena and apparently her uncle, who sat at the dining alcove in the kitchen. Uncle Terence, her father's senior by six years—sixty years old to her father's fifty-four—huddled in his bathrobe across the table, a well-used handkerchief held to his mouth. Poor man, he looked like death warmed over, but he'd braved the worst of his flu and now was starved for real food.

"Ahh, smells divine."

"Serve it up, my darling girl."

Pleased that one of her two favorite uncles anticipated her beef stew, she ladled out several scoops per bowl and took them to the table. A basket of sliced French bread already awaited the sopping up of the thick brown gravy she'd added to the stew. Just the way her uncle liked it. She was just about to serve her own bowl when her cell phone buzzed. The screen warned her to keep it private.

"Sorry, a call from D.C. Go ahead, Uncle. Don't wait for me." She answered it as she walked into the living room across the central hallway. It was Detective Ochoa.

"Hope I'm not interrupting," he said, "It's noon here, my lunch break."

Athena's heart pounded. Had they caught the serial killer? Did she and her mother's clairvoyance really help to catch this man?

"No, not a problem, Detective."

"Palomino wanted me to give you an update, for courtesy's sake. Is your mother there?" She told him no, but she'd be in touch with her that night. "Okay, that's fine. What we've learned from the skipper of the Baltimore Bullworth is this: Our Person of Interest, whose real identity I still can't reveal to you—sorry. When the skipper learned of our subpoena to detain his crew member and search his stateroom, he told the man. Who, the skipper then reported back two days later, jumped ship in Johannisburg and is now in the wind. So our only recourse was to put out a BOLO with Interpol and the South African state police. This guy's too smart to pull this kind of disappearing act, which screams *guilty*. We're completely baffled, didn't expect this. If you and your mother have any dreams, visions, whatever about this jerk, let us know, okay?"

Her hopes for a resolution to this case plummeted. "All right, Detective, will do. I'll call you if and when we get anything."

When she joined her uncle at the table, he noticed her look.

"Oh? Bad news, Athena?" Terence Butler asked, his spoon pausing mid-air.

She remembered her father's disapproval of her and her mother getting involved with police cases, and so she just shrugged. If Uncle Terence knew, then within hours her father would know. "Just a friend at the Institute. Her boyfriend broke up with her and she's upset."

Lying was not her forte, but apparently, she sounded convincing.

"Well, too bad, that is, but everyone gets his or her heart

broken at least once in a lifetime. Isn't that true?"

Uncle Terence, a retired solicitor and widower, wiped his sweaty brow and scooped up another helping of stew. "If I recall correctly, your father had his broken several times before he met Anna. He seemed to fall in love every month or so."

That tidbit made Athena smile. "So Father was a softie at heart . . ."

Terence tore a thick slice of bread in two. "Chris recently informed me of his string of disappointments with the opposite sex. He, unfortunately I might add, has taken after his old dad. Shameless romantics. Crocodile hides but marshmallow hearts."

Athena smiled. "I like that. Marshmallow hearts and crocodile hides. I know someone else like that. A friend in California."

"More's the pity," chimed in Uncle Terence. "You and Anna, the frail females of the Butler family, are proving to be anything but. Wouldn't you agree, Athena? Our women—you and your mother—are as tough as nails. Your hearts are not so easily broken, are they?"

Her uncle's piercing blue eyes—a trait of the Butlers—connected with Athena's. Her thoughts ran to Tony, her former co-worker, and how he'd tricked his way into their condo and probably a little into Athena's heart. Maybe she wasn't as tough as Uncle Terence thought. Immediately, her chest twisted and she thought of Kas Skoros. How could their brief meeting and fleeting sexual fling have affected her so much? She had a crush on him, that was true, but nothing more. Surely! And that nonsense of cousin Lorena's, about their future together, was just that, nonsense. Bollocks, as Max would say. Outright bollocks.

"I've gotten tougher with each year, Uncle Terence. And I imagine by the time I'm thirty, I'll be an iron maiden."

Her reference to the medieval torture chamber, obliquely implying how she'll be treating the opposite sex, apparently finally sank in.

Her uncle burst out laughing. "Iron maiden, indeed. Well done, Athena, a *double entendre*. However, I don't believe it for a minute. You just haven't met the man who deserves you. The man you're meant to be with."

She smiled, then dove into her stew. Her uncle was such a fan of hers. Would he continue to be if he and her father knew all of the lies she'd told them, all of the secrets she'd withheld from them? Her latest escapade with Max?

Her mind turned on a quid note. Mikela had texted her while she was preparing the stew. Her friend's New Year's Eve party sounded like so much fun. She could text Kas and ask what he was planning to do New Year's Eve. If he couldn't go with her—after all, why should he fly all the way across the North American continent just to go to a party with her? If he couldn't go, why not ask Dan?

Wait a minute—she was stuck in London, nursing Uncle Terence back to health. She looked up at his thinning pate of gray hair. "Uncle, if you're well enough, will you be going out for New Year's Eve?"

He smiled as he dabbed another piece of bread in the stew's gravy. "My club is having a men's night of gaming. Free drinks if one buys into a poker tournament. Why? Is there something you're yearning to do? A pretty young woman like you, surely you have a date. Oh, but your date's in Washington, is it not?"

"Yes, sort of."

She blew on her spoon filled with beef. Mustn't look too anxious. Did she have the money to fly back to D.C.? Of course she did, thanks to the Skoroses' generous birthday gift.

"I thought, there's a party in Washington. Maybe I could

fly back there early? If you're feeling better?"

He smacked his lips and downed the bread in one gulp. "Of course, I'm feeling better. Mrs. Hughes can fix me something before I run off to my club. Her roasts last me for days. I owe her a Christmas present, anyway. You know how women are about such things. They like to be remembered. You make your plans, Athena. You're young only once, dear. Just make certain your parents know you'll be flying back early."

She jumped up, went over and hugged him. He waved her off, typical English prudence winning out over sentimentality.

"Don't, my dear. Wouldn't want you ill next."

She hugged him anyway.

CHAPTER TWENTY-THREE

Forty-eight hours later, Athena pulled to the curb at the Reagan Airport Arrivals terminal. She turned off the ignition and stood up by the driver's door. Then she saw him. He was looking away, gazing at the queues of cars.

Her heart somersaulted as she took in his appearance. Kas Skoros cleaned up well. He was tall and suave in a sky-blue sweater, a dark gray sports coat, and gray slacks. His brown hair slicked back, he was clean-shaven, almost shiny with good looks and robust health. What happened to the rugged, whiskered mountain-man of Thanksgiving week? Today he looked like a Capitol lobbyist. With anticipation, she hoped to see all the faces of Mr. Skoros. More importantly, were they going to finish what they'd started a month ago? She certainly hoped so.

She called out his name and waved. Soon he was tossing his large carry-on bag into the back seat of Athena's sedan. Rather, the four-door Ford sedan that her father leased, mainly for her mother's sake, during their long posting in D.C.

He leaned over and gave her cheek a peck.

"This was a great idea, Athena," he said as he buckled up. "I was looking for an excuse to see you." He noted the cast on her left arm. Although hampered a little, her left hand held the steering wheel while her right hand worked the gears. The pain had subsided to nothing. The full-arm cast was cumbersome but tolerable.

"I heard what you did to help the FBI catch those guys.

You're a real pistol, Athena Butler."

"The Embassy's security detail planned the trap. I just went along, and things happened. Just got unlucky with a ricocheted bullet."

"Or maybe that was the luckiest day of your life."

She smiled and shrugged, wanting to change the subject. Her right hand flipped up and down before she pulled into the flow of traffic. "Your family didn't mind your leaving on the spur of the moment?"

The smile he shot her had an edge to it. "They don't rule me. Except for the work I do for Skoros Enterprises, I come and go as I please. Father's doing fine and the others are all in town, and I haven't had a vacation in over a year. Don't you think I deserve a five-day break?"

"Of course," she glanced over, "But you live with them, as I do with my parents. It's different, don't you think?"

"Athena, you probably wouldn't know this, but I live in a condo in downtown Sacramento, near our corporate office. I go home to Loomis only when the Search and Rescue Team calls me or something special comes up. Jeez, I keep forgetting how young you are, how tied you are to your mother's apron strings."

That stung a little, though what he said was true. The traffic slowed to a crawl, so Athena turned to face him. "I'm trying to cut those strings. That's why I'm here instead of London."

He grinned. "This can be just a sightseeing trip with you as my tour guide." A pause when his eyes met hers. "Or it can be something totally different. It's still up to you, sweetheart. I'm wading into dangerous waters here."

Athena had to laugh. Was Kas so afraid of her and that booze bottle he'd alluded to before? "Kas, you make me sound like a man-eating shark."

He laughed, too. "You're too young to be one . . . yet.

Look, I'm booked into the George Washington Hotel. Never been there, but I read it's a stately old remodeled hotel and a block or two from the White House, prime location, close to everything. I want to see a couple of Smithsonian museums while I'm here. The Capitol building, the Lincoln Memorial, the Mall, whatever else I can squeeze in. I want to see them with you."

By the time she turned the corner and stopped in front of the entrance of the George Washington, her mind was made up. She'd packed a bag just in case . . .

She told him, "I'm going to the parking garage two blocks away. Meet me in the lobby, okay? Give me fifteen minutes."

The look he returned made her want to laugh. She'd caught him by surprise. Kas Skoros, man of the world, underwent a series of expressions. The last one showed a fine set of straight, even teeth, making him look more boyishly handsome than usual.

"Okay, hurry."

"I will."

She wanted to jump in the air and kick up her heels.

Yeah!

Two hours later, they were lying in his queen-size hotel bed, completely naked, the perspiration cooling on both their bodies. Reveling in the way he stared at her bare breasts and shoulders, Athena left the sheet at her waist. She'd cleaned up a little and, though her genitals were throbbing a bit, she felt wonderful. Awesome. He was gentle and loving, even solicitous towards her. Every step of the way, he'd put her feelings before his galloping desire. She lay on her stomach, propped on her bent, casted left arm and cast and braced against his side. Her right hand snaked across his chest and tugged gently on his chest hair.

"Are you okay?" he asked her.

"You didn't hurt me, Kas. We can do this again, can't we?" She looked up and caught his lop-sided grin.

"As often as you want, babe. Just as soon as I get some room service and get recharged. I brought a pack full of condoms, that's how hopeful I was."

She hadn't yet begun taking the Pill, so she was relieved by his initiative.

"You traveled all night. Do you want to take a nap?"

"Oh, hell no." Kas reached for her and cautiously rolled Athena over onto her back. His dark hair tickled her as his mouth found her breast. She turned off the images that flooded her mind, seeing what he intended to do next. Pleasure swamped her ordinary senses, so much that nothing else was needed or mattered. She closed her eyes and sighed as she rode another wave of pleasure.

His bravado lasted four more hours before he finally crashed. Athena slept, too, curled against him in a safe, loving cocoon.

In addition to the leisurely walk they took around the circumference of the White House grounds one morning, they took a one-day tour of the city inside the Beltway. The remainder of Kas' five days, they were content to talk and make love. Athena forgot all about Mikela's New Year's Eve party as she dined with Kas at the hotel's rooftop restaurant that night. They made no plans for the future, preferring to live and love in the here-and-now. They ignored their cell phones and didn't answer the hotel phone in their room.

On Sunday afternoon, Athena took Kas to the airport. They held each other for a long moment, then kissed. She had no idea when she'd see him again.

Nevertheless, she refused to cry as she waved him off.

Chapter Twenty-four

Two weeks later, Athena was knee-deep in school projects, and everyone in her family had returned to their normal routine. Chris was back at the boarding school in Virginia, her father was putting in long days at the Embassy, and her mother had another translation job to finish in the study. On Friday night, Athena dedicated herself to finishing Alex's portrait.

Her mother paused at the living room's threshold to wish her goodnight.

"I want you to know, Athena, that I'm not judging you for your . . . what shall we call it?"

Good grief, she couldn't keep anything a secret from her clairvoyant mother. Now she understood the resentment of others, the *normal* people who didn't have their powers. How did her mother find out? Had she read a thought, a memory as she casually touched Athena during daily life? Probably. Had Lorena picked up something from her son? Probably. Had they put two and two together? Most likely. She, herself, hadn't breathed a word. Of course, living with her mother, such a normal thing—verbal communication—wasn't at all necessary.

Athena put her brush down and turned to face her mother. "Let's see, the Americans call it a fling. The French call it a *liaison*. You Italians call it *una relazione*. I call it an awesome five days and four nights. And I might never see him again."

Her mother frowned and picked at some lint on her sweater. "And if you have your heart broken? Lorena foresees that it's impossible . . . at least, for some time."

"Then so be it." Athena huffed and turned back to Alex's portrait. "Now, may I return to this painting?"

"You used protection?" her mother persisted.

Athena held her breath and counted to twenty, marshaling all her patience. Her mother was just being . . . a mother. She couldn't help herself. But if Athena could protect the precious moments with Kas from becoming the subject of a family rumor mill from D.C. to California, or fodder for Chris' mockery, then she would. With all the power she possessed.

"Protection? What's that? I've never heard of such a thing—"

Evidently, her mother didn't appreciate the sarcasm. "Buona notte." Then she was gone.

Relieved, Athena took up her brush. She had to get Alex's smile just right. She didn't know what, but something compelled her to finish the portrait that night. She wouldn't go to bed until she was satisfied with his smile.

Hours later, she dragged herself to bed after applying the finishing touches on Alex's face. When the oils were fully dried, she'd spray the canvas with a varnish fixative before Fed-Ex-ing it to Kas in California. It was early Saturday morning, two o'clock. Her eyes closed almost before her head hit the pillow. She slept soundly for an hour or two. Then the dream began.

This had never happened before. She found herself in Kas Skoros' mind without having to touch him. How could this be? No matter, for she wanted to be there.

He was at his favorite watering hole in the old gold mining town of Placerville, up in the Sierra Nevada foothills. Alex was hosting an engagement party and all the guys were downing beer, bumping elbows and knuckles, full of themselves and jokes about marriage. The ol' ball and chain. A prisoner of love chose his own cell with the words, I do – the most hated words in the English language. Falling in love was a kind of insanity, and marriage was the cure. On and on they went, rubbing it in while Alex laughed and good-naturedly took it all. Irony reigned, for the only one to remain silent was Kas, the only single man among this crazy bunch.

Single and free but even he was sick and tired of casual sex. Meaningless physical couplings, lacking in emotions other than a mild fondness or a lusty attraction. No woman he'd ever want to wake up and have breakfast with, anyway. Except for Athena Butler.

While the men joked and laughed, Kas thought of his time with Athena in Washington. His mind was recalling every moment, every day, every night, from the time he'd arrived to the Sunday afternoon when he kissed her goodbye. Playing it over in his head like a video loop, meanwhile feeling the pleasure, the thrill of discovery – she constantly surprised and challenged him. Discomfiting moments when doubts beleaguered him, when he felt she was too good for him, too young, too inexperienced.

Time droned on and he was downing his, what, fifth or sixth bottle of beer. He got up and wove his way to the men's room, barely got to the urinal in time. Zipped down, relieved himself, zipped up. Washed his hands and looked into the mirror. What he saw made him scowl at himself. The new furrows on his forehead, the first gray hairs at his temple. God, he was only twenty-eight! His brothers all married – even Alex was looking forward to getting married in one month, the date all set, the Greek Orthodox church and hall booked for the grand event. His fiancée, Nikki Theopoulis, the daughter of wealthy Abe Theopoulis, his father's business partner. Pretty thing, but shallow and selfish. Poor Alex couldn't see through her. She was going to drive Alex insane. Hey, shit happens. What could he do? Nikki was pregnant. There was no reneging on such a compact between families, even if Alex wanted to. And poor besotted Alex wasn't saying no to anybody.

Back at the table, slurping down another beer. This time, his eyes began to cross, his vision blurred, everyone swaying, the whole room listing left and right. Like a goddamned ship in a storm. His brother stood up and insisted on taking him home, his shoulder under his arm, steering him to Alex's sports car in the side parking lot. His mind a swirling blank and everything spinning around him. That was strange, everything was strange. Otherworldly.

A moment later, his stomach lurched and his intestines felt on fire. He made it to the men's room in time but just barely. Minutes later, Alex found him on the floor, hugging the toilet and muttering nonsense. Kas knew what he was saying.

"Bad beer . . . bad peanuts . . . bad something . . ."

He passed out. Still, his mind churned and delirious dreams swirled around his head. They were in the boathouse at lakeside. Athena, that strange girl, was struggling with her wetsuit. He went over to help her and his fingers grazed her back, her neck. Why couldn't he have her? He wanted her, ever since he saw her that first day at the airport. He'd noticed her tall figure, slim in all the right places, plump in all the right places . . . oh yeah. Then he'd looked into her eyes, that sea green. He sensed the depth of her mind, the fullness of her heart. Wanted to hold her, possess her, claim her as his own. But no . . . not possible, his mother had warned him. Why not? He was needed for something else. Fuck the something else!

Nope . . . not possible, not now.

In his delirium, she dove into the lake and swam away. He jumped on the jet ski and tried to find her, but she'd disappeared. Into the depths of the cold lake.

No, no, no!

Would he have another chance with her? He had to get his act together, do something great with his life. He'd go to her when he was ready, when he had something to offer. Not just money. Something else . . . if only he knew what. His chest constricted as if a band were squeezing his heart and lungs.

Somebody was gently slapping his face, then carrying him. Eyes closed, he felt a car move. Cold outside, but Alex always kept his car warm inside . . . funny guy, his older brother . . . the women loved him . . . even Athena had spent more time with Alex than she did with him . . . but she'd called him to come to D.C., not Alex. She looked at him a lot and smiled.

He laughed aloud. "'Thena, you read my dog's mind!"

Then the car jerked, swayed violently. He opened his eyes and looked at Alex at the wheel, fighting for control, swearing and screaming, "No-o-o! Dammit, no-o-o!"

The car was flying now, airborne. Reflexively, Kas brought his arms up to shield himself. Something exploded into his face, smothering him, pinning him down, as the front of the car hit something hard. He felt the back of the car lurch up and then come crashing down. The wheels bounced a few times before Alex's car came to a halt and settled down.

The airbag deflated and cleared his head and chest. He gingerly moved his neck. His whole body ached, his neck felt on fire. He slowly moved each of his limbs. Nothing is broken – hell! A scorching pain shot up his right leg. He gagged, then bent over and vomited. What the hell happened? Was he still dreaming?

Gradually, his head cleared and the nausea subsided. He cautiously turned his head. Alex wasn't moving, his body angled towards the driver's window, bloody smears already visible among the cracks in it. So much blood. Where did it come from? Alex's airbag, where was it? Why didn't it deploy? Kas reached over and placed his hand on Alex's shoulder.

"What the hell just happened?"

Alex sat there, still, frozen. One short moan before a whoosh of air escaped his mouth. Then silence.

Kas screamed, "Alex! Alex!"

Over and over, until his own voice died away.

Athena awoke and lurched to a sitting position. She covered her face in her hands, her breath coming and going in jagged sobs.

Noooooo, please no . . .

Chapter Twenty-five

Athena tore her gaze away as the two eldest Skoros brothers closed Alex's casket. People began to leave before it was lowered into the rectangular pit. The Skoros men and all the other male relatives and friends wore black armbands over their jacket sleeves, the women, including Lorena and Anna, in black dresses and pantsuits. Although she hated the tradition, Athena too wore black trousers and a black sweater on which she'd pinned a bright yellow daisy. For that was how she remembered Alex—a brightly colored flower in the midst of drab winter grays and browns.

The older white-haired Greek Orthodox priest had read from the Divine Liturgy, the Orthodox holy book. Everyone who spoke Greek had bowed their heads and repeated the prayers in traditional Greek while the majority present followed the younger priest in English. While the casket had been open, mourners approached to kiss the cross lying on Alex's chest and to murmur the words *Memory eternal*. She'd watched Kas hobble over on his crutches, his right leg in a thigh-to-ankle cast, his head held stiff by the neck brace he wore. With his two elder brothers' supporting him, he bent over and kissed Alex's cross, his face crumbling, accompanied by the two brothers' own naked expressions of grief. Athena had to turn away to avoid gasping aloud. Lorena and Phillip Skoros followed, each helping the other in their darkest moment to say goodbye to their next to the youngest son.

Athena felt numb and dry, all cried out. Her brother,

Chris, holding it in for days, now wept by her side. She hugged him tightly, his skinny frame almost reaching her height as he buried his face in the crook of her neck. Her mother hugged the two of them as the three Butlers formed a little island of sorrow amidst the sea of grief at the gravesite.

Stoical Lorena looked over at them, nodded and smiled. Since the moment they'd arrived, she seemed to perk up, as though having her cousin Anna there, and Athena, fellow clairvoyants, made all the difference. They were all slaves to fate, and their presence appeared to reinforce Lorena's own belief. She'd done all she could to prevent this family tragedy, and in the final analysis, she'd known it would never be enough. Fate would be served, she had told them, as all humans would recognize eventually at the hour of their deaths. Now, Lorena comforted the grandchildren at her side, smoothing the dark hair of George's eldest, also named Alex, already grooming him to fill the void in their hearts for their much-loved son.

Sitting with another group of mourners, the Theopoulis family, Alex's fiancée, Nikki, handled her own grief by dabbing at her eyes with a black lace handkerchief, the diamond on her ring finger sending out flashes of light every time she moved her hand. She clutched the sable mink collar of her black coat to her body, showing an occasional black-tinted leg, uncovered to well above her knee. A fashion plate, she wore her reddish-auburn hair upswept in an elaborate hairdo, a fascinator made of feathers and rhinestones perched along one temple, askew as was the latest look. Athena knew Kas thought she was shallow and self-centered—but also very pretty. And she was. Narcissistic Nikki Theopoulis. Alex had deserved better.

Self-consciously, Athena straightened her black beret and tidied her sprawling blond hair. In comparison to fashion plate Nikki, she would be found lacking in chic, to be sure. Oh well, she was what she was . . .

Uh-oh, Kas was on his way towards her as the mourners turned to leave the gravesite. In the two weeks since the car crash, he'd had neck surgery to fuse two badly herniated disks and leg surgery to fix the two cracks in his femur. She hadn't spoken to him on the phone, but he'd texted her often while in the hospital. He'd wanted her to come to Alex's funeral if at all possible. Of course, she, her mother and Chris wanted to pay their respects, while their father was unavoidably detained in London for some top-secret meetings with the Foreign Office ministers.

As much as Athena was over-the-moon mad about him, Kas Skoros was impossible. She never knew where she stood with him. Were they long-distance lovers? Was he trying to be a friend with benefits? Even when she'd read his thoughts that awful night of the crash, he'd been drunk as a skunk. Or half drunk and half sick with a stomach bug. Did anything he thought about her have any real meaning? He was an enigma. What she wanted was an uncomplicated boyfriend, someone to do things with. Go to galleries with, movies with, go clubbing with, walk along the river with. Was that too friggin' much to ask?

What she had with Kas was so complicated.

He was maneuvering his crutches over the uneven grass with difficulty, his face a study in sorrow so deeply etched, she was certain he'd never lose the premature lines. His eyes were swollen and red, but he appeared composed enough to speak. She greeted him with an awkward hug, her casted arm moving aside so that she could press herself against his body. So strong and solid, his physique seemed to engulf her. He embraced her for a long moment, then disengaged enough to pull Chris into their hug. Her mother patted their shoulders and went off to join the main Skoros contingent, extricating Chris in the process and holding onto his arm for support.

Athena found herself alone with Kas for the first time since they'd arrived the evening before. Only then did she gaze into his eyes, continuing to touch him but turning off her third eye. There was no need to read his mind, nor did she want to. She couldn't absorb any more sorrow that day, so filled to the brim was she.

"Looks like we're both the walking wounded, only you earned yours. I was just stupidly drunk and sick. I guess I won't be doing any more Search and Rescue for a while." He smiled that boyish grin of his. "You're looking great."

Basking in his praise, she felt almost tongue-tied. "Thanks."

"Oh, Athena, I've missed you. You have no idea."

The hurt of his absence and neglect surfaced. "Really? I wrote you two long letters and all I got were a few texted messages. In one month."

He lowered his dark blue eyes to look at the ground, but he kept his arms around her while he balanced against her body on one leg. His crutches lay on the ground.

"I'm sorry. I'm not much of a writer." He attempted a grin. "A day hasn't gone by when I didn't think of you. At the oddest moments, day or night. You were always there, in the back of my head."

"I know," she said, "I was in your head—I swear I don't know how it happened. I dreamed about you that night, the night of the crash. I was in your head, thinking your thoughts, feeling your emotions, experiencing the whole thing. You were sick, I could see that. Food poisoning."

He flinched visibly. "Yeah, the bar'd put out rancid peanuts. I was the only one in our group who ate them that night. The doctors said that's what probably saved me—I was so limp and wiped out. God, how it happened—I don't even know exactly what happened. One moment we were in the car and driving down the road. We both forgot Mom's warning—we just weren't thinking. All of a sudden, we were flying through the air and hitting a tree. We were half a mile from home—the family compound. On that winding country road off the highway. They think a deer caused Alex to swerve off the road, he lost control of the car and—" His voice caught. "His airbag was defective, they said."

"I know. I was there . . . or at least, some part of me was there." She paused, recalling that dream at the exact moment it happened in Pacific Standard Time. A shudder of horror passed through her. Still, the wonder of it made her try to explain. "Kas, that's never happened to me before. Jumping into somebody's head like that, miles away, thousands of miles away. I didn't have to touch you to jump into your head."

He stroked her face and ran his hand down one long lock of her hair. "We have a special connection, you and I, 'Thena. I can't explain it, but I felt it from the moment I first saw you. That's never happened to me before. You know, you can jump into my head anytime—only next time, choose a more pleasant moment."

She stiffened away from him as she pictured him at the same local bar, this time with a woman. Jealousy overwhelmed her as she bent over and helped him pick up his crutches.

"Oh yeah, when would that be? When you're in the arms of another woman?"

He silently tucked the tops of the crutches under his arms, stood there shaking his head.

"Okay, I was waiting for this. The physical distance between us. My mother keeps telling me it's too soon for us. Okay, so she's psychic, foretells the future. We don't have to let fate or Lady Luck or the gods—whatever you want to call it—control us. We control our own destiny."

"Do you really believe that? After what's happened to Alex?"

"Yes, I do," he said, though she heard the wavering in his voice. "What do you want from me? Tell me and I'll do it, say it, make it happen. If it's humanly possible."

She walked alongside him, mute in the face of such a pointedly blunt question. Indeed, what *did* she want from Kas Skoros? A bi-coastal friendship? A romantic relationship? A sexual one? Oh, sure, how was that going to work? They led such different lives, and she had at least one more year of art school ahead of her.

"That's it," she finally admitted, feeling stupid, "I don't know."

"What if I flew out there once a month, would you meet me in a hotel for a weekend? Like we did over New Year's?" He'd stopped on the gravel path under a giant oak tree and was now studying her face. People were getting into their cars, the Skoros family waiting for them to join them in their long, black limousines. "Would you like that, Athena? A once a month rendezvous, sex and champagne, flowers and Valentines? Are you up for that? Is that all you want from me?"

The heavy irony of his voice told her that was all he thought she wanted. A girl's hot fantasy. No more reality-based than an erotic romance novel.

"I don't know." Her lame reply served only to harden his expression.

"Look, the Aftermeal is a Greek tradition, lots of food and oozo, wine and song, a celebration of Alex. Literally, Greek singing and dancing, everyone joins in. Then there's a meeting of the Skoroses and Theopoulises, some kind of summit meeting. Don't really know what that's about, but I think it has to do with Nikki being pregnant with Alex's child. What a mess that is." He bent over and brushed her forehead with his lips. "Five o'clock tonight, at dusk, meet me in the boathouse. We'll talk some more. Meanwhile, think about what it is you want from me. If it's possible, I'll make it happen."

Two limo doors opened. Kas, with help, climbed through one and Athena the other. Her mother, Chris, and George, his wife and their three children all gave her speculative looks. Then, like shutters, down came the blank looks of grief.

Tables throughout the dining room and kitchen seemed to groan under the weight of platters of food. The bar in the family room ran an unending parade of people drowning their sorrow in booze. A disconsolate Phillip Skoros, paler than usual, his face a haggard wreck, sat ensconced in his favorite easy chair, Abe Theopoulis at his side, both patriarchs of their families and Chairmen of the Boards of their respective companies. Athena learned from her mother that the Theopoulis Enterprises empire reigned over the port of Stockton and thereabouts and had partnered up with the Skoros Group on several shopping centers between Sacramento and downtown Stockton. In the works at present were two commercial buildings in Emeryville, the headquarters of a digital movie company, a potential buyout from Disney. A *triple net lease,* whatever that was. The two family empires, apparently, only took breaks from business at funerals, weddings and christenings. However, according to Kas, something big was up for discussion at their afternoon meeting.

Outside on the terrace, where Athena had wandered with Chris, male and female dancers in Greek costumes were spinning and weaving, the music of a small band of musicians keeping them going. One of George's daughters passed around bracelets of blue beads, the concentric blue and white *eye* of each bead meant to ward off evil spirits, or the *mati*, the Evil Eye. Another child wandered around holding a tray of red-dyed Easter eggs and a cake called *tsoureki*, symbolizing the rebirth of spring and the continuation and renaissance of the soul.

It was a lovely idea, but one that Athena couldn't believe in. If her mother was correct, all the souls of past living humans merged into The Flow, the river of humanity. Whether they were ever recalled to join the humans on Earth for another chance at mortal life, her mother wasn't sure. She'd never met one who'd come back from The Flow. Neither had Athena.

She felt Kas' body ease up behind her, his mouth at her ear.

"What do you think? The way Greeks celebrate life and spit in the face of death?"

"Hmm, so different from the English. I like it."

His face was clean-shaven today and she could smell his aftershave lotion. Her heart tripped a beat or two, and she realized how much she'd longed for his physical presence. In many ways, he looked different than he had during Thanksgiving week two months before, younger and more vulnerable than he'd looked over New Year's, too.

It was a shock to her that she wanted Kas Skoros more than as a once a month lover, much more than just a long-distance friend. Although why the sudden revelation shocked her, she didn't know. Was she so repressed or so busy with school and work—not to mention crime solving for the Metropolitan Police and intelligence gathering for the Embassy's security force—that she hadn't allowed herself to consider any relationship seriously?

Kas was standing against the house, supporting himself in part by the exterior wall. She slowly backed up until her rump nestled against his upper thighs and found the dip of his crotch. Immediately, his arms surrounded her waist, his hands laced together in front to lock her in. Together, they watched the next dance and half listened to the music, their own voices concealed somewhat by the haunting music of the ancient Greek instruments. The twang of a string instrument, the trill of a flute.

"You don't mind generating some gossip?" he murmured against the side of her head.

"Do you?"

He chuckled, a deep-throated, light chuckle that thrilled her, made her glad she could draw him out of his grief, even if only temporarily.

"According to Mom, Alex and I have been the only source of family gossip for years now. I think Alex would approve my carrying on in his—" He broke off, the heaving of his chest pressing into her back. "He'd approve of this, you and me. Funny, Athena, that first time you came, I thought you might've fallen for Alex."

"You don't know jack about women." She felt his face nuzzling the crown of her head and smiled.

"Guess you're right. Let me make up for it. I'm hoping you'll teach me—" His teasing remark was cut short when George sidled up next to them. A head shorter than Kas, he leaned into Kas and whispered something. The look he gave Athena before moving off held a trace of something . . . Pity? Regret?

Kas gently eased her forward so he could put his full weight on the crutches. Nevertheless, he bent his head and brushed his lips against her temple.

"Gotta go. Summit meeting with the Theopoulises. Five o'clock, boat house, okay?"

She nodded and shot him a slight smile. Her heart was beating like a hummingbird's wings. Just a few hours from now, she was going to take the biggest plunge of her life. She was going to ask him for a commitment.

What kind of commitment, she wasn't sure.

Chapter Twenty-six

In her guest room on the third floor, Athena put a last touch on an attempt to make up her face. A hint of rouge, a little eyeliner and mascara, a pale coral lipstick. She gathered her long tresses into a high ponytail, her bangs and side hair drawn back severely. Diamond stud earrings completed a look that she hoped would lend her a little sophistication.

The black trousers and sweater would have to do, for she'd brought very few clothes on their brief visit. She wondered what Kas would think when he saw her, a little more dressed up than usual. Whatever . . . she felt different, older, more worldly. He'd mentioned weekends in a hotel. He'd fly all the way from California to meet up with her and have a secret liaison. It sounded illicit, thrilling . . . forbidden. Her mother would never approve and neither would her father. No matter how rich the Skoros family was, or how kind and friendly they'd been to Athena and her mother.

All the more exciting!

She checked her watch. Five o'clock. Not the least bit cold, she ignored her leather jacket and skipped down the back stairs, found an exit door by the garage and made a detour around the side to avoid the terrace and main part of the mansion. It was dusk, and the shadows along the trail were long. She breathed in the cool night air, enjoying a balmy California wintry night. Night birds chirped and even an owl hooted in a nearby tree. Lorena had said they'd spotted a mountain lion on a granite escarpment crowning a nearby hill, so the flashlight in Athena's hand was meant for both illumination and a possible defense weapon. The ten-minute walk was refreshing and, fortunately, uneventful.

A light in the boathouse greeted her. Good! He'd come, just as he said he would. Was he as excited as she was?

The door was ajar.

"Kas?"

"Athena, come in." His voice sounded anything but excited.

She found him sitting on an old patio swing against the far wall, near the third boat berth, the jet ski hanging from its winter harness above him, blocking his upper body. As she approached, she could see him, folded over, elbows on his knees, his hands clutched together and pressed against his mouth. He looked up. The same gravesite expression blanketed his face.

"Good grief, what happened?" Alarmed, she went and sat next to him. He continued to gaze at nothing, his sapphire blue eyes glazed over with pain.

She waited patiently while he inhaled deeply before slowly turning to face her.

"The summit conference, it was about Alex. And Nikki. The baby. The reason for their sudden wedding plans." He stopped and looked away.

"It's bad, I get that," she said, beginning to tremble. A sudden chill darted through her that she knew would eventually ice up her heart. "Just tell me, Kas. Get it over with."

He exhaled heavily. "Nikki's six months pregnant. Alex's child, so she claims. Actually, I believe her. I think she was head over heels in love with him . . . in her own way. Alex was so excited about the child. A kid himself, he'd bought the baby—a boy, by the way—all kinds of toys that he knew he'd love to show the kid how to play with. You know Alex."

Kas' voice cracked and he swallowed back a sob. Athena

leaned over, touched his shoulder and nuzzled the side of his face. She waited until he regained his composure.

"So Papa Theopoulis is faced with a dilemma. How can his only daughter avoid the shame of a child out of wedlock? Jeez, that's how they talk, these traditional Orthodox Greeks. A bastard child of Alex's and Nikki's, a child out of wedlock. Unthinkable. The shame, the scandal. In the old country, she'd be driven out of the village or stoned. My father kept saying *he's a Skoros male.* Old Abe kept weeping and saying *no Theopoulis has ever been so disgraced, so dishonored.* They looked at me. *It's all his fault. He was drunk. He let Alex get behind the wheel. After all the warnings."*

"Oh, Kas, it wasn't your fault," she said, hugging him to her.

"Want to know how they solve this sort of problem, these old-fashioned Orthodox Greek-Americans?"

She sat up straight and stared at him. Already, she could see him drifting away. He noticed and seized her hand. Resignedly, she let the mental barrier down and read his mind. Her mouth dropped open. Her stomach rolled over, a kind of pit-of-your-stomach free fall from the top of a skyscraper. She squeezed her eyes shut.

"No-o-o! How-how can they ask that of you?"

"My father and Abe want the child to have the Skoros name, to be legitimate. For the family's sake, for Nikki's sake, in honor of Alex and to honor his commitment to the Theopoulis family. His child should have his surname. I'm the only single Skoros male. If I go along with this marriage, it'll cement our family's legal and moral attachment to Alex's child. My parents want that for their grandchild." He rattled it all off so rapidly, as if it couldn't hurt them if he said it quickly. "Athena, this'll sound crazy . . . but I think Alex would want that, too. He would want his son to have his name, the Skoros name."

"Did your father threaten to disown you?" Athena

opened her eyes and struggled to understand all the ramifications, for she knew it was a *fait accompli.* So much for her fantasies of a hot rendezvous in D.C. So much for her and Kas, period.

"Oh, god no, he'd never do that." Kas' face remained shuttered in pain, but he was using logic and persuasion to make the fathers' case, just as she knew they'd used it, themselves. "It was more, you have to do this, son, for the sake of the two families. For Alex's son's sake." His gaze locked with hers. The pain in his eyes was unbearable. "The Theopoulises are as close to us as blood relatives. Alex would want this. Can't you see the logical solution in this? Your mother says you were meant to stay single for just this very reason. Maybe it's my moral obligation to Alex. If I hadn't been so out of it that night, none of this would've happened. It's my fault. This is my way of making up for what happened."

She shook her head in denial, unwilling to understand why he would think and feel this way. Still, their solution and Kas' agreement to it outraged her emotionally.

"It's not fair," was all she could manage. Then Kas' very words returned to haunt her. "What about *they don't rule me, Athena?"*

"It's only temporary, only they never said that. I'm telling you this, Athena. It's only temporary."

Abruptly, he encircled her in his arms and kissed her. She returned his kiss, holding onto him for as long as she could. The kiss drew out, long, wet, full of angst and passion and all of the emotion they'd denied themselves for weeks. When she didn't resist, he lingered, planting warm lips to her face, neck, ear. She shuddered with her need of him.

"It's only temporary," Kas whispered. "We can still meet. I'll fly out there as often as I can. We'll make it work, make it happen. I want you, Athena. This is not a game to me."

Dazed and heartbroken, she knew he was grasping, trying to catch and hold onto a dream as gossamer as a misty night on the lake. Lorena was right. She saw it all. Their timing was lousy. And it sucked big time.

Somehow, Athena found the strength to push him away. She let the heartbreak and outrage into her mind and accepted it for what it was, a fate that she had no power over. She couldn't fight it any more than Lorena could prevent it.

"Please, Kas, don't ever try to see me. Or write me or call me. I can't stand it, it's too much. As long as you legally belong to another woman, I can't see you. I can't love you. I won't thumb my nose at the vows of marriage, and I won't stand between you and what that child will need, a father. I won't do this, not for you, not for any man." She stood up and moved away.

He pushed himself up to a standing position, holding onto the swing's arm and trying to grab her at the same time. She eluded his outstretched arm and walked towards the door of the boathouse.

He called out to her. "Athena! You know as long as you're walking the earth I won't be happy with any other woman." His voice broke into a million pieces as he gasped and swore to himself. He fell back onto the swing as she turned away.

Her mind formed into a glacier—that was how she felt inside. More the fool she was, falling for men who were either con artists or hapless pawns of fate. She took one last look at Kas Skoros, a sob stuck in her throat, her eyes stinging with welling tears. Struggling to find the strength, she turned away. She wanted to tell him goodbye, that she wished him the best, but she couldn't. The words choked her up.

She left the boathouse.

Lorena had scheduled a formal unveiling of Alex's portrait for seven that night. Everyone, all the members of the Skoros and Theopoulis families, including other distant cousins and close family friends, gathered in the vast living room. Both Lorena and Phillip Skoros had asked Athena to make a few remarks, so she stood by the huge, sculpted limestone mantelpiece, over which the unframed twenty-two by twenty-nine canvas stood, propped against the wall and covered by a cloth. The previous painting had been taken down to make room for what would become a sort of family shrine to honor Alex's memory.

Athena took a deep breath, purposefully not scanning the room for Kas' presence—she'd already sensed him standing by her mother and Chris. She could feel his intense blue-eyed stare, as if he were trying to thaw her out and make her change her mind.

Ain't gonna work, as Mikela would say.

"I've never unveiled one of my portraits before today," she began hesitantly, uncertain whether to keep her tone light or somber, then decided just to be herself. "I usually just show the person who's commissioned the painting and hope he doesn't groan from disgust when he sees it." There was an appreciative titter of laughter that rippled about the room. "I've painted all kinds of things, still lifes, landscapes, even abstract art. But painting the portrait of another human being is a special challenge."

She took another deep breath, recalling the portrait she'd done of Kas in his deputy's uniform. She'd taken a photo of the completed painting before sending it to California. Ironic, but that was all she'd have left of Kas. That portrait of Kas was now hanging in the Skoros' family room.

"As an artist, I have to try to capture the person's personality and character, not just his appearance. His soul, his philosophy of life. Basically, what makes him tick. I hope I've accomplished this with Alex. It's been a great honor to have had this opportunity to paint a man I admired very much."

At her nod, George Skoros carefully removed the cloth draped over the painting and stood back. No one had yet seen it except for Alex's mother, Lorena, and she'd insisted on this formal unveiling. Athena knew she was more than pleased with her portrayal of the family's irrepressible son. She was moved in ways that only a mother could be.

The room as one rose in a collective gasp of delight and awe. There he was. Wise-cracking, charming Alex Skoros, leaning against the mantelpiece in almost a swaggering pose, his handsome face split with a wide-open smile. As though he were in the middle of a joke and about to tell the punch line.

Phillip Skoros exclaimed, "Oh my god!"

Nikki could be heard gasping aloud.

Athena snuck a quick look. Even somber Kas had erupted in an open-mouthed look of delight.

Spontaneously, the assembled families and friends broke into applause, which continued for much longer than Athena had ever imagined possible. Whether for Lorena's and Phillip's benefit or her own, she wasn't sure, but it was tremendously gratifying, all the same. Maybe Alex's soul was grinning down at them all, pleased by what she'd captured in the portrait.

Lorena came to her and embraced her. Telepathically, the bereft mother expressed her deepest appreciation and gratitude. Then what transmitted was overflowing sympathy and an apology for what had to happen, Kas' obligation to both families. The woman knew the arranged marriage would ruin any chances for her and Kas. She had foreseen it all. The car crash, Alex's death, Kas' family obligation, Athena's and Kas' doomed relationship. But even for Lorena, everything was beyond her control.

One by one, people came by to congratulate Athena. The eldest son, George, wanted to commission a portrait of his wife, himself and their three children. Others wished her well in her career. Several approached her mother to commend her for raising such a talented daughter.

The two patriarchs, Phillip Skoros and Abe Theopoulis, stood together, gazing up at Alex's portrait, their hands on each other's shoulders, as though congratulating themselves for solving a difficult problem. They both appeared pleased, wistful and saddened. Pretty Nikki Theopoulis would marry Kas, and her baby son would be legitimized by the Skoros name. There would be no scandal, and the Skoros family would forever be linked with their new grandchild.

Would Kas eventually learn to love the mother and the child?

Perhaps. That, too, was beyond Athena's control.

She saw Chris drift off onto the terrace where a firepit drew the children for a marshmallow roast. Several elderly Greek-Americans held long skewers of lamb over the fire. Only Kas stood apart in the living room, his plaintive stare boring into her but leaving her coldly resigned to their fate.

Too bad, Kas. You had your chance to stand up to them.

And you chose duty over love.

CHAPTER TWENTY-SEVEN

Under the cloudy dark skies of a winter's evening, Athena emerged from the Art Institute. She'd been back in D.C. a month. Winter Quarter brought Painting Still Lifes, Art History of the Renaissance, another Western Civilization course, and thanks to the largesse of the Skoros family, she was able to take a fourth class, European Literature. At this accelerated pace, she'd finish her bachelor's in one year. Her cast was off and she'd quit her job at Starbucks.

There was a little bounce to her step, also. Dan Grantham had called—several times, in fact—and they'd arranged to meet for dinner that evening. He kept asking about her Manet pastiche, for it was overdue by two weeks. According to Dan, Martin Larsen, on behalf of his company, Genuine Pastiches of the Great Masters, had pressed him to find out the progress of her painting, implying in the process that there was another painter who wanted to tackle Manet.

Before her, however, sat *Max* at the helm of a black Range Rover. She went over to the curb.

"Sorry to spring this on you, Athena, but there's an important meeting we'd like you to attend. It's rather an emergency. If you don't mind."

There was no question whether she minded or not—this was a British Embassy security chief asking for her help again. The PM's visit had been postponed a month as the security detail continued to investigate who had hired Tony and the Serbians. They appeared a little closer to answering that question, according to her father. So what could she say? *Sorry, I have a date with a fellow painter. I can't help you prevent the attack on the PM's life and countless others, including my own father.*

She frowned and got into the back seat, the passenger seat in front already taken by Max's team mate, *John.*

"Where are we going?" she asked.

The prime minister's visit in one week had set everyone on edge, especially her father. She and her mother had learned from her father one evening after their return from California that Max had translated the Arabic message left in Winston Blake's gym locker that day. "We gave you what you demanded. Now it's your turn." Of course, they couldn't discount completely that Winston had gotten involved in a private matter, but if so, the message implied he was a blackmailer.

On a worse note, he was a traitor. The content of that secret message implicated her father's own secretary in a plot to kill the PM and others, implying that Winston Blake was paid for supplying inside information to the PM's whereabouts and secret plans during his visit to the U.S. If the attack was imminent, then at what point during the visit was this attack meant to take place? Where, when, how—those were the big questions.

And when they'd returned from Alex's funeral, her father had made it very clear that he was angry at Athena for getting involved in the whole business and upset with her mother for encouraging her to use her clairvoyance in these matters. And furious with himself for not protecting them from the cruel world. To which, she and her mother said nothing but just hugged him for his lovely and manly sentiments.

That was her father. The perennial boy scout and gentleman.

When Athena asked why Winston Blake hadn't already been interrogated, her father had explained. The ambassador himself had decided against interrogating their prime suspect or inside man. Instead, the security team administered polygraphs to the entire Embassy staff, not wishing to reveal their trump card, but Winston's and a few others' results were inconclusive. Sir Richard was morally opposed to torture of any kind and felt that, inevitably, good intelligence would save the day.

Well, good luck with that, Athena thought.

"To Old Town Alexandria," supplied John, "to meet your father and mother . . . and the ambassador."

Her pulse skipped. She wasn't dressed for a meeting with Sir Richard, or anyone else important. Startled, she met Max's gaze in the rearview mirror.

"We want your sense of a few things, that's all," he said, "Nothing to stress over."

She harrumphed. "Easy for you to say. What if I get it wrong? What if I can't see anything? What if I draw a blank?"

"Then your mother will help fill the void. Remember, Athena, you were the one who had that vision of Blake's gym locker, the secret message. You led us to him, and you were spot on. Sir Richard doesn't know what to think about you, your . . . talent, shall we say. We've convinced him that what you see is good intel. That's what we need at this point."

She nodded, her mind jumping to her date with Dan, whom she'd just stood up.

"Shit!" She reached for her cell phone and sent Dan a text, apologizing profusely for the change in plans at the last minute. Waited for a reply, cringeing meanwhile. *There goes another one. First, Tony, then Martin, and now Dan. Kas, well, we won't go there. Too fucking painful . . .*

"You're sounding more American these days," commented Max, his wry sense of humor reminding her of more important things than dashed love affairs.

"You should hear the way I think," she retorted. Her cell phone buzzed and she read Dan's text.

I'm sorry. Here I'm sitting at Luigi's, having a glass of Chianti. I know you're involved with the British Embassy—good for you. Other things in life besides painting. How's the Manet going? I'd like to see it.

I'll be working on it tomorrow, eight am. Fifth-floor painting studio. Come and see it. It's almost done.

Will do. What's your coffee drink?

Skinny hazelnut macchiato. Thanks.

See you then.

Athena smiled, her chest feeling lighter than it had in days. She sighed. *Life goes on.*

Wharfside was the kind of restaurant that was an Old Town Alexandria destination, wood-paneled and glowing with old-style brass ships' lamps and the best seafood in town. The loyal clientele included the Who's Who of Washington politics, who often crowded the red-leather stools at the long bar and the banquettes along the walls. There were private dining rooms for lunch and dinner meetings. She followed Max, John bringing up the rear, into one of these dining rooms.

The British ambassador, Sir Peter Willcott, was already seated next to her father and mother, the three nursing cocktails, her mother sipping a favorite of hers, a vodka martini—Athena could tell by the shape of the glass—her father swirling a Scotch whiskey, no doubt. Two other men, whom Athena didn't know or who looked vaguely familiar, sat on the other side of the ambassador. She approached shyly, intimidated by the company present at such a meeting. John had joined the other two guards standing by the dining room threshold, big, bulky hunks in oversized suit jackets.

Armed and exuding no-nonsense, they kept their vigilant gaze roaming the area constantly.

Max introduced her and she smiled shyly, wondering if she should curtsey. *No, ninny, just nod your head.* Sir Peter wasn't a royal, or even born into the aristocracy. He was a self-made man, a Cambridge man from a middle-class family, just like her father. Her mother reached over and took her hand. The telepathic message was *They don't know about me. Let's keep it that way, for your father's sake.* Athena didn't know what that was about—other than her father's fear and concern over what people in the Foreign Office would think. Nevertheless, she nodded slightly in consent.

To cover the moment, her mother said, "'Thena, there's no need to be nervous. Sir Peter called this meeting, in part, to thank you for your role in that ambush."

Athena looked at the ambassador, noted that he was pointedly acknowledging her left arm, and smiled. When everyone was seated and had drinks—Athena got a diet soda—all eight of them, Sir Peter began the meeting.

"I've called you all here for this unofficial meeting of the Embassy grounds for two reasons—actually, three reasons. The first, to recognize Athena Butler's courage in volunteering to be the bait in Max's successful operation in December." He paused while the others applauded appreciatively in Athena's benefit. She felt her face warm with the unexpected accolades.

Then Sir Peter went on, "We all sincerely hope your arm has healed thoroughly with no long-term effects, and we've been told that you're mending nicely. Secondly, to keep our latest findings as secret as possible, I have limited the number of people who are now privy to the security team's ongoing investigation of Mr. Blake. We all agree that further investigation is warranted and due process must go forth. However, in light of the prime minister's visit next week, we must add haste to our investigation of a possible insider's leak and betrayal. With that in mind, the somewhat dodgy implications of Mr. Blake's inconclusive polygraph, and with the security team's recommendation, I would like to try something unorthodox with our young friend, Athena Butler."

With the exception of her parents, Sir Peter, Max and his two security men, the two Foreign Ministry officials looked somewhat perplexed. Max meant to reassure her by patting her arm and grinning at her in encouragement. Instead, she read his thoughts. *God, if this doesn't work, I'm royally fucked.* Her eyes widened at his worry. Max was putting his career on the line—that was how desperate they were to uncover Blake's plot and expose his accomplices. Evidently, the FBI's interrogation of the Serbians had led nowhere. They were in prison awaiting trial and deportation.

Which meant the pressure was all on her to use her clairvoyance and get correct results. Her mother stared at her and silently cheered her on. Athena understood why her mother refused to help in this case. If Athena was wrong or couldn't see anything of value, Trevor Butler wouldn't be blamed. But a wife who represented her husband—well, that was a different story.

Sir Peter now indicated that his cultural attaché should take over. Athena's father opened a manila folder and took out a stack of papers held together with a metal clip.

"These are copies of the PM's schedule for the seven days he will be on the East Coast. The security team has already seen the daily and hourly schedule, as has everyone else here except my wife, Anna, and my daughter, Athena. With his approval, Sir Peter would like Athena to handle these papers and look over the details of each day's schedule. She has already, in everyone's view, proven her loyalty to Queen and country, and therefore we trust she will keep confidential whatever she sees. All of us present here tonight agree that whatever happens at this meeting must never be spoken about. Tonight never happened."

"Agreed," chorused the group.

"Jolly good. Well then, Athena, take these papers and let us know what you think. Take your time."

At first, she didn't understand. Then it dawned on her. Of course, Winston Blake had overseen the copies made on the office copier, had handled the papers himself and had probably passed on the information to whoever was planning the attack. Maybe Blake had even recommended the date, time and venue for the attack. He would know the numbers of security assigned for each event, for that was detailed on the printout as well.

Athena took the slim stack of papers and placed it on the table in front of her. Closing her eyes, she smoothed her right hand over the top sheet before touching the clip and rifling through the other sheets. When nothing came through, save a sense of Blake's quickened pulse and queasiness in his stomach, she began to turn each page and run her hand down from top to bottom. Nothing more transmitted, except Blake's increasing anxiety. His heart was pounding by now, hammering hard in his chest as he studied each block of days in the PM visit's schedule. She sensed him looking hard at the motorcade's route to the Smithsonian's Natural History Museum before moving on to the next page.

He had discounted the PM's White House Dinner, too many uncertain variables, too many unknown security details. On and on, page by page, she ran her hand over the sheet, occasionally pausing on a page when she felt Blake's anxiety heighten.

Finally, she reached a page and a sudden spike in Blake's mind and pulse rate, followed by an abrupt release of anxiety. He'd found the most likely event that heralded success. *Yes, this is perfect! Minimum security for the guests. The wireless perimeter alarm system on the Embassy grounds would go off for intruders only. There would be more than perfunctory checks on the catering staff and the musicians already booked for the occasion. They would be thoroughly vetted.*

Centerpiece deliveries. A lot of controlled chaos. Strangers milling around, entering and exiting in all directions. Trucks allowed in for superficial inspections. No more than a crew of six needed with automatic assault rifles and rocket-propelled grenades. Incendiary and concussion bombs. Maximum damage and fatalities. Two hundred of the Washington elite. The greatest prizes of all, the PM and the American president.

Athena heard him snicker, heard his evil thoughts. *What's not to love? And if half those buggers are killed, so what? They don't expect to escape. More martyrs for jihad. Who cares? I've got ten million in Cayman. I'll claim PTSD, like my ol' pa, quit the Foreign Service and disappear. Live like a bloody king for the rest of my life.*

Athena opened her eyes and looked down at the page. The event, an Embassy hosted formal dinner-dance in the mansion's ballroom. Sunday, March tenth, seven to twelve pm. The one that her parents had been invited to. Sir Peter and his wife, Max and his security team, everyone at the table would be present. But what kind of attack? Bombs, grenades, machine guns? Blake considered several possibilities but didn't commit. No other details came across. She closed her eyes and let her hand linger a minute or two longer on that page.

Nothing more.

She shut it down and looked up, blinking her eyes as her mind made the transition from Blake's mind in the past to her reality in the present. Slowly, she turned to Max beside her and tapped her forefinger on the page which described the event's details.

"This is the target event," she told him. Morosely, she shook her head. "Mr. Blake doesn't care about anyone. He truly doesn't care." Then she looked at her parents. Tears sprang to her eyes immediately. "The dinner-dance on the tenth of March."

Max and his team had one week to prevent a catastrophe.

CHAPTER TWENTY-EIGHT

Eight o'clock sharp the following morning, Athena climbed the Art Institute's steps, remembering that Dan Grantham had said he'd meet her. Sure enough, there he was, sitting on a ledge, two Starbucks cups of coffee in his hands. He grinned widely when he saw her. The last time she'd seen him was on a visit to her hospital room over a month ago. He'd brought her flowers, and she'd apologized profusely for what had happened. His friendliness to her had earned him a frightful experience with bullets flying about and men with guns shouting in their faces. He'd said it was the most exciting thing that had happened to him in years, so no problem. She had to smile.

"Hi, Dan. I didn't know if you'd come." She'd reached his level on the steps and stopped beside him while he stood up. He was at least six-foot-two, nice and tall. Her weakness, tall men with great smiles and lots of hair. Dan's was dark blonde, thick and straight, cut just the right length, a little on the long side. He looked like an artist in his black turtleneck and jeans under a long, wintry wool coat of gray and black herringbone tweed—but not a starving artist. He seemed the perfect blend of artist and businessman. It was time to get to know him better.

Upstairs in the large, open studio, flanked by tall windows and lots of light exposure on this cold but sunny day, she pulled her canvas out of her locker slot and set it up on a nearby easel. Two other students had acknowledged her and Dan's arrival with nods but then had refocused on their own work, but they were out of earshot. It was probably best not to let others know she was painting pastiches. Even though Professor White was doing it, the other staff members might not approve. In any event, she'd committed herself to trying it.

Carefully, she removed the cover cloth and stood back with Dan. For a few minutes, he studied the work-in-progress with a thoughtful gaze, comparing the large colored print that she'd clipped on a side easel. He drank the rest of his coffee all the while. Finally, he began to point at various places on the canvas.

"Okay, I think I know what's needed. Your thalo blue is too vivid here, needs to be toned down, maybe with pale gray or federal blue. Her face needs to be brought up, high-lighted with a lighter tone of flesh beige, maybe a tinge of mauve around her neck. One cheek is very florid, so pick that up, too. The white diagonal slashes on the mirror need to be toned down, but not by much. Maybe a few more small, flat patches of color in that corner over there. Brush strokes appear accurate. You know the French Impressionists used fairly aggressive strokes that stood out. The conservative art critics of that day considered them a sign of poor technique. The painters knew what they were doing, and you certainly do, too. Overall, Athena, it's a wonderful copy. You've actually improved on Manet's original." He looked at her fully then. "I'm damned impressed."

For reasons she didn't understand, his frank appraisal and praise made her tear up. The welling of emotion spilled over and the tears rolled down her face. She tried to cover her emotions by turning aside and sipping her coffee.

Dan obviously saw through the cover but misunderstood. "I'm sorry, I was just nitpicking. Don't be upset," he urged, looking crestfallen.

Athena smiled and wiped away her tears. "I'm not—it's

nothing. I'm happy you think it's good. Do you think Martin and his partner will accept this?"

He gave a mild snort. "I have no doubt. But do those touches, spray with the fixative and let it dry. Leave it alone for a few days, then go back to it. Touch it up some more if you think it needs it. There's a meeting next week at the gallery. Martin'll be giving us new assignments, so it's a good time to show it."

"In front of the other painters? What if Martin rejects it?"

"He won't. Trust me. I wouldn't be telling you it's good if it was really lacking. If you want me to take one last look after you make those tiny changes, I'll do that. I'm free this coming weekend. What about Saturday or Sunday?"

The Embassy dinner-dance was Sunday. She was attending the affair, but not in the usual role, as part of her father's table. But she wasn't about to tell Dan about it. He'd think she was a lunatic. Or a danger-seeking adrenalin junkie, which was probably worse in his book.

"I can't on Sunday. Tell you what. I'll be finished before Saturday. Let me buy you dinner Saturday night as a thank-you for advising me. And to help make up for—"

"The gunfight at the OK Corral?" He chuckled and placed his hand on her right shoulder. "Sounds good to me. If you're buying, how about Ming's in Georgetown?" His teasing tone provoked a return smile. She liked the feel of his hand on her shoulder. They continued to stare into each other's eyes. "How's your arm?"

"Almost back to normal." She didn't tell him that her gifted mother was advancing the healing with her own brand of what her biology major friends called electro-magnetic energy infusing, but which her mother called *spiritual vibrations.*

"Really, it took just two months? I broke my arm when I was fourteen, a really bad compound fracture. It took almost six months to heal. I thought the bullet really messed up your bone."

Athena just shrugged. "I guess the damage wasn't as bad as they thought. So, shall we meet at Ming's? It'd be out of your way to come all the way down to Alexandria . . ."

He removed his hand while his gaze roved over her hair, face and upper torso. He paused for a split second at the deep vee-neck of her lavender tee-shirt before lifting his focus. "I don't mind. I'll pick you up . . . if that's okay with you."

"Okay, it's a date."

At least he's not gay. Thank God!

And he doesn't live in California. And he's not married.

For the first time since her last visit to California, she felt a weight lift off her chest and a bubble float up in her mind. A bubble of hope lessened the deep emotional pain of losing Kas —the man she'd never had but still yearned for. *Ninny!*

For now, that little bubble of hope was enough.

Chapter Twenty-nine

Athena hadn't heard from Max since the meeting with the ambassador at the Wharfside restaurant. She hadn't seen her father in days, since he'd involved himself in the security end of the PM's visit. The only thing she'd heard was that the Embassy was adhering to his planned schedule, known by at least one hundred people on the staff—including her father's secretary, Winston Blake. But only the seven present at their dinner meeting that night were privy to the heightened security risk of Sunday evening's Dinner-Dance in the mansion's main ballroom.

At least, those who had believed her assessment of the situation. Counting her parents and probably Max and John, that made four. She couldn't blame the others, including Sir Peter Willcott, for discounting her voodoo clairvoyance tricks. They were skeptical, and why wouldn't they be? Why should they believe her? She'd proven her courage in being the bait for the Serbians' ambush but hadn't proven to the ambassador her clairvoyant abilities. Max and her father had nixed the idea of *reading* the ambassador and possibly exposing secret thoughts or memories better kept private. Humiliating the man would not win him to their side.

Late Sunday afternoon, getting ready for the dinner-dance event, her mother had laid out her beautiful royal blue chiffon gown and was now singing in the shower. Chris was upstairs in his room on his computer doing who knew what, while her father had taken his evening clothes to change into at the mansion. A car would pick her mother up, and her father would meet her at the mansion entrance at seven sharp.

The relative peace and quiet was heaven-sent, it seemed, so she took advantage of it. For two hours, she sat on her stool in her corner of the living room, putting the finishing touches on her Manet pastiche. Her cell phone jangled two bars of Miley Cyrus' *The Climb.* Her stomach leapt—was it Kas? Had he told his father and Abe Theopoulis to shove it? That he loved Athena and wanted to be with her?

Then it fell when she learned it was Max.

"I need you here as soon as you can possibly make it." When she said nothing, he added urgently, "Athena, this is no joke. Winston called in sick, said he's got the stomach flu. Like hell, the bugger. He's getting ready to run now that the attack's all set up. We know it's tonight, but from who? From where? We've vetted everyone concerned without his knowledge. The orchestra members, the caterers, the florist, the car parkers, limo owners and drivers. The fireworks people. We haven't overlooked anyone. If any one of those people had so much as a parking ticket, we've checked him out. Weeks' worth of background checks, and nothing."

Her thoughts ran to her mother and father, the ambassador, the prime minister and his wife, the president and his wife . . .

A chill ran through her veins. *They've overlooked*—suddenly, the picture of the Greeks' Trojan horse sprang to mind, straight from the pages of her Western Civ tome.

"Athena, this is no joke. Blake's got something up his sleeve and we haven't found it. We need your help!"

She blinked. A Trojan horse? She held up her paint-smeared hands and arms and groaned. "Max, I've got paint all over me."

"Clean up as best you can. I'll send John for you, and I'll get Winston down here if I have to go there and grab him by his collar. On second thought, pick up some soup and bring it with you. We'll pay him a visit. We've got eyes on him, and he's still in the Residence, playing sick."

"Okay, give me fifteen minutes."

"You have ten. John's at your curb as we speak."

She understood what Max was going to have her do, bring some soup to the man on behalf of her father. Winston Blake, like many of the single men and women among the approximately two hundred-odd diplomats and over one hundred additional staffers who worked at the Embassy, lived on the grounds in a five-story residence hall. Somehow, she knew Max wanted her to make physical contact with the traitor without alerting him to their suspicions.

After one long, lingering look at her pastiche, she wrapped up her brushes in foil—she'd clean them later—tore off her painting smock, and ran upstairs. Her mother was still showering. Why bother her? Athena planned to be back before her mother, all dolled up for the evening, left in their rented limousine. She washed up as best she could, redid her ponytail and changed into a clean turtleneck tee top. Her jeans were smudged with paint but there wasn't time to find something else. On her way downstairs with her jacket, she peeked into Chris' room.

"Chris, tell Mum I've gone to meet Max at the Embassy."

His back to her, engrossed in his electronic game, he raised a hand and made an "O" with his right thumb and forefinger. "Gotcha." In Chris' lingo, that meant *Roger that.*

Skipping down the stairs, she considered how lucky Chris was not to have been burdened with a mental power like clairvoyance. He didn't have a broken arm, did he? He wasn't called away on a moment's notice to help his father's security team, was he? He didn't have to worry about offending his dates by reading their minds, did he?

There were definite advantages to being normal.

Right on the dot, John screeched up to the curb in one of

the black Range Rovers that Max's security team seemed to live in. She was barely strapped into the passenger seat when he took off in a roar.

In all the rush, she'd forgotten the soup. When she said as much, John just shrugged. He'd stop and pick up something at a deli in Georgetown.

The Embassy of the United Kingdom nestled among groves of trees in a gargantuan estate of acreage and manicured lawns. The compound, situated at the northern end of Embassy Row, or Massachusetts Avenue—the Americans called it Mass Ave—northwest of Dupont Circle. The compound included the ambassador's residence and the old and new chanceries, the old chancery having been converted into staff quarters and offices. In the forecourt of the mansion stood a statue of Winston Churchill, his right arm raised in his once famous speaking gesture. The flag of the European Union flew alongside the Union flag but flapped lower on the poles than the Union Jack, a symbolism not lost on anyone who visited there. The British wanted the world to know which came first in their hearts and minds. This compound, for all intents and purposes, was Great Britain.

John showed his credentials at the gate and Athena showed her ID. She noted the extra security at the heavy wrought iron gates. Royal Marines lined the front entrance, more than she'd ever seen before at the Embassy. Cleared, John steered the Range Rover onto the cobbled roundabout driveway that skirted the forecourt and Churchill's statue. In one hour the limos would begin to appear, taking their place in the long queue that would stretch all the way back to the massive entrance gate, always well-guarded by Royal Marines but now a veritable fortress. Their task was to scrutinize each driver and passenger, each guest in turn, visually and manually, referring to the list of guests already vetted and approved.

Athena noted the extra security on the grounds, too, a mixture of Royal Marines and plainclothes agents like Max and John, all holding their positions and all armed to the teeth. Barring a rogue airplane aiming for the mansion, she didn't see how an assailant could possibly break the security barrier.

By stealth. Trojan horse.

The words kept running through her mind. Plain ol' intuition was telling her that a plot was already in action. John gestured to the white panel trucks, already cleared by the guards at the gate. The florist and catering trucks had arrived and were winding their way to the rear of the mansion, about to disgorge men and women in mostly black and white uniforms. She saw three trucks stop along the side entrance and within seconds, an army of workers vanished into the mansion, burdened with enormous displays of bouquets, candelabras and other table accoutrements.

John took the side road that led to the Residence building behind the mansion. Athena had always found the mansion breathtakingly beautiful. The building reminded her of Chatsworth, the Duke of Devonshire's country home, which she'd visited once with her family years before. Almost hidden among the copses of tall, mature trees, the three-winged and five-storied building held its own Edwardian-era charm. Constructed of pale-yellow stone and brick, the Residence beckoned with an entrance framed with sculpted pediments.

If her father had been single, he most likely would've lived there. The building was finer than their modern brick and glass condo building, and his commute would've been five minutes instead of close to fifty. Reminders of her father were everywhere. The lawn where he'd played a friendly cricket game—the diplomats versus the staffers—and on which she'd cheered him on as a thirteen-year-old, while nine-year-old Chris got to clean the balls and wickets.

She glanced over to the mansion, partially hidden by the trees but lit up like a birthday cake. Her parents had brought her and Chris, all dressed up with shining faces, to several events there over the past six years of her father's posting in Washington. She wondered if her parents would find it difficult to leave when the time came to move on. Talk at the dinner table had proved to her that they *were* ready to move on. Europe, preferably Italy or Switzerland, were high on their wish list. Her mother wanted to be closer to Nonna in her waning years, and Como, where Nonna and her Uncle Giancarlo lived, was one hour's drive from Milan. Even Rome was just hours away. Her father had already applied for a new posting.

John had opened the door and was waiting for her. She'd been lost in a kind of nostalgic reverie. She shook herself and jumped out of the Range Rover. Tonight's mission struck her to the heart. She had to uncover Winston Blake's plot. He'd been clever and careful enough to keep it hidden these past five months. Obviously, an attack on the mansion while he feigned illness at the Residence.

But from whom?

"Third floor, room fourteen," said John, patting his red windbreaker under which his shoulder holster and pistol rested. "I'll be in the hallway out of sight. Here, wear this." He fastened a large pin—in the shape of an American flag and the Union Jack crisscrossed at the bottom—to her jacket lapel. "It's a micro transmitter. I'll hear you and Blake. Any trouble, you let me know." He gave her the plastic deli container filled with now lukewarm soup. She didn't even know what kind of soup it was.

"How? What should I say? Some code word?"

"Just say *bloody hell.*"

While it wasn't original, Athena figured it would probably do the trick. John looked more than ready to bust Winston Blake's butt.

The Residence appeared half deserted, most of the staffers helping with the arrangements in some way, some of them, according to her father, doubling as greeters, escorts and ushers. Outside of Winston Blake's room, she stopped. John had slipped into the men's restroom at the end of the hallway to wait. For a moment, she organized her thoughts, then rapped loudly on the door. It opened shortly, a hesitant Blake blocking the entrance.

"Hello, Mr. Blake, Do you recognize me?" she said with false cheer.

He frowned. "Mr. Butler's daughter. Yes, hello. I apologize but I'm not feeling well, have a touch of stomach flu, I believe." He was fully clothed in slacks, button-down shirt and sweater vest. "May I help you?"

"I'm so sorry to disturb you. My father said I should peek in on you and see how you're doing." She held up the plastic container. "I brought you some soup. Or maybe I can bring you something from the mansion's kitchen. Some hot tea and biscuits? I just came in to help with the floral arrangements." Maybe she was talking too much, in her nervousness.

"You're not attending the dinner-dance," he stated flatly, then appeared to remember the reason for her visit. "That's very kind of you, but I can quite manage on my own. I need to lie down and rest."

"Yes, of course." It looked like he wasn't going to budge from his stance between the door frame and the half-open door. He certainly wasn't going to invite her in for a cup of tea. Her mind raced for another excuse. "I-I . . . Yes, lie down, rest . . . I think . . ."

She feigned a swoon, followed by an immediate lurch into his body. The container of soup went flying, the lid flipping off and chicken-and-noodle splattering on Blake's sweater and slacks. He hollered and staggered back, the door to his room swinging widely open. She stumbled into him and held onto his right arm, like a poor swimmer hanging onto her lifeguard. The floor, filled with soup, made her slip and slide. She collided into him and down they crashed onto the floor.

"What—" Blake cried out.

She began making loud, retching sounds as if she was about to vomit. She turned her head aside but continued to hang onto his arm. Visions came through but none of them helpful. He was too focused on her and what she was doing.

With a shriek, she rose to her knees on the floor, then rolled to her back and moved her head from the side like a woman in the throes of childbirth pains. She'd seen enough such scenes on television to fake her way through this. This time, like those women in childbirth, she clutched onto the nearest man's arm. She wasn't going to let go until some vision came through.

"What on earth is wrong with you?" he asked, annoyance lacing his voice. He yanked his arm away and rose to his feet. No trace of compassion or concern apparent, he stood over her, his arms akimbo. "Look at this mess! Soup all over. My good sweater vest—"

Athena moaned and rolled her head on the floor. "H-help me into a chair. P-please." *Yeah, please, you bugger!*

Her eyes closed as she moaned again. A moment later, she heard him swear under his breath. Blake pulled on her arm to a sitting position.

"W-water," she begged as she bent over her splayed legs like a ragamuffin doll. She needed to keep touching him.

He went to the basin in his room and drew a glass of water. "Miss Butler, are you quite all right? You must leave now."

"N-no," she moaned, but shakily held the glass up to her mouth and drank a little. While she drank, she grasped his arm again as he remained crouched over her. Other visions flowed through. Troubling ones to her, but she bet that John and Max would find them interesting.

You dirty, rotten traitor.

After a few more sips, she got to her feet, still holding onto his arm. He shook her off and stepped back.

"Miss Butler, are you well enough to leave on your own? I'm quite ill, myself."

She swayed a little on her feet and quickly scanned the room. There were two cell phones on his desk by the large window, where he had a partially obstructed view of the mansion. One of them was his contact phone with the attacker. He was awaiting a call. The assassin was already inside the compound.

"Miss Butler? You must leave. I need to lie down."

She stared directly at him and turned on her Brit-speak. "Yes, I think I can make it downstairs. So sorry, ol' chap. Don't know what came over me. I might be getting the flu, too. Or something." At the door, she looked back. "Goodbye, Mr. Blake."

Enjoy your prison cell, you scumbag.

Halfway to the Range Rover, John relayed what Athena told him. By the time they climbed back in, two of Max's security men passed them on their way to Blake's room. There, he'd be handcuffed and guarded until one of the Embassy's solicitors could file charges against him. The link between the attacker's cell phone and Blake's would solidify the case against him. Blake would never get to enjoy the ten million pounds stashed away on Grand Cayman, courtesy of the wealthy Arabs who'd financed the attack.

"We tracked the money wire to Blake's Cayman account to several front organizations tied to Hezbollah and Al

Qaeda in the Arabian Peninsula. Payback for helping the Americans in Iraq and Afghanistan, no doubt," said John on their way back to the mansion after he'd explained to Athena the genesis of this atrocious plot.

He screeched to a halt beside one of the catering trucks. On the far side of the rear parking lot, the concert band members were rolling out their instruments from six gray vans. In small groups, the musicians filed into the rear of the mansion, ascending the back staircase to the large second-floor dressing room, adjacent to the Grand Ballroom. In one hour, they would begin playing, but as they moved into the mansion, they appeared in no hurry.

She and John stood counting the musicians, John occasionally speaking into the miniature radio mic clipped to his sports jacket. Max and several security guards were upstairs, roaming the ballroom and its two large terraces. They would greet the musicians in addition to the caterers and decorators, doing last minute screening and searching.

From the absence of string instruments, the musicians appeared to be members of a concert band of about thirty-five musicians. They were moving up the stairs towards the big dressing room, where the musicians would remove instruments from their cases. Based on her past experience at such events, large jugs of water would be made available for them and there were staff restrooms nearby. Athena knew the music was due to begin after most of the guests had cleared the gate. They would then climb the grand staircase at the front of the mansion to the lilting strains of music.

Five musicians and eight band crew members brought up the last of them. Amid the forty-odd catering helpers bustling about, entering and exiting the rear service entrance with carts and food containers, these stragglers could have easily been lost in the crush. Athena's gaze fixed on one dark-haired man, clean-shaven and smiling. His furtive eyes weren't the only thing that alerted her. He was carrying a very large case, at least five feet long, and a second case almost as long as the first. He placed the two cases on the graveled ground by the front of the van and followed the others.

"He's the euphonium player," she said quietly to John, "Or supposed to be. I think there's a weapon inside that case." She watched the man disappear inside the rear service entrance with the other musicians.

"The what player?" John asked, his head averted, ready to convey the message to Max upstairs.

"Euphonium. It's like a big tuba. What kind of weapon would fit in a case that size?"

"A shoulder-held rocket launcher. Maybe an RPG—a rocket-powered grenade launcher." He turned away, his back to the musicians' van and spoke. His voice, thin and strident, conveyed his controlled anxiety. He ended up with an urgent, "Get down here."

"He's going to slip away. There's a second man, John," she said, looking up at the tall, second-floor-to-ceiling windows of the Grand Ballroom. John ran to the rear service entrance and vanished, leaving Athena alone in the parking lot by the Range Rover.

She watched in horror as another dark-haired man came out of the same door. He was one of the band's crew members, whose job it was to help the musicians carry the instruments and set up. That same man had carried in the keyboard stand, she recalled. She'd overheard him say he'd come back down for the rest of the instruments. The second man was going to set up the weapon, dealing with anyone who got in his way. He carried a pistol with a sound suppressor, she knew, for she'd seen the plan flash through Blake's mind like a fast-forwarded film.

A rocket launcher the size of a Euphonium could shoot

ten exploding grenades per minute. Enough to shatter the glass windows in the mansion's ballroom and kill or maim hundreds of people. In minutes, her parents and the other diplomats who lived off the compound were scheduled to arrive, followed by the first of the guests, who'd be greeted by a long reception line at the base of the grand staircase. That included Sir Peter, and her father and mother would be assembling soon.

The cell phone inside her shoulder bag shrilled but she ignored it. *Not now, Mum, Father. Busy trying to save the day.*

The earbud receiver nestled in her left ear suddenly crackled alive. It was Max, assessing the situation based on her reading of Blake. They'd detained the first guy and had searched him, finding nothing.

Her pulse pounding, she turned aside and spoke into the crossed-flags pin.

"Bloody hell, bloody hell! Goddammit, bloody hell!"

The return message: "On our way. ETA, one minute."

One minute? She had to do *something*. Now!

Pasting a smile to her face, she approached the second dark-haired man, who had moved the two cases behind the van. He was bending over them and had begun to open one of them. Music stands were resting against the panel doors. She supposed he'd come down on the pretext of getting them.

"I saw you with those big cases. Can I help you? Maybe take those cases? Or these music stands?"

For one nerve-racking moment, he stared at her. His right hand let go of the case and went to his tuxedo jacket pocket.

"Really, I'm stronger than I look," she added rapidly, widening her fake smile, "I've been assigned to help. I can carry the music stands."

Something passed over his face and he relaxed. "Sure, take those stands. I'll get these cases." He stood up and handed her the two music stands.

"You play trombone?" she called out, grasping a stand with each hand. He'd already turned back to the cases.

"No," he said gruffly. He stopped and waited for her to carry the stands inside. She had no weapon, couldn't shoot a gun if she had one, anyway, and her shoulder bag with the pepper spray was on the back seat of the Range Rover. Lot of good it did there.

Athena nodded, then proceeded towards the mansion.

"Wait!"

Athena froze. Oh god, had he seen through her charade?

Was he going to shoot her? Then kill her parents?

Chapter Thirty

Slowly, she turned around. Already bending over the large, oblong cases, the man called to her half distractedly. His dark eyes burned with intensity when they turned them on her. His deep voice almost barked out the command.

"Tell the guys up there I'm having a smoke. I'll be up in a few minutes."

"Okay."

The man spoke English with an American accent, she noted. They'd recruited an American assassin to kill the English PM? Bewildered and horror-stricken, Athena fought to keep a clear head as she climbed the service stairs. Halfway up, she met Max, John and four of their security men on their way down. They all wore black bullet-proof vests, helmets with mics attached, and all six carried assault rifles and wicked-looking pistols in holsters on their hips.

They looked like a British S.W.A.T. team.

"Athena, luv, what are you doing?" Max asked. He directed his men past him as he stopped beside her.

"John told you? The man—he's got a pistol and some weapons in those cases."

"Yes, we figured that. Stay here." Abruptly, he left her side and clomped down the stairs.

She didn't have a chance to tell him what she saw when the man had passed the stands to her. What else was planned? The music stands in her hands were not as important as the message she needed to convey to Max and his men. The music stands made an awful clatter when she dropped them on the landing. No matter. She spun around and dashed back down.

Halfway down, she heard popping sounds coming from the parking lot. When she emerged in the sunlight, she immediately searched out the musicians' van. Max, John and the rest of their team surrounded the man, who was lying prone on the ground. She ran towards them.

Oh God, what if she were wrong? What if they shot and killed an innocent man? It would be her fault!

She reached the security perimeter that Max's men had made around the man. An automatic weapon lay on the asphalt next to the man's body. Max was speaking into his mic and interrupted his call when he saw her. He said something to John, a monosyllabic command, and the nearest team member turned around and grabbed her. She watched in dread as Max opened up one of the oblong cases. Inside, a metal-gray rocket launcher lay in two tubular sections, each section about two and a half feet long. Max leaned over and retrieved one section which had a pistol-grip assembly and an aluminum tube with a sight and heavy metal guard. The men's excitement morphed into a flurry of exclamations in their own military-style code.

"Crikey, that's an M-18. Ten rpm."

"Look at that wire shoulder support. Made it lighter."

"Yeah, I figure six kilos max."

"I'll wager seventy-five millimeter."

"So who's this bugger?"

"Ask bloody Blake."

At the mention of Winston Blake, Athena tore her gaze away from the blood-drenched body of the American assassin. She felt hot bile rise in her esophagus, but she swallowed it down. Max looked occupied as he opened the second case and two of the men gathered around it. She had to get Max's attention, and fast!

She looked at the guard holding her at bay. "Tell Max there's another attack coming. The main group. This guy was just the—the distraction."

John overheard and came over.

"What's going on, Athena? You were supposed to stay inside."

She took a deep breath, exhaled and forced out the words. "From the park!" She pointed to a vast expanse of woods, Dumbarton Oaks Park on the other side of the New Zealand Embassy. "The rocket attack! Dumbarton Oaks!"

Max frowned. "You sure?" She nodded and pointed in the direction of the woods—southwest of the Embassy grounds.

Max barked out an order to one of the men, then spoke into his mic. "Better go check out Dumbarton Oaks Park."

A loud whistling sound flew overhead. Then, in the grassy area beyond the border of tall trees, an explosion. Everyone ducked and Athena fell to her knees and huddled into a ball. No more than fifty feet away, dirt and grass clods mixed with metal flak flew in all directions and tree branches snapped and became projectiles. They hit the trucks and vans in the parking lot. Athena screamed as John covered her with his body.

When all grew quiet again, John was up and grabbing her before she could get to her feet again. She stared at him for a moment. His vest had caught a metal object and it stuck out right over his heart. He was busy, getting Max's attention and pointing back at her. In the eerie silence that followed, Max shouted to her.

"Athena?"

She yelled back, "I'm okay. They're not on the grounds. They're in the park over there!" Deafened and disoriented by the explosion, she wasn't sure anybody had heard her before the attack.

Max and John spurred into action. They and three others climbed into John's Range Rover and peeled out of the lot. Athena watched them cut through the grassy field towards the side gate, skirting the mansion's main driveway and forecourt. One well-armed security guard remained by the assassin and the RPGs, calling on his radio for backup.

Another explosion sounded on the far side of the mansion, north of their position, closer to the building than the first explosion.

"Get over by the trees, Miss Butler. Stay down!" The guard collected the assassin's automatic pistol, tossed it into one of the cases and closed them both up, ignoring the dead assassin at his feet. He placed both cases in the musicians' van and then began running, pushing her towards the wall of trees. They had to hop over debris, and one branch tripped her. As she began to fall, he scooped her up and kept her going. Two more explosions hit the north corner of the mansion.

Athena could hear the screams of people caught in the middle of the attack as some were arriving in their limos and others were climbing the front entrance's main staircase. She cowered beside one oak tree while the guard stood nearby, his assault rifle at the ready. His head kept turning from side to side, as though he expected attackers to appear out of nowhere. It was dusk, and shadows merged into each other. The darkness around them made her breathless with dread. As if each tree would become an attacker and begin to move.

As skeptical as her mother was religious, Athena nevertheless closed her eyes and prayed. As hard as she'd ever prayed in her life. *Please, God, spare Mum. Spare Father. Spare them all! Don't let Max get hurt! Or John or any of them!*

In the distance, she heard gunfire. The lights in the mansion went off. More shouting and screams ensued. More gunfire. One more explosion that rocked the mansion. Then silence. The explosions had stopped.

The security agent beside her held up his radio as it crackled to life. He listened for a long moment before pulling her to her feet.

"They got 'em."

CHAPTER THIRTY-ONE

Two hours later, Athena found herself riding home in her parents' limousine. She sat between her mother and father, holding their hands, tears running down her cheeks. Chris sat facing them, his focus glued to the news helicopters that filled the sky. Their limo exited the Embassy's main front gate, flanked on both sides by news vans and televisions crews. Photographers snapped flash photos on the site. The dinner-dance had been canceled, of course, the ambassador apologizing to everyone. Max and his team would debrief the Embassy staff in the morning.

Athena felt safe for the first time all day. Her little family, cocooned inside the dark limo, was safe. She'd thanked God a hundred times in the past hour since she'd reunited with her parents and Chris.

"What's going to happen, Father?"

Both parents sat, still dazed and exhausted from the evening's stress and excitement. Fortunately, according to her father, the president, his wife and the PM and his wife hadn't even broached the front gate when the first explosions erupted. Their limos and security vehicles had whisked them away and back to the White House grounds.

Her parents, standing in the long receiving line, had sought shelter in the basement along with everyone else by the grand staircase. Half the law enforcement on the Embassy grounds had converged at the site in the park where the mortars had been launched. Three men were killed outright, another one arrested. Her father expected the investigation into what had gone wrong would continue for months, if not years. But he wagered, in typical English understatement, that Winston Blake would be compelled to give sufficient insight into the assassination plot.

The plot that almost succeeded.

Her father squeezed her right arm. "Thanks to you, luv, this horrible plan did not succeed."

"Who was behind this?" she asked.

"I can only speculate, luv. Maybe the Iranians. They hired the terrorist group, Hezbollah, to bomb the American Embassy in Beirut in nineteen eight-four. From what MI-six has heard, they were behind the Benghazi disaster, when American ambassador Stevens and three other Americans were killed. The Iranians tend to hire other nationals to do their dirty work. Also, they showed me the bodies of the would-be assassins. They all died with the jihadist hand salute, the four-finger Rabiya gesture. We'll find out for certain, rest assured."

"Yes, you will, my love," her mother said softly.

In the limo's gloom, she felt her father's growing fury. He demonstrated the four-finger gesture to her, and it struck a chord. She'd seen that gesture in the first attacker's mind, as his thoughts skittered to his fellow assassins at the park site. At the time, she didn't know what it meant.

"One thing we've learned," her father added, "the vetting process held up but the admittance through the gate did not. The gate guards should've had ID photos in addition to the names. Those two assassins with the band had forged papers, but photos would've excluded them. Why the photos were omitted from the protocol lists, I have an idea Blake was involved."

Athena patted her father's leg. He was blaming himself and making a vow that such an attack would never happen again on British sovereign soil. He was also worried that this security failure would alter the upward course of his diplomatic career.

"I should've done more," Athena murmured lamely, "maybe to help you vett some of those people. I should've helped you with those background checks."

"Your mother helped me. She had no way of knowing two musicians would substitute at the last minute. Without my knowledge or Max's knowledge. We should have taken Blake into custody sooner, but we had no concrete evidence of his betrayal. Just a supposition that an able barrister in a court of law would've shot down."

Her mother said very quietly, "Let's just be thankful no one other than the assassins was killed."

Athena nodded solemnly. Max and John hadn't been hurt. Only one of their men had suffered an injury, and he was going to recover. The Trojan Horse she'd seen had materialized, but only as a distraction. She hadn't seen the entire picture until it was almost too late. This failing bothered her.

She'd have to remember that her clairvoyance wasn't infallible.

One corner of the mansion was destroyed, but fortunately, the attackers, all British nationals, were stopped before they could perfect their aim with their mortars. The second story Grand Ballroom with a full exposure of twenty floor-to-ceiling windows never suffered a direct hit.

Her mother leaned over and kissed her forehead. She kept sighing deeply and audibly, as if that were the only way she could contain her emotions.

"*Bella figlia mia,* don't blame yourself. You could not have done more. But now you see the absolute good you can do with your God-given gift. You can see what others cannot. That is a gift not to be taken lightly. You saved lives today, remember that. You can continue to save lives. Do you not see it now? The importance of this remarkable gift from God?"

Athena could only nod.

But still, she wished she wouldn't have to use it again, at least not in the near future. She wasn't cut out to be a soldier like Max and John. Too scary. Too nerve-racking. Too . . .

Too much responsibility.

Chapter Thirty-two

Strangely enough, Athena's nerves hummed like electrical wires, more so even than during the attack on the Embassy. She was sitting next to Dan Grantham, watching intently as each pastiche was unveiled on its large tripod stand. There were four, ready to be viewed and either criticized or praised by the artists present today.

Dan held her hand and smiled at her encouragingly as Martin Larsen and his partner approached the stand to her painting's left. It held Dan's latest pastiche, Paul Gauguin's self-portrait in his old Breton clothes. An anonymous client had commissioned it and was willing to pay dearly for it. Athena had seen it during a private unveiling in Dan's apartment the day before. The painting's colors were bold, as were its brush strokes and daring outlines. And it was a magnificent copy.

"No etchings tonight?" she'd asked flirtatiously the day before as they lingered in his living room. He'd smiled and shrugged.

"My bedroom etchings? Just waiting for you to give me the go-ahead. As you English say, I don't want to get the wrong end of the stick."

They'd kissed goodnight later when he took her home after dinner. She'd tousled his silky dark blond hair. No doubt about it, their friendship was heating up.

He wasn't Kas—*no, don't even go there*. In her mind, she scraped off all memory of Kas Skoros with her trowel, like a mistake in paint from one of her canvases.

She turned her attention instead to the unveiling. With a flourish, Martin Larsen unveiled the Gauguin pastiche and the assembled painters in the Visions Gallery's private backroom all murmured their approval. A few even gasped their admiration aloud. Everyone there applauded and approved it unanimously. If a copy didn't pass muster with the pastiche painters, it was rejected and the painter could either toss it or improve it.

Dan, grinning from ear to ear, clicked his crystal flute of champagne against Athena's glass. "Good," he said. "That took me a hundred hours of painstaking work."

"Perfection," she said to him. While everyone applauded, Dan stood and, a little embarrassed at the attention, modestly nodded and sat down.

Martin now approached Athena's pastiche. Three had passed inspection with Martin's pastiche painters, and they were not about to let down their standards.

"Let's take a look at our newest candidate's pastiche. Edouard Manet's The Waitress by our youngest painter, Athena Butler."

Martin's brows rose in anticipation. He hadn't yet seen her painting and so Athena was bracing herself for criticism and a possible flat-out rejection. He might soften the blow with suggestions for how she might improve the masterwork copy, but mostly she guessed the five thousand dollar check would be considered enough compensation for her time and effort.

Martin turned around and carefully removed the cloth cover. Hums of surprise and approval followed as the entire painting came into view. She'd reworked the main colors and brought up the light in the girl's face, which lent the waitress' expression an air of wistful youth. Exactly what she thought Manet had intended, as though the girl was thinking *do I have to do this the rest of my life? Maybe I can be a showgirl instead. Or just get married.*

Athena empathized with the master's subject, a young, pretty French girl stuck in a thankless, dead-end job. Like the girl, perhaps, she wanted to excel at something that she was passionate about.

Painting was her passion. She wasn't passionate about her clairvoyance. In fact, she'd kept it secret from Dan, too. That was all she needed to end another relationship, a young man freaking out and thinking she was crazy or delusional. She'd read him enough to know he liked her very much and wanted her . . . badly. Making love with him—heck, would she ever do that again? Intimacy set a person up for heartbreak. In that, her mother had been correct.

Was she willing to take that giant leap . . . again?

Kas—*No, that's over and done with. Ah well, if you can't be with the one you love, then love the one you're with. Isn't that how it goes? Good ol' practical American logic.*

Martin was clasping his partner's hand. They shared a mutual expression of joyful surprise.

"I think we've finally found our Manet painter," Martin announced to the group, motioning for her to come up.

"This is superb, divine, so exacting that I'm blown away. Athena, welcome to Genuine Pastiches of the Great Masters. We're honored to have you join us, and we have a contract for you to sign if you accept."

Athena smiled and shook Martin's offered hand. Then she accepted his hug. When he let go, she saw in his blue eyes genuine admiration for her talent. But she read in his heart, fear. Fear of what, she didn't know.

Distracted, she turned around to face the room full of applauding fellow artists. Her gaze around the room paused at Doctor White. Her painting professor at the Art Institute, herself the Cezanne specialist of the group, was beaming with pride. They nodded at each other. What could be more complete a triumph than this, Athena thought. Her heart burst with unfettered happiness.

Yes, this is what I was born to do. Not read minds.

Well, maybe both.

Her fellow artists approached and wished her well. When most of them had drifted away towards the refreshment table, Martin and his gallery partner waited for her at a big desk. Briskly, Dan appeared in front of her.

"Congratulations!"

"Stay with me, okay? Make sure the contract's good. In case I have any questions."

"Sure, and after this I want to buy you dinner. French, in honor of Monsieurs Manet and Gauguin? Or steaks, to fit our appetites?"

She smiled up at him. Thank heavens he was nice and tall. And handsome. And not afraid to speak his mind. A fellow artist who would understand what it took to fall in love with something and never let it go.

"Steaks. I'm famished. Then later, you can show me your bedroom etchings."

Understanding lit his face. His hand stroked Athena's shoulder as he leaned over and kissed her cheek.

"I kept wondering when you'd ask."

To be continued . . .

YOU MAY ALSO ENJOY THE FOLLOWING FROM eXTASY BOOKS INC:

Born to Sing
Donna Del Oro

Excerpt

She was needed at home. Desperately. Dear God! What if . . . But she mustn't think about that now. She had a guest, so Eva assumed the role of polite hostess.

"I'm so pleased you could find the time to see me, Miss Villa," the young reporter said, shaking hands and then sitting down abruptly. "My editor said he's a big fan of yours, has seen you on stage many times." The woman looked down at her notebook, already poised on her denimed knee. She was wearing a black turtleneck and green wool blazer with her jeans. Her neck was wrapped up to her chin with an impossibly long wool scarf and hiking boots. Eva suddenly felt overdressed in her teal wool trousers and matching sweater and jacket. Even the long string of pearls she wore seemed inappropriate. "He said you're retiring from the stage after twenty-five years, and you sang your last opera last night."

It was already apparent to Eva that the girl—her name was Serena Suarez, a fellow Latina like herself—knew little about the opera world or Eva's role in it. But what did it matter? The interview would help pass the time until she was scheduled to leave. The young woman reminded Eva of herself at that age. Young, naïve, a little socially gauche even, but very, very determined to succeed.

Despite her fatigue and anxiety, Eva smiled at Serena and invited her to help herself to the coffee on the buffet. Delighted, Serena jumped up, went over and did just that.

Eva sighed as she sat down on the sofa. She was tired and wanted to fly home. He needed her, much as she knew he hated to admit it. Patience, she told herself, have patience. In five hours, she'd be on that plane and on her way home. HOME. Where she belonged. Her past two months in New York—the ovations, accolades—were already history in her mind. This interview was but a fond farewell to the city that had welcomed her with open arms.

"My editor said you were great in—" The girl broke off to consult her page of notes. "Uh, as the star in Rodelinda."

"Yes, Handel's Rodelinda. A wonderful role. The Met's done a superb job bringing that production to light, promoting it. It's not that well-known, even in the opera world. We closed last night. Last night's fund-raiser for the American Cancer Society was a huge success."

"I see. Uh, he told me—I've learned, Miss Villa, that you've had an illustrious career singing opera . . ."

"And concerts. Recordings. I've been Artistic Director of several regional opera companies in Texas, including Visiting Artistic Consultant the past year with the Met."

"Oh, I see."

The girl looked nervous now, poor thing, thought Eva, so out of her depth. Terrence, the Tribune's Entertainment and Arts editor had attended last night's performance and was putting together a feature story on guest artists at the Met. Oh, well, he probably wanted to test Serena in some way. And he knew Eva would be kind and help her out. Give her the goods on a silver platter. Give the girl experience with interviewing minor celebrities.

Why not give her a scoop? The biggest story of her as yet short journalistic career! Eva's true story had never been told despite the attempts of that biographer last year. D.J. had told part of their story in his memoir, which the girl reporter most likely had never read. But it was mostly his story, not hers.

The memoir. D.J.'s memoir, Eva kept with her at all times. Her link to their common past and a period of time in her life that influenced everything else that followed. Reading D.J.'s words as he wrote them, himself, always thrilled her, amused her. All those bittersweet memories, he'd managed to put into words in his own inimitable style. A blend of manly humor, Texas plain talk and deep sensitivity. He'd given her a special, autographed copy, accompanied by a bouquet of roses. So typical of that man. D.J. was a sensitive man who had a voice that had always resonated with something inside herself that she could never quite verbalize. It was . . . too visceral. But she could never put him out of her mind. He was etched there for all time.

For Eva's lifetime, anyway. And for D.J.'s.

The girl reporter was staring at her. Consciously, and with an actress' consummate skill, Eva wiped clear her stricken expression and smiled politely.

"Would you like to hear how I got started in the opera business? Who influenced me? What made me decide to devote my life to this incredibly challenging but fascinating world? Well, other than singing in the church choir and coming from a long line of musicians and singers. One of my favorite hymns includes this verse . . ."

Eva cleared her clogged throat, shook her head clear of tears and began to sing from her position on the sofa in her hotel suite. When she concluded with the verse, " . . . the gifts we have, we are given to share," the girl reporter was awestruck.

Had the girl never heard a lyrical soprano's voice before,

Eva wondered. No, probably not, not live and in the same room, anyway. Her role model was most likely Beyonce or JLo. Come now, Eva, she scolded herself; let's not be a prima donna cum snob. That's what he jokingly called her these days, ever since he began recording what their agent called "pop op". But she wasn't really a prima donna; she wasn't even a diva. Not anymore, anyway. Maybe she never would be again.

Somehow, the joy of singing . . . was gone.

Oh, please help me, Eva prayed. If I can't sing, I can't breathe. If I can't have him, I can't sing . . .

"Th-that's beautiful," the girl breathed, her eyes wide with sudden appreciation.

"It's an old church hymn," Eva explained. The lovely melody helped to stem the rising sorrow inside her. "I was singing it one day in church—I must've been about twelve or thirteen. I was their soloist and all of a sudden it struck me. I had a gift and I needed to share it. I was obligated to share it. And so when I got a scholarship to UT—"

The girl looked perplexed.

"The University of Texas in Austin—I got a music scholarship and began to plot my course to the opera world. My parents were poor East Texas farmers and it was my only way to get there."

Because the girl looked genuinely interested now, Eva sat back and relaxed. Would it be so difficult to pass a couple of hours reliving her romance with opera . . . and her romance with the man who influenced her singing career the most?

The girl bent over her notebook, pen tightly in her fist. She looked up curiously when Eva hesitated.

"Are you a Tejana?" Serena asked. A Latina born and raised in Texas?

"Yes. Would you believe it, one of my ancestors was a lieutenant in Captain Juan Bautistia De Anza's expedition party . . . oh, sometime in the eighteenth century? He left California and came to Texas. His name was Francisco Beltran de Villalobos. Yes, house of wolves. I always wondered where that came from. My Uncle Manny thinks he fled some danger in Spain and assumed a new identity under De Anza's command. Anyway, my family's been in Texas ever since. Farming, doing a variety of work but mostly farming and ranching. Lots of us there in Texas. Proud to be Tejanos with a long history. We go back to before Texas became a republic."

"I'm from California, myself," Serena said, "So Cal."

"Why did you come to New York?" Why would anyone leave the warm beaches of Southern California for the wet snow and gray winter days of the Big Apple?

"My boyfriend, mainly. He's a grad student at Columbia. Secondly, to further my career."

Eva nodded and took a sip of hazelnut-flavored coffee. Now that her stage career was over, she could afford to indulge in a few extra calories. Gracias a Dios!

"Good for you," she said to Serena. And meant it. It was important for a woman to have a career to fall back on. In case the men in your life let you down.

That was something she knew about.

The journalist whipped out a small digital recorder. "Mind, Miss Villa?"

Eva shook her head absently. Already, her mind was wandering back to the past.

"My path to singing opera involved a man, not just classwork and auditions. I was a music major, a Voice major. He . . . well, he was majoring in Women and Fun and Booze. At least, that's how he started. By the time I met him—in our junior year at UT—Darren James McKay was slowly resigning himself to a different path in life. The exact opposite from the one his father wanted him to take, of course. But that was the McKay family. Bull-headed, filthy rich, owned a goodly portion of central Texas—"

Eva broke off as the girl shot her an astonished look and stopped writing.

"Darren McKay, the singer? Wow. You went to college with HIM? My mother has all his CD's. She absolutely a-DORES him. Has a MAD crush on him. He's not bad looking either, uh, for an older guy."

Eva smiled knowingly. "He's fifty now and, yeah, not bad looking for an older guy. Twenty—ah, let's see, twenty-six years ago, he was ten-times more gorgeous. He was as handsome a Texan as you'll ever find. I think you'd call him hunky or studly. All the coeds were crazy about him." Eva giggled, and amazed herself. Good lord, when was the last time I did that? Giggled?

"You see, I can't tell you my story without telling his as well. We were . . . let's say, linked . . . for a long time. And then we came apart and then—well, let me tell it one step at a time. Is that okay, Serena?"

"Yes, of course!" the reporter enthused.

"Is it okay if I tell you my story in my . . . own way? The whole truth—" Eva smiled broadly— " . . . and nothing but the truth?"

The girl reporter was nodding excitedly now, for it was obvious that she realized she'd stumbled onto a possible celebrity scoop. She blinked rapidly and nodded.

About the Author

A retired high school English teacher, Donna loves to read, write, travel with her husband. She also sings in a Northern California women's barbershop chorus. She has been writing stories since childhood.

Made in the USA
Lexington, KY
20 July 2019